GLITCH

Copyright © 2020 Chrome Valley Books
All rights reserved.

Glitch

Written by Andrew Mackay

Edited by Ashley Rose Miller and Aly Quinn

*Cover Design & Images:
ViknCharlie / Andrew Dobell / Freeeda (Shutterstock)*

**ISBN: 9798662872752
Copyright © 2020 Chrome Valley Books**

This is a work of fiction. Names, characters, places and incidents either are products of the author's imagination or are used fictitiously. Any resemblance to actual persons, living or dead (or somewhere in between), events, or locales is entirely coincidental.

No part of this book may be reproduced in any form or by any electronic or mechanical means including information storage and retrieval systems, without permission in writing from the author. The only exception is by a reviewer who may quote short excerpts in a review.

Chapters

Chapter 1 1

Chapter 2 17

Chapter 3 29

Chapter 4 55

Chapter 5 73

Chapter 6 97

Chapter 7 115

Chapter 8 123

Chapter 9 141

Chapter 10 163

Chapter 11 179

Chapter 12 195

Chapter 13 209

Chapter 14 249

Author Notes 255

Acknowledgments 260

Get Your FREE ebook 261

About the author 263

Chapter 1

"Mom?"

"Yeah, honey?"

"I'm scared."

"Why?"

"I don't want to be alone all by myself. Can I sleep with you and dad tonight?"

An interesting, if frequent, proposition from an eight-year-old boy with a genuine look of concern on his face. The soft, powder-blue eyes pinned around such a cherubic face was hard to refuse.

"Honey?"

"Yeah, mom?" came the expectant reply from the boy.

"You're going to have to learn to sleep in your own bed, you know. Be a big boy. Remember all the little accidents you used to have?"

The boy lowered his eyes and did his best to adjust to defeat. "Yeah. I don't do that, now, though."

A pale, white hand brushed over his brow as his mother's voice waded into his ears. "That's right. You grew out of it. And you'll grow out of this, too."

"But, mom—"

"—Rex, honey. Listen to me. I want you to lie back. Close your eyes. Take a few deep breaths. Eventually, you'll fall asleep. In the morning you'll wake up and be very happy you were being so brave."

Unsure of his mother's answer, little Rex Milton shuffled back and pressed the back of his head against the spongy pillow.

"There. That's the first step."

Rex averted his eyes to the top of his mother's legs as she slid forward and allowed him some room to straighten himself out. It seemed as if the ass inside the jeans was about to lift and exit the room.

"Don't go."

"I'm not going anywhere, honey," the voice came from way above Rex's eye shot. "I'll leave your door open, okay? I'll leave the hall light on, too."

"If something bad happens can I come to your room?"

A resounding pang of confidence enveloped the response. "Of course you can, honey. But *only* if something bad happens. Okay?"

"Okay."

"Now, close your eyes."

The little boy did as instructed. Both eyelids pulled down the front of his eyes, cutting out the light flooding into the room from the hallway.

Mom stood up straight and rolled her shoulders. A flock of blood-red locks fell down her back and licked the small of her back.

A voice crept from behind the door to the master bedroom. "Kara? Are you coming to bed?"

The woman didn't dare tear her eyes away from her child's face.

"Wait a minute," she whispered to nobody in particular. "He's falling asleep."

The cute, snorkeling rumbling through Rex's nostrils signaled that he had drifted off, and far quicker than anticipated.

The sides of Kara's mouth widened, forming a maternal smile of protection.

"Sleep tight, honey."

She reached forward and went for the thumb panel on the night light sitting on the bedside table. Before her thumb connected with the synthetic plastic, her attention was drawn to Rex's cell phone.

It seemed to buzz without moving.

Buzz... buzz... buzz...

A vibrating sensation erupted up her right thigh. Quick-thinking, she grabbed at her own leg and felt the rectangular device in her jeans pocket.

It was *her* phone, and not his.

Nobody was calling Rex, but someone was demanding her attention at this godforsaken time of night — 9:45, as displayed by the infrared holographic projection on the bedroom ceiling.

Kara knew who was calling.

Those damn floorboards.

They creaked each alternate step along the upper landing as Kara moved past the bathroom and approached the master bedroom.

Her cell phone vibrated in her hand as violently as her heart in her chest.

"Kara?" came a voice from the bedroom.

"Yeah, I'm coming."

A final creak, and Kara stopped stone dead in her tracks. The phone needed answering before she walked into the bedroom. She swiped her thumb across the screen, introducing a bright blue glow which illuminated her face.

A grid of texts that should have disappeared long, long ago were still present, much to Kara's surprise.

"Shit."

In the fumble to conceal the content, she nearly dropped the phone on the plush carpet next to her bare toes. She caught the tumbling object in her chest and breathed a sigh of relief.

In only the way those who are suspicious do, she lifted the phone from her chest, lowered her head to the screen, and continued the chat.

Denton: *I need to c u.*
KM02: *I can't right now. I told you not to instig8. It's too risky.*
Denton: *Sorry.*
KM02: *Call u in 5.*
Denton: *OK*

Burn: *5… 4… 3… 2… 1…*

The messages evaporated before her very eyes. The green and white logo of the app she was using whizzed up and out of her view as she slipped her phone back into her pocket.

Now hurried by her promise to the person on the other end of the exchange, she darted into the master bedroom and caught her husband climbing into bed.

"Hey, Ian."

"Ian?" her husband chuckled. "We're on first-name terms, now, are we?"

Kara feigned a mild and humorous agitation. "Yeah, uh, I'm sorry. I'm not feeling too good."

Ian pulled the quilt over his legs and patted her side of the bed. "Oh, no? Lying down might help?"

"No, no—I think I need some water, or something. I'll go downstairs and take a breather. Chill out for a second or two."

"You sure?"

Kara attempted to smile and conceal her true intentions, wondering if her husband would bite. "Yeah."

Ian relaxed into bed and clapped his hands together. "Okay, I'll watch some TV. Just holler at me if you need me, okay?"

"I will."

Kara squinted at her husband and found herself staring - and wanting, and suffering and, ultimately, saddened. Ian was a handsome guy, kind-hearted and devoted. Deep down inside she hated him for putting her in the position she found herself in.

The feeling had lasted for years and showed no sign of improving.

So lost was Kara in her thoughts of abandonment, she waved her cell phone - the very device she was using to threaten their marriage - to suggest everything was okay. Then, she moved out of the room with the same confident grace her husband might have expected.

"I'll be right back."

The faint chatter of news whirled around the room as Ian snapped his fingers. The glimmer from the TV screen at the foot of the bed reached up the white linen sheets.

Two characters on screen turned out not to be on screen at all. Their chests bulged forward, producing a holographic 3D effect, which slid towards Kara as she turned around.

Seconds later, she walked right through the image as the volume grew louder.

Kara was gone, leaving a red-eyed Ian to watch the holographic image of the woman speak at him.

"—Which has been dubbed the revolutionary technological marvel of the century. The Synthetica program, brainchild of Xavier Manning, is due to launch tomorrow morning and change the way we live forever."

The reporter's name blinked by the reporter's knees - *Dana Doubleday*.

"For SNN Sense Nation News, I'm Dana Doubleday. Stay tuned for my exclusive look at the future being history in the making, next."

Kara trod carefully as she descended the stairs, using the glare from her cell phone to guide her.

Dana's voice echoed behind Kara's ears and faded away as she reached the bottom step. Another glance at the app on her phone, followed by a mental miscalculation of how many steps were left to be taken, had Kara stumble to the ground. She gripped the handrail and prevented herself from serious injury.

"Jeez."

An inch farther, and her left knee might have been impaled on the table to the right of the front door.

But *nothing* could outdo the deliberate carelessness being perpetrated on her phone right now.

It was all her fault, and she knew it.

The kitchen was the farthest room on the ground floor from the stairs, which provided fertile ground for a quiet chat.

Relieved to find the evidence of her exchange had deleted itself, she opened the green-and-white app on her phone.

Badum-boom-ding.

A friendly, familiar chime accompanying the cartoon cupid and its bow and arrow fired to life.

InstaBate:
Life's Too Short Not to Fuck Around.

Kara hated that logo with a vengeance usually reserved for lynch mobs. It popped every time she opened the damn app. Each time she'd use it, she'd forget to roll down the volume to silence the stupid chimes - and each time she got away with it, though only just.

Badum-boom-ding.

Practically every bastard on the planet knew the app's opening tune, what with the frequency of the commercials. Most joked about how daft it sounded, and others' ears pricked up if they ever heard it coming from their friends' devices. Kara's often suggested that men became aroused by it.

Bullshit.

Kara was no different in that respect to many of her friends, both male and female.

The stupid cartoon cupid climbed out of the white halo, threw the user a cheeky, knowing wink, and sauntered off screen - leaving the easy-to-use dashboard lighting up the user's face.

The screen light grew harsh and blinding for Kara, so she snapped her fingers and stood with her back against the stove.

Kara pupils adjusted to the light in the room as she scanned the screen. It was a dashboard she knew well due to the interface's ease of use.

Option #1: Text chat.

Option #2: Video call.

Option #3: Contacts.

A quick check at the sliding kitchen door was all it took. Nobody was awake enough to want to venture down the stairs and check after her.

She whispered into the handset. "Call Denton Rossco."

Biddip-bing.

The call sign bounced up and down like an overexcited child expecting a sugary drink. The three seconds it took for Denton to answer felt like an age for Kara. She cleared her throat and, as was usual before a sneak, opportunistic video call, fluffed her bright red hair and adjusted the camera to her good side - the one that reduced the amount of skin under her chin if she lifted the camera just a touch above her neckline.

The bouncing icon vanished into the thin air, to be replaced by Denton - a handsome-looking young man with a goatee and glasses.

"Hey," she whispered.

"Hey, hey, hey," the man said. "Where are you?"

"In the kitchen, listen—uh, now's not a good time."

Denton leaned into the lens so far it seemed as if his forehead would burst through her phone. "Is everyone home?"

"Keep your voice down," she hurried. "Shit. I knew this was a bad idea."

Denton smiled and licked his lips. "That's not what you said the other night."

Stern-faced, Kara snapped into the camera lens. "You can't message me like this. Okay? Stop fooling around."

"Stop fooling around? Now that's ironic."

"Very funny, asshole," she spat in all seriousness. "I swear to God you're gonna get me busted. I message you, okay? Not the other way around. My husband nearly caught me."

"Okay, I'm sorry."

Denton stepped back and sat at the edge of what looked like his double bed. The cream-colored walls and mirrored dresser just off to the right of the screen. Kara held her breath and tried to block the last time she saw the mirror, and the events that reflected back in her eyes.

"I miss you, that's all," Denton said. "I wanted to hear your voice. See your face."

Kara felt her heart turn to stone as she bit her lip. The feeling was very much mutual. "I know, I know."

"What I really want is to smell you. Just rest my cheek on your thigh, close my eyes, and breathe you in."

Kara bit her lip and allowed a shudder to roll down her spine. "Christ."

"Crazy to think you're just a couple miles away. So close, yet so far. Shit. I'm going out of my mind without you here."

Kara widened her eyes as Denton's lens tilted down between his legs.

"I want you to see what you're missing."

Kara's jaw dropped at the image presented on screen. "Jesus, Denton."

His voice bled through the speakers as he moved the lens on his phone closer. "I know, look at the effect you have on me."

"Stop it," Kara whispered back. "Not now, uh—."

"—That no-good husband of yours in bed sleeping, is he?"

Kara tried her best to allay the desire to jump through the phone and ravage the man to within an inch of his life. "Denton, please. Don't—"

"—Can't you sneak out for an hour?" Denton said. "Come to my place and let me tear you up like the little princess you are."

"No, I c-can't—"

"—Oh, come on," Denton huffed, near to anger. "You'll be in and out. Or, rather, I will be. And then you can leave and sneak back in without waking anyone up?"

"No, Denton. Please."

"What are you wearing right now?" he asked. "Lower the camera. I wanna see your legs."

On the verge of saying no, Kara was ready to hang up, but couldn't deny her feelings. The added risk turned her on and made her cave in.

She lifted the camera lens down to the golden buckle on the belt across her jeans.

"See? I'm clothed—"

"—Pull the zipper down," the voice instructed. "Then open it out, I wanna see you."

Kara leaned forward and gave the request some serious thought. She barely knew the man she was speaking to, but in the Biblical sense she was an expert.

For once in her life, she felt like she was in control. No longer would she be playing the submissive to a man who could dominate her.

A shuffling noise came from her phone's speakers, which could only mean one thing. Denton was enjoying the show a little too much.

Denying her guilt, Kara felt an overwhelming shower of control power down her spine. A quick tilt of the cell phone up the length of her midriff, and then to her face, meant she was looking down on the man.

"You want me?"

"Yeah-huh, I want you," Denton grunted. "Give me some, princess."

A check to the left revealed the backyard. A check to the right, and the door to the kitchen was still fully open.

Nobody about.

Kara bit her lip and pinched the zipper on her jeans between her thumb and forefinger.

"Yeah. That's right, you dirty little bitch," Denton whispered. "Show me what's under—"

Kara closed her eyes and let the lukewarm chrome-plated zipper edge chew down the train track covering her panties.

One by one, the zipper teeth pinched open, and peeled out like a budding rose to reveal what lay beneath.

Pink cotton material, parts of which had stuck to her skin, folded into Denton's view.

"You like that, don't you?" she whispered. "I can't give it up tonight, but it'll keep you going."

Denton didn't respond.

Typical man, Kara felt, swallowing everything but his pride and ability to speak in the heat of the moment. Even his grunts seemed to be more aggressive than usual.

"Guh—guh," he grunted, suggesting a lustful fire of rage might be blowing out through his nostrils, which only exacerbated Kara's desire to tease him further. "Guuuh."

She hooked her thumb through the front of her underwear and threatened to leave nothing to his imagination. Before she reached that point, she took a second to enjoy the moment with her clandestine love and ran the side of her knuckle between her legs.

"Mmm," she whispered just loud enough for her voice to reach the handset two feet away between her legs. "Do you like what you see?"

"Yes. I do."

Kara flung her head back so violently she nearly snapped her neck in half.

The fact that Denton's voice had changed was lost on her. As far as she was concerned, she was the only person in the room right now.

"I gotta say, I really like what I'm seeing," the phone said. "I guess I was right."

Kara moved her finger between her legs faster. "You were right?"

"Uh-huh."

"Oh, yeah, princess. Let me show you."

The kitchen lights blew out. Each bulb rattled as pure darkness smothered the room, leaving Kara masturbating in the spotlight produced by her cell phone.

She yelped as she lifted her left hand and blinked three times. "What the fuck?"

Slam.

The electronic kitchen door rolled along its casters and sliced shut, sealing her inside the kitchen. Three green lights flashed on and off, threatening to keep the door shut.

Bzzz. Bzzz. Zip.

Kara moved the screen to her face and was about to scream, but was too terrified to move.

Denton's blurred face had frozen solid due to some technical hiccup.

"Kara?" his voice rocketed from the cell phone's speakers. "H-Help m-me—"

His paused face pixelated into thousands of tiny squares. The pure white walls of his bedroom snapped to black, producing a peculiar negative-effect.

"Denton?" Kara stammered through her terror. "What's h-happening—"

"—I c-can't b-breathe—" his voice growled into an evil baritone. "K-Kara—I—I—"

"M-My God."

The screen sparked in her palm and produced an image of an egregious white, blue, and red skull in place of Denton's head.

The jaw lifted up and down as it produced a godforsaken laugh.

The Skull shimmered through the static. "Are you K-Kara M-Milton?"

"Huh?"

The Skull twisted around and zoomed so far into the screen, it nearly head-butted the phone out of her hand.

"Goddamn it, are you Kara fucking Milton?" the floating, electronic skull head asked. "Answer me."

"Yes," she squealed, beyond terror. "I am, I am. Wh-who are you?"

The Skull tilted diagonally and appeared to squint at her with suspicion. "You *have* been a naughty fucking girl, haven't you?"

Kara hyperventilated and clutched her chest thinking she was suffering a stroke. "Whuh—whuh—"

"—Yeah, it's you all right," The Skull's jaw chattered in time to the eerie voice. "Hold your phone tight. Watch *this*."

Bzzzzzzz—fitch.

Denton's agonized face snapped back on screen, paused, half in motion.

Kara Milton?

She looked around to see where the voice was coming from, although it could only be from her phone. "Yes?"

The angry, electronic voice pounded against her ribcage.

I don't have time to fuck around, unlike you.

"Wh-what d-do you mean—"

Shut up and watch.

Denton's face flew across the screen and smashed against the mirror. His two front teeth punctured through the glass and snapped away from his gums as his forehead slammed against the floor.

Denton Rossco. This piece of shit is about to help me help you understand that I am not fucking around. Keep watching.

"No, don't," she squealed. "You're hurting him."

Come here, big boy.

The walls of the room careened from left to right, indicating that Denton had dropped his phone onto the floor. Now at a slight angle, it showed the large TV screen on the dresser opposite the mirror.

The electronic skull burst onto the TV screen and grinned.

Hey, Rossco. Stop lying around and get busy, asshole.

Kara watched on in horror as Denton rolled onto his back and used the edge of the bed to pull himself to his knees.

"My G-God," he shrieked at the image on the TV. "What the hell is that?"

The Skull's jaw moved up and down and flung back, encouraging the man to approach him.

Rossco. Come here.

Terrified, Denton glanced at his phone and staggered across the carpet. "Kara?"

"Denton!" she screamed.

Hey! You two lovebirds shut the fuck up and watch. Come here, Rossco.

The view from Denton's phone showed a bare-naked Denton reach the screen and gasp at The Skull speaking to him.

Denton Rossco, 108 Sears Road. Born October 14th.

"Y-Yes?" he said to The Skull.

InstaBate User# 155770.

"Wh-what do you want?" he asked the sneering, talking skull.

You look like shit. You're missing your two front teeth, too.

Kara calmed herself down and felt her eyelids practically lift over her scalp in fear. "Denton, run!" she screamed at her phone.

Don't you dare fucking run.

The electronic skull fizzled with anger. Somehow, it magnetized the man in front of it to stay perfectly still and hold his right hand to the screen.

Touch my face.

"No," Kara screamed. "Don't—"

The second the skin of his palm touched the screen, the skin of his hand singed and burned, glued to the plastic.

"Aggghh."

The Skull roared with laughter as the barbecue effect tore through the man's forearm, past his elbow, and set his shoulder ablaze.

Kara? Do you see what I'm doing to your well-endowed boyfriend?

"Please, stop," she said through her tears. "You're killing him."

Denton's entire naked body burst into flames, shooting a deathly smog of cooked flesh racing across the ceiling.

The bed and carpet caught fire as the TV exploded, which had no effect on the laughing skull on screen.

Die, motherfucker, die.

The jaw of The Skull expanded and bulged through the TV screen — when it left the contents of the television set, in the real world, the image turned to pixels.

The Skull inflated and chomped on Denton's abdomen, cutting him clean in two. The top half of his body split apart between The Skull's pixelated teeth as the image slid into the television set.

The bottom half of Denton's corpse fell to its knees, expelling its distended organs around his ankles.

Ha!

The flames engulfed the scene as The Skull flung back into the TV set and disappeared from view — and right back onto Kara's cell phone.

Have I got your attention now?

Kara held her phone in her hand and stared at The Skull. She didn't dare move - or breathe, or speak.

Good.

The Skull flew around the screen like an impatient ghost, bucked the lower half of his head, and vomited out an electronic rendition of the top half of Denton's body at the bottom-half of her screen.

Be careful. You don't want to get his guts on your fingers.

"Gah!"

The phone sprung from her clutches and into the air.

Don't drop your phone, either. You're gonna need it.

Kara stepped forward and caught her phone in her left hand and wiped her brow with her right shirt sleeve. "What the hell is going on?"

The Skull enlarged and tilted its head at the poor woman who had soiled herself not two minutes ago. It stared her dead in the face, apparently examining her fear, and feeding off it.

There was plenty of it to go around.

Listen carefully to me.

Kara's eyes focused on The Skull, resigned to the fact she might be next on this crazy apparition's hit list.

I'll take your silence as acceptance that you believe I am serious.

A flurry of static rippled through the contours of The Skull's barren eye sockets.

I know you, Kara Milton. I know everything about you. Every dirty, unprotected detail.

Kara's stare of terror quickly turned to one of fury. A second longer, and she might have snapped her device in two, were it not for The Skull to deliver the final death knell.

And if you want your secrets kept hidden, then you're going to do exactly as I say…

Chapter 2

Manning Inc. Headquarters
~SiliChrome Valley (West)~

Earlier That Day.

Three people sat behind the birch table at the far end of the room, expecting someone to answer.

George Gilbertson, the man on the left by the green desk lamp, looked at least twenty years-older than the other two. Sporting wire-framed spectacles and gray mustache, George looked somewhat out of place for such a young company.

The guy in the middle couldn't have been older than thirty, and judging by his confident and upright manner, he was definitely the leader of the pack.

Of course he was.

His name was Xavier Manning — the CEO of the corporation.

His personal assistant, the charming Leanne Vickers, had introduced herself before the interview began, and was known to the interviewee.

All three kept staring forward.

The awkwardness got to the point where George felt he had to peruse the papers on the desk once again.

"So. Evan Cole?" he said, "Why did you apply for this position?"

Sitting opposite them in a basic office chair was a man of few words. His gaunt visage suggested vitamin D was a luxury commodity. The guy couldn't have made any less of an effort if he'd tried, what with his loose-fitting jeans and silver jacket.

"Because I can do the job," he said,

George sniggered and returned to the papers in his hand. "Is that right? It says here you've spent time in the pen."

"So?"

The response surprised the three on the other side of the table. They weren't used to this kind of attitude. Many of the employees at Manning Inc. could best be described as sycophants, and would sell their grandmother for the chance to work for such a prestigious organization.

Evan stretched his legs in such a way that suggested he was interviewing them.

Leanne chimed in with her calculated and somewhat rehearsed response. "Can you tell us more about what happened?"

"I could, but it's not really relevant," Evan said.

Xavier couldn't help but grin at the cheek of the guy. The loner sitting opposite him presented a challenge, and if nothing else, trying to get inside the guy's mind would be a fun exercise.

"Evan?" Xavier said.

"Yeah."

"You *do* know who I am, don't you?"

"Yeah," he said. "I know all about you."

Xavier cracked his knuckles and lowered himself to Evan's obnoxious level. "Doesn't surprise me. I have a question for you."

"Shoot."

"Tell me everything you know about *InstaBate*."

Evan sat up straight and took the challenge head-on. "Formed three years ago, on October 14th, two weeks ahead of the Halloween launch, which took place right across the hall in the arena. First day's download figures were nearly half a million, and before Thanksgiving, the app peaked at #1 on both the popular download charts—"

"—I'm impressed," Xavier said.

"I haven't finished yet."

Evan reached into his jacket pocket and pulled out his smart tablet.

"By the time Christmas was done, InstaBate acquired one-point-six million users, with a three-to-two ratio of men and women which, at that time, was unthinkable."

Leanne and George's ears pricked up as they watched Evan speak and slide his thumb over the screen on his device.

"InstaBate is free to download, use, browse and communicate with other users, which is a first for what was, at the time, a secret fuck-buddy service."

The skin of his thumb peeled away from the screen to reveal a white-and-green logo with a cartoon cupid basking in the middle of it.

"As of today, there are north of sixty million users all hooking up behind their spouse's backs, and getting up to all sorts of nasty shit," Evan said as he pointed to the picture profile of a regular good-ol' girl in her thirties. "A user can filter by hair, face, including cheekbone structure, jawline, neck, breast, and waist size, height, and a whole host of interests, both social and sexual—"

"—I think we've got the general picture," Leanne said, none-too-happy with where the answer was going.

"No, Leanne," Xavier said. "Let him speak. Go on, Evan."

Evan scrolled down a list of what seemed like a thousand settings. "From there, you can filter their sexual desires. This girl, for example, has ticked every single box. I mean, whoa, there's nothing this broad won't do."

George pressed his hands together and stared the interviewee in the face. "Have you used the app, personally, Mr. Cole?"

"I have, yeah."

"How did you like it?"

"It was okay," Evan grinned. "I had a few hookups. Well, let's put it this way. *InstaBate* is a nice place to visit, but I wouldn't wanna live there."

"Oh, really?" Xavier interjected with an acute curiosity. "And why's that?"

"Because the app isn't designed to match-make."

"It isn't?"

"The strap line is *Life's Too Short not to Fuck Around*. I don't think that strikes the right note for those looking for anything other than a one night stand."

Xavier folded his arms and relaxed into his chair, celebrating the forthcoming argument in his mind. "We've had many success stories over the past thirty-six months, of course. Long-term arrangements."

Evan scoffed and pretended to take offense. "Yeah, and you've made damn sure the media knows about it. Any hookup app like this is bound to have a *success* story. It's just a matter of chance."

"I guess I can't argue with that."

Evan was about to speak when he noticed, to his amazement, something that had escaped him until now - a giant watercolor painting of a man who looked eerily like Xavier. It wasn't *quite* the man he was engaged in intellectual combat with, but it was damn close.

"Who's that?"

The three heads on the other side of the table turned up to the wall to the left of Evan's chair.

Xavier cleared his throat. "That's my father. Alexander Manning."

"Where is he now?" Evan asked.

Could it be that Evan Cole had pushed his luck a little too far, and ventured into personal territory? He didn't much care, and Xavier couldn't deny the kinship that was developing in the room.

"He's dead."

"Dead?"

"Yeah," Xavier said. "Like, no longer alive."

"What happened to him?"

"He was killed. Slain in the pursuit of creating the perfect companion."

"Let me guess," Evan snickered. "It was a woman, right? It's always a fucking woman. They screw everything up eventually."

"How the hell do you know that story?" Xavier barked.

"Ooh. Touched a nerve there, didn't I?"

"You certainly did."

Evan mocked the man who'd accosted him and pretended to shiver with fear.

"Tell me, smart-ass, why us?" Xavier asked. "Huh?"

Evan chuckled quietly to himself and flicked the screen on his tablet once again.

"Why InstaBate?" Xavier continued. "If you're so good for the job, why play the asshole like this?"

"Because if you hire me, I'll tell you how I did *this*."

Evan lifted the tablet up and hit the red button at the edge of the screen. A sensor beamed to life and projected a 3D holographic image of a list of tens of thousands of names blanketing up and down the watercolor image.

"My God," Xavier said. "How did you do that?"

Evan smiled at the man knowing damn well he'd impressed him. "A simple XPS strike. *InstaBate* has a severe security flaw in its coding. It's surprising you haven't been the subject of a simple hack by a five-year-old."

George's collar tightened so hard he felt the blood rush to his head. "Jesus Christ."

"No, please, call me Evan."

George thumped the desk and yelled. "That's not funny, you little shit."

"I'll tell you something else that's not funny, too. See this list? That's every user in the west side of Chrome Valley alone."

Xavier waved his hand and turned his head away from the image. "Turn that off."

"You get the picture, now?"

"I said turn it off."

"You're the boss."

Evan switched the screen off and put the device in his jacket pocket, making damn sure everyone could see the self-congratulatory look of satisfaction on his gaunt face.

"You're right," Xavier said. "I am the boss."

"Uh-huh."

Xavier could barely stave off the stench of defeat. "Evan. I'm not technical. I don't know how any of this works, but we're looking for someone who knows."

"This is all very last-minute," Evan said. "What happened to your previous lead programmer?"

The three interviewers fell quiet and glanced at each other. Eventually, George gave up the information.

"He, uh, had to leave."

"Why?"

"His face didn't fit," Xavier said, clambering to his colleague's defense. "We won't bore you with the details. Suffice it to say, the right guy for the job is going to be very well looked-after."

"I hear you."

"When can you start?" Xavier snapped, much to the chagrin of Leanne and, more especially, George. Both turned to Xavier in astonishment.

"Xavier, shouldn't we—"

"—Shut up, George," he said, before turning to Evan for a final answer. "Don't make me ask you again, Cole."

Evan placed his hands behind his head and basked in the glory of victory. "Well, lemme think… there's no time like the present. So, how about tomorrow morning?"

"Fuck that. You're going nowhere. You're starting *now*."

Seconds later, George had just about managed to pull his overexcited colleague outside the room for a hearty one-to-one.

"Are you out of your fucking mind?"

"What?" Xavier snapped.

"We've three more candidates lined up to interview," George said. "We can't just turn them away without having had a face-to-face."

Xavier pointed to the window on the door to his office, all the while keeping his voice down. "I want this guy."

"That rude-ass ex-con?"

"Uh-huh, yeah," Xavier said. "He's perfect. You saw his resume. You know what I'm talking about, right? You know?"

Xavier cast a knowing eye across his friend's face and followed it up with a friendly, but hard, bop on the back.

"Ugh."

"I'll have Leanne cancel everyone else, and call those we've seen to tell them no."

George reached up to his cheek and scratched his fingernails along his stubble. Xavier caught the man's sleeve before it ran any further down. "Careful."

"I'm not sure about him, Xavier."

"It's not for long. He sees everything, and we have an alibi, or at the very least an answer."

George snorted, still unconvinced. "He better not fuck around later today when we come for the Rubicon."

"He'll be a sitting duck. We have precisely what we want. He's a genius. I'm a genius. Put two geniuses together, and who knows what will happen. Am I right, or am I right? I'm right. Right?"

George huffed with resignation. He knew Xavier was onto something, but felt they were moving a little too fast.

"Right."

"Good. Now, pull your zipper back up and let's get back in there and welcome our new friend to the fray before show time."

Leanne didn't know where to look with just her and Evan in the room. They'd spent the best part of five minutes in each other's company without saying a single, solitary word.

The time for empty platitudes and small talk had truly passed them by.

Leanne had spent much of the time with her arms crossed on account of Evan sneaking the occasional look at her blouse.

"So. How long have you worked here?"

She sighed with relief at the dispelled silence. "Oh, nearly six months."

"You like it here, do you?"

Leanne thought of a way to avoid any awkward questioning. "Yeah. Have you heard about tomorrow's Synethetica launch? We're all very excited."

"Right, that's the updated MAVIS droid from a few years back?"

"Uh-huh. It's quite remarkable."

"But that's not what I asked," Evan grinned. "I asked you if you *liked* working here? You know, for a company that promotes infidelity."

She smiled and ignored his nasty inference. "It's a nice place to work. Everyone's very friendly."

Evan smirked, deliberately throwing an air of suspicion into the room. "Yeah. *Right.*"

Confused, Leanne unfolded her arms and protested. "What do you mean by that?"

"You think working for a company that encourages screwing around is rewarding, do you?"

"Well, I guess I hadn't thought—"

"—Thought, yeah, it seems that you haven't thought," Evan said as he slipped into a ferocious tirade. "Giving no consideration to the families that have suffered, right? The broken homes. The destitution, the break-ups—"

"—No, I—"

"—Not to mention the suicides," Evan said. "They asked me about app numbers earlier, but they don't seem to give much of a shit about the numbers of people who've killed themselves—"

"—No," Leanne thought aloud before producing an innocent, sweet smirk. "Anyhow, I don't really get involved in all that kinda stuff."

Evan produced a cheeky smirk and squinted at the harassed girl sitting a few feet from him. "You're not on the InstaBate app too, are you?"

"No," she said, sternly. "I would never—"

"—Because I can find you with a swipe of a finger, you know."

"I am not. It's not my thing. And besides, I have a boyfriend."

"How do you know *he* isn't using InstaBate?"

Leanne lost her patience and threw a look of evil back at Evan. "Because I look after him. Okay? That's the whole damn point. Guys won't fuck around if their girlfriends get the job done."

"Or get the job, *period*."

"Very funny," Leanne said with a pinch of sarcasm and disgust. "I think you've charmed the pants off my employer—"

"—You think so?"

"Yes, I do. And I think you've probably landed the job—"

Just then, a deafening silence befell the pair. Evan knew he'd crossed the line, but that was part of the plan. Having taken clean advantage of Xavier's impatience, and George and Leanne's resulting concern on such matters, Evan had well and truly won the argument. There was no use in prolonging the misery, or even bothering personnel with the boring details.

Time was of the essence, it seemed.

Leanne folded her arms and scoffed at Evan. "Let he who is without sin cast the first stone."

"Ah, you're religious, too," Evan said. "That's too bad. You're kinda hot—"

The door swiped open on Evan's sentence, cutting his joke short.

George walked in first with a renewed vigor on his face and shook Evan's hand. "Congratulations, Mr. Cole."

"What?"

Xavier took the man's hand and gave it a good squeeze - one which signaled that he meant business and wasn't to be messed around with.

"Congratulations, Evan. You've got the job. Uh, can I have a quiet word with you?"

"Sure."

Xavier walked Evan to the corner of the room and made sure the other two couldn't eavesdrop.

"Listen, Evan. I got a bit of an issue right now, and I thought I'd just come out with it right off the bat."

"Sure."

"I'm not one to get personnel involved, and us having to wait fucking days and days to get you in on the action. I dunno if you noticed, but George is a bit apprehensive. I've talked him round. I just, uh, need you to get started. Meet the team, and get right the fuck *on* with work. Especially on patching up the app."

Evan grinned. "I had a feeling you might say that."

"I know we're on the same page. So we'll get you tooled up and you signed in—"

"—I could sign myself in. I'll just hack my way right into the mainframe and activate my own card."

"Yeah," Xavier chuckled - and then stopped, when he saw Evan wasn't joking. "What, really?"

"No," came the fey response. "I can code, and re-code the app, but I'd need at least five minutes to break into your security system."

Xavier placed a well-positioned hand on Evan's shoulder and exhaled. "Fuck. Evan, you know, if you weren't a dude, I'd jump your bones right about now."

Evan chanced a joke. "Fuck you."

"Ha. Not if I fuck *you* first."

Evan didn't see the humor in his new employer's statement. "Can you take your hand off me, please?"

"Sorry."

Xavier removed his hand and cleared his throat. "We have the launch of Synthetica tomorrow morning."

"Yeah, I know all about it."

Xavier squinted at the man. "Is there *nothing* you don't know or can't do?"

Evan thought about his response. "Um, no."

"Thank the Lord for small mercies. Okay, let's get you to work right away."

Chapter 3

Xavier took the ID pass from the receptionist and handed it to Evan, who couldn't tear his eyes away from the beefy security guard. The name badge on his jacket read *Big Ben*.

Evan raised his eyebrows as he slung the ID card around his neck. "Are all the security guards identified by their physical stature?"

Big Ben overheard the comment Evan had made and grunted at him.

"Ha. No, sometimes it's just pure coincidence. Ain't that right, Ben?"

Big Ben checked the ID of a passing visitor and let them through. "Yes, Mr. Manning."

"Anyway, enough about the lackeys. You have some work to do."

"Sure."

Evan extended the lanyard and looked at his stupid mugshot on the laminated plastic. "I look like a goddamn serial killer."

"Yeah, well," Xavier said. "Well, not too far from the truth, huh?"

"Don't make me show you you're right."

"Ha."

Unamused, Evan followed Xavier to the turnstiles and gave the security guard the thumbs up.

"Hey, Big Ben."

Ben kept his eyes on the new guy and spoke with a monotonous drawl. "Mr. Manning."

"Don't worry about Ben, here, Evan. He's not as knuckle-dragging and violent as he looks."

***

The ride in the elevator to the seventh floor was speedy yet slow at the same time. The pressure in the cage pulled the gravity so far down Evan's legs he felt that his jeans might slip down.

Ping.

"Seventh floor. Have a nice day," announced the chirpy speakers in the metal cage.

The doors opened and allowed Xavier and Evan out and into the sprawling corridor that led to the Manning Inc. offices.

"We occupy the entire level, here, as you probably already know. Hell, you probably know my inside leg measurement, too, right?"

"I guess you'll have to find out," Evan smirked as he watched Xavier place his own ID card to the plate on the wall.

Swish.

The doors slid open.

Xavier walked through and Evan followed noticing, for the first time, just how hi-tech the entire set-up was.

Giant TV screens lined the reception desk, displaying a white, female android sporting a face with streaks of blue neon down both sides of its face.

"Is that what I think it is?"

"Yep. That's Synthia," Xavier said. "The launch tomorrow."

"Oh, yeah. The sex doll."

"Hey, now. Synthia is no sex doll. Well, that's not all she is. She's so much more than that. Perhaps I'll give you a sneak preview of her before the day is out."

Evan couldn't shake the feeling that something was very wrong about the way Xavier spoke.

Maybe that's just the way the ultra-rich start-up kids talked these days, he decided. Actions spoke louder than words, after all.

Evan cleared his throat and felt the urge to further impress his new employer. "How's she different from your father's MAVIS iteration? I presume there's an upgrade, somewhere? A new operating system?"

Xavier offered a wry smile. "I'm impressed. Yes, before my father passed away, my mother had George take over and hold the fort. The Synthetica program took over, and erased all the nonsense."

"You really think there's a market for this, now?"

Xavier turned to the man with a cast-iron look of seriousness on his face. "You know the InstaBate numbers, right?"

"Right."

"I know what you're talking about," Xavier said. "Where my father went wrong, these days, your common user wants more than just an authentic vagina and an on/off switch."

He admired the image of his work and rubbed his hands together. "It's all about companionship. Good ol' Synthia, here, is far more than just a simple machine. She's going to change the world."

Evan stared at the image of the curvaceous droid body. White arrows sprung up around her limbs, face, and torso, annotating her specifications.

"Wow."

The admiration wasn't lost on Xavier, who nudged the man out of his daydream.

"You like that, don't you?"

"That's pretty advanced stuff," Evan said. "Sixteen teraflops of data? Synthetic amalgam, and a Titanium-based endoskeleton? A perfect replica of human skin?

"And a self-cleaning vagina, anus, and throat, too."

Evan blinked and threw Xavier a look of disgust. "You had to go there, didn't you?"

"What's not to love, Cole?" Xavier grinned. "InstaBate is on its way out. Nobody will want to hook up after Synthia breaks out of her cage."

Evan lowered his head and pined for the death of civilization at the hands of the ultra-rich man ushering him into the brave, new world.

"The future is history in the making, Evan."

Xavier walked off into the main office area, where a giant grid of walled-off cubicles around five feet in height housed the technical team.

A large and imposing Manning Inc. placard adorned the wall, hanging over anyone foolish enough to forget just how influential the company really was.

"So, most of the admin staff are stationed here," Xavier explained. "You won't be interacting with them, though. It's effectively a giant call center, so nobody of any particular interest to you."

An ocean of huddled faces and eyes scanned Evan, ostensibly afraid of Xavier, it seemed, as they walked on by.

"Get back to work," he shouted at them. "Come on. We have a launch to prepare for."

Evan caught up to Xavier and chanced a question. "Do you always treat your employees like shit?"

"What?" Xavier chuckled. "Hell, no. We're a team. Every single employee here is just as valuable as the other. Only, some are more valuable than others. If you get my meaning."

"You read a lot of Orwell, do you?"

Xavier grinned. "Well read, too. I'm impressed."

Just then, a scrawny-looking young guy with spectacles approached Xavier and Evan. "Hey, hey, hey."

Xavier smiled at the man and held his hand out at Evan. "Hey, Bobby."

"I heard we have a new LP?"

Evan squinted at the guy. Much like Xavier, Bobby appeared to be fresh out of college, and all out of shaving cream.

A five o'clock shadow ran under his neck, which underpinned his somewhat bohemian get-up: brown corduroy pants, a faded *Once Upon a Time in Chrome Valley* t-shirt, and sneakers that should have been consigned to the recycle bin at least two years ago.

Bobby offered his hand to Evan. "Hi. Bobby Chariot."

"Evan Cole."

Xavier rubbed his hands together. "Well, this is where I leave you, I'm afraid. I'm sure you two lovebirds can get acquainted and do the necessary."

"The necessary?" Evan asked, offended.

"Not like *that*. I mean, you know—" he tailed off and winked at Bobby before waltzing off to his office. "Bobby, Evan will fix everything. Just show him where the bodies are buried."

"Sure."

Bobby smirked as he watched Xavier sprint through the grid of cubicles. "Pfft. Prick."

"Huh?"

Bobby shook his head and retrained his attention to his new colleague. "Sometimes I wonder if I shouldn't just throw myself out of the fucking window and be done with it."

"What do you mean?"

"So," Bobby said, changing the subject with a sneaky abruptness. "New guy, huh?"

"It would appear so, yeah."

"Come on," Bobby said as he surveyed the cubicles. "I'll show you where the magic happens. We should get out of here before one of the Karens complains to the manager that we're blocking her fucking sunlight."

THE BLUE SKY ROOM
~*Central Control*~

A never-ending series of server machines snaked into the distance.

Rows and rows of whirring and beeping devices produced an intense heat. The noise emanating from them produced a damn near invasive atmosphere.

Bobby swiped the door open and lifted his tablet as he walked into the room. "So, this is where the magic happens."

"Abraca-fucking-dabra."

Evan scoured the machines and recognized most of them instantly.

"What system are we running on here?"

"In their infinite wisdom, Manning cheaped-out. Standard 607X NT Octo-Core processors.

"How very 2020," Evan scoffed. "You'll be telling me all these machines are running on XP, next."

"Yeah, close to ten years on, and we've barely made an improvement. Ripe for hacking. I just hope their insurance coverage isn't as shit as their genius decision to use substandard tech."

"Octo? Doubling up to sixteen-core processors?" Evan asked.

Bobby slammed the larger of the machines in the fourth aisle. "One point above. We're essentially running on fucking fumes, here. Overheat, overclock, most of this shit is raid-array, anyway. It's just a matter of time before one of these pieces of junk gives up and takes us all with it."

Evan turned over his shoulder. "Please tell me that fucking door is fireproof."

"Nope."

He turned back to Bobby with a look of horror on his face. "What?"

"Well, it's *supposed* to be fireproof. The LP before you never had it replaced—"

"—Hold on a fucking second," Evan snapped. "I know it's not in the job description, but you mean to tell me the lead programmer before me never reported the fire hazard to Manning?"

"Nope," Bobby said, casually. "Besides, that's health and safety's job, not—"

"—OSHA don't know their ass from their nutsacks," Evan quipped as he inspected the next machine. "Right, I want all overclocking dialed down to one point over threshold. At least till we can get in and calm everything down."

"Okay."

Evan raced over to the giant machine on the far wall. On his way there, he noticed the giant rectangular window that stretched across the wall.

It offered a superb view of the west side of Chrome Valley - a sight Evan had never seen before in his life.

"Nice view."

"Yeah, it's okay."

"I can see my apartment from here," Evan joked, and then turned to the green machine and gripped the right-hand door. "Is this the mainframe?"

"Yeah, they call it The Grid."

Bobby moved forward and pointed to the ports at the front. "One of three machines in the valley actually directly linked to the international network. Whatever gets in here can go viral, big time."

"How often does the 6G go down?"

Bobby smirked. "About as often as your mom."

Evan exploded with laughter at the joke. He hadn't expected such a dry response. Little did Bobby know that his new colleague wasn't so much laughing at his wit than at his spurious and bleak outlook on life.

"Ha, yeah," Bobby said. "Nah, seriously, though. It goes down *a lot*."

Evan wondered aloud and tutted. "How the fuck did they ever get an app up and running? Let alone build that synthetic android fuck-machine thing they're launching tomorrow?"

"It's amazing what you learn behind the scenes. Stay here long enough, and some of the stuff you'll discover will make your nose bleed."

"Oh yeah?" Evan chanced, quickly. "Like what?"

"Well."

"Well?" Evan asked. "Tell me."

"You clearly know your stuff, Evan," Bobby said. "You know about the Undernet, right?"

The mere mention of the word sent a chill down the back of Evan's neck. "Yeah. Yeah, I know about that."

Bobby's mood soured to match that of his new colleague's. "Some fucked up shit going down there. You've seen the reports of all those youngsters going missing, right?"

"I've seen them."

"It's a fucking outrage," Bobby said. "My wife and little girl are terrified of leaving the house. Same goes for our friends, too. Way to keep us all in fear, huh?"

"Fear will keep the sheep in order."

Bobby shook his head and swallowed. "Look, I'm sure a genius like you doesn't need five nanoseconds to figure out that the same people who created *InstaBate* are also involved in some super nasty shit, too."

Evan placed his hands on his hips and acted dumb. "No, you're right. It wouldn't surprise me."

"All those rich billionaires who've never had a bad card dealt to them their whole lives? With their space projects, eco-friendly cars, and child-molesting friends with their own private islands?"

Evan cast Bobby a wry eye. "Are you saying what I think you're saying?"

Bobby swallowed his speech and tried to change the subject. "Nah, I'm just playing with you."

Suspicious, Evan returned to The Grid and absorbed every nook and cranny on the super-technical machine.

"Do you have your work device on you?"

Bobby reached into his jacket and pulled out an ultra-thin tablet. "Yeah. Such as it is."

Evan glanced at the ancient hardware and scoffed. "Manning hired me to patch this motherfucker up. So, let's patch it up, and worry about the antiquated hardware they're issuing, later."

***

Three men in suits occupied an elevator all to themselves.

Each carried a suitcase in their right hand, and each of them faced forward in silence.

There was just one thing that made them look out of place - their lifelike animal masks.

The first man had a dog's mask, complete with a rubbery wiggle of its lips.

The third sported a peculiar ram's head, complete with two horns.

And the leader of the pack in the middle resembled a rabbit with two goofy teeth poking under its rubbery top lip.

Second floor… third floor… it would be just a matter of a few seconds before they would arrive at their selected seventh level.

"Security was fucking easy," Dog said in his guttural, broken English, an inflection that suggested he was Eastern European.

Bunny tilted his head left, then right, and ironed-out the crick in his neck. When he spoke, his voice came across as modulated. "Be quiet. Don't talk unless you have to."

He gripped his throat and shifted his jaw around. "Goddamn voice alternator," he said. "I sound like a fucking Dalek from that TV show."

"Funny, because you look like a rabbit," Ram said.

"Shut up."

Ram's voice muffled under the rubber as he spoke. "How easy was it to leave the basement and bypass reception, anyway?"

Bunny unclipped his suitcase and readied himself for action. "And we're about to prove it. Let's see how much a billion bucks really cares for its users."

Dog stepped forward and readied himself to exit. "Nearly there. Get ready."

The sixth level light flashed as the cage slowed to a halt.

"Remember, no names," Bunny said. "And don't speak unless it's to order some prick to behave."

Clip-clip.

Bunny held his suitcase to his stomach and pressed his knee against the side. It opened up to reveal two loaded shotguns. He caught the first and threw it to Dog, who caught it in his right hand. "Don't point it at anyone you like."

Dog inspected the barrel of the gun and felt the firearm's heft in his hands. "I will not."

Bunny took a step forward and spied Ram holding the shotgun in his hands. "It's showtime, gentlemen."

Ping.

"Seventh floor. Have a nice day."

Ram smirked as he walked out of the elevator with his colleagues in tow. "Yeah. You too."

The doors to the office loomed at the far end of the corridor.

Ram and Dog chased after Bunny as they arrived at the glass doors. None of them had an ID card in hand.

Bunny's idea of brute force was one they'd decided on before they arrived.

"Gentlemen?"

"Stand back."

Leanne looked up from the reception area and saw a suited dog poking around behind the glass.

"Huh?"

Dog produced a shotgun and aimed it at the doors.

"Oh, shit."

Blam—smash.

The doors exploded off their hinges and slammed against the wall in a haze of dust. Leanne hit the deck just in time for three pairs of pristine shoes belonging to the bad guys to surround her.

"Please, d-don't hurt me," she squealed.

She opened her eyes to find the dog looking down at her. His white, human hand slid towards her face.

"Woof, woof, bitch."

Just then, Leanne felt her scalp tighten. Dog gripped the back of her hair and lifted her to her feet.

Bunny stepped forward and placed his index finger to his lips. "Shh."

"What d-do you want?"

Bunny tapped the side of her face. His electronic voice put the fear of God into the poor girl. "Take us to Mr. Manning."

Ram took Leanne's ID card from her chest and pulled it apart. "Do it quickly."

"Okay, okay."

It was inevitable that those in the cubicles would see three grown men dressed as animals walk across the hall towards Xavier's office.

Most of them giggled amongst themselves, until they witnessed the bizarre sight of a flustered Leanne being frogmarched towards their boss's office.

Nervous, one of the cubicle workers whispered to their neighbor. "What do you think is going on there?"

"Dunno," came the response. "Probably Xavier preparing for tomorrow morning. You know how he likes to play around."

"Hmm."

Knock-knock.

Xavier looked up from his computer desk in haste. He wasn't expecting anyone.

Xavier slammed his laptop lid down and carefully removed it from the table top and slid it onto his lap. "Hello?"

No response came from the person knocking, which was extremely unusual.

As each second of nothingness passed, Xavier's anxiety compounded further and gnawed away at his chest.

"Leanne?" he shouted. "Is that you?"

The handle on the door dropped down, and then pushed open.

Leanne stepped through having been pushed by someone standing behind her. The pained expression of on her face matched Xavier's

"Leanne?"

Instead of replying, she just nodded, barely able to speak. Her arms were half-outstretched in such a way that suggested she had been taken captive.

"What's wrong, Leanne?" he asked. "Why are you crying?"

He needn't have asked.

A man-sized bunny rabbit dressed in a suit shoved her out of his way and waved at his colleague, the dog, to shut the door behind them.

Whump.

Xavier went for something underneath his desk, but the bunny caught him instantly.

"I wouldn't do that if I were you," Bunny said.

Dog lifted his right leg and kicked Leanne over to Xavier's desk. "Get over there, bitch."

He swung his shotgun at her, which encouraged the ram to aim his firearm at Xavier.

Bunny nodded at the desk. "Hands above the desk where we can see them."

Leanne burst into tears and held her arms above her head.

Xavier held his arms out and steadied the unseen laptop on his lap. "It's okay, Leanne. It's okay."

"Oh, it's *far* from okay, Manning," Bunny said through his electronically-altered voice.

"What do you want?"

"Thank you for not raising the alarm," Bunny said. "Because if you had done that, then we'd have to raise hell, and the last thing we want is to have to shoot anyone."

Bunny adjusted his collar and took three steps toward Xavier. "Perhaps I should tell you the *first* thing we want."

Xavier's concern elevated to pure anger in an instant. He eyed his oppressor with venom and sneered. "What?"

Bunny looked around the desktop and saw a monitor, keyboard, and mouse, but no device.

"Your laptop. Where is it?"

"Fuck you."

Ram and Bunny cocked their shotguns and vied for the first to shoot the man's head clean off.

"Please, don't kill us," Leanne said.

Bunny yelled at Leanne so hard that his voice box almost exploded. "Shut the fuck up, *bitch*," he shouted, and then pointed at Xavier's head. "The laptop. Now."

"I swear to God, motherfucker, I'll find you."

"Look at me, asshole," Bunny said. "I'm a rabbit. I love carrots."

"Wh-what?"

"Now, we *could* try the carrot and stick approach. I take a carrot out of my suitcase and *stick* it up your ass and take your fucking laptop, anyway. Or, we can try the *nice* way, which is where you just hand it to me."

Defeated, Xavier reached for his lap and grabbed the device in his hands. He lifted it onto the desktop and snorted with disdain.

"If this is all you want, then take it. And leave us."

Bunny turned to Dog. "Take it."

"Woof woof."

Dog stepped to the desk and swiped the laptop into his suitcase.

Ram kept his shotgun aimed at Xavier's face. "Get the fuck up, asshole. Do it."

"Now, now, Mr. Ram," Bunny said. "Be nice. Nobody ever got anywhere by being rude, did they?"

"Yeah, but I wanna blow a hole in this cocksucker's forehead."

Bunny sniggered and shook his head. "Aww, I should apologize for my associate's behavior, Mr. Manning. He's a bit of a hot head."

Xavier didn't find the joke funny.

Bunny chuckled. "Must be the *horns*."

Again, Xavier wasn't amused.

"Okay, let's get this charade over with," Bunny said. "We're gonna walk out of here, and you're gonna take us to the server room, and you're going to give us access to the central mainframe. It won't take long for us to get what we want, then we'll leave, and the rest of your life is your own."

"Fuck you."

Ram stormed forward and yelled into Xavier's face. "Open your fucking mouth."

He shoved the end of the shotgun between Xavier's lips and threatened to pull on the trigger. "Let me execute this piece of shit right now."

"Hmm," Bunny said. "Let me think about that."

He turned to Leanne for a reaction. "Should we blow your employer's head off, or not?"

"No, p-please," she wept. "Please don't."

"Every PA's dream, isn't it? To see their boss suffer?"

Bunny leaned into Ram's neck and lowered his voice. "Take the gun out of his mouth. I think he gets the picture."

"Fuck."

Resigned, Ram booted Xavier in the stomach. The man sputtered as he stepped back and crouched down in pain.

"Okay, is everybody clear on what we're doing?"

Ram and Dog placed their weapons inside their suitcases and snapped them shut.

Bunny grabbed a fistful of Xavier's hair and threw him towards the door to the office. "Get the fuck over there. We're gonna do this nice and calm."

Whump.

The door to Xavier's office sprung out and slammed against the wall. He was the first to sprint across the main walkway with the three masked men in tow.

For all intents and purposes to those in the cubicles, it seemed as if a hastily-constructed meeting was in process.

Xavier didn't look at a single employee as he made his way to the back of the open-plan office.

Bunny turned to those closest to him in the cubicles and nodded his head. "Good afternoon," was all he bothered to say, but somehow, the empty gesture put those who were watching at some ease.

Dog spoiled it by following the platitude up with a snappy "What the fuck are you looking at?" to the very same people who stared back at him.

***

Bobby Chariot had seen many unusual things in his time working for *InstaBate*, but witnessing a man with a missing pinkie finger wasn't among them.

Evan stood before The Grid and smiled at Bobby, who tried to feign a similar response.

"What the hell happened to your finger?"

Evan smirked. "It's a long story."

Bobby marveled at the human-machine infusion that occurred just above the corresponding digit's knuckle. Where his pinkie finger might have been, instead, it resembled a stick of metal.

"You wanna tell me about *that?*"

"Sure, watch."

Evan extended the stick and inserted it into the port in The Grid. "Uploading now."

"Uploading what?"

"The patch for the chink in InstaBate's armor."

"Okay, this is some fucked-up futuristic shit I don't wanna know about," Bobby said. "You mean to tell me your *finger* is transferring data? The patch?"

"Yep."

"How the hell—"

"—Maybe one day I'll invite you back to my place and you can see my setup, and just how crazy a genius I really am."

Evan used his free hand to tap the top of his head. Where Bobby expected a light thud-on-hair, a distinct sound of metal clanged from within the man's head.

Bobby's jaw nearly hit the floor. "Are you even human?"

Evan glanced at the flashing green light where the fingernail on his pinkie would have been. "Ha. No, it's a standard plate. I had an accident a few years ago. Made a deal with the devil to stay alive."

"Really?"

"No," Evan half-joked. "Not really. But the plate in my head is real, I assure you."

"Like a cranioplasty?"

"Yes. That's exactly what it is—" Evan said, before his eyelids shimmered and caused his jaw to shudder. "Ugh."

"Huh?"

"Sorry about that," Evan said. "Every now and again I get this twitch. Only lasts a few seconds."

Evan returned to his finger and acknowledged the blinking strip light up the side of his metalized pinkie.

"Okay, all done. You got your device?"

"Yeah."

Evan wiggled his pinkie and retrieved his tablet from his jacket. "Right, let's synch up. Make sure it's working."

"Okay."

Bobby held his tablet up and swiped across the screen. The *InstaBate* logo flashed up, showing off the ridiculous cupid cartoon. "I'm in."

"Okay, I'm with you."

Both devices connected via the fanned WiFi symbol. Evan typed a name into the search box.

"I don't have an account. I'm using a dummy one. Let's check this worked."

"Okay."

"Okay, go to filter, and sort by sex."

"Gotcha."

Bobby's screen blinked and the dashboard slid to the right to reveal a series of settings. Another swipe of the thumb scrolled the image down to sex.

"Male."

"Male."

"Set it to *sexual orientation*, gay," Evan said with no hint of humor. Bobby snickered and thumbed the option. "Done."

"Good. Don't go getting any ideas, now, okay?"

"Fuck you."

They both chuckled as Evan returned to his screen. "Not if I fuck you first, my gay little friend."

"I can see why Xavier hired you on the spot," Bobby said. "Your quick-wit and affability."

"Yeah, it'll take me some time to match your sarcasm, though," Evan said. "Okay, type my name. Evan Cole."

Bobby typed the name with the on screen keypad. "I'm way ahead of you."

"That is reassuring, just don't go expecting any dick pics."

"If you do take any, make sure you're set to landscape," Bobby joked. "Okay. Yup, found you."

Bobby held up his screen to Evan. A picture of a freaky, goth-like skull sat in place of where a user would usually put their real-life photo. "I mean, I presume this is the correct Evan Cole?"

"That's me, all right."

Bobby scoffed at the ugly, skeletal avatar. "Are you *sure* you didn't make a deal with the devil?"

"That's for me to know and you to find out."

Bobby shifted his eyes from The Skull picture, to Evan's face, and back again. "Hmm. Yeah, I see the resemblance. Miss three more meals and it'll be spot on."

Evan looked over his shoulder, his attention drawn to a small commotion at the far end of the Blue Sky room.

Bobby focused his attention on the dummy profile Evan had set up. "It says here you're into INXS, collect butterflies, and despise capitalism?"

Curious, Evan slid his tablet into his jacket pocket and moved alongside the banks of servers. "Did you check the patch?"

"Yeah, it's tight," Bobby said. "I dunno how you did that, but it's—"

Beep-swipe.

Evan raised his eyes as the sound of a connecting device from behind the door. "Bobby?"

"Yeah?" came the calm and collected voice from behind the machines.

Evan planted his foot on the carpeted floor and froze still. The walls around him were silent, the air broken by the incessant humming from the banks of servers that surrounded him.

"Who knows we're in here?"

"Who cares?" Bobby's voice seemed to sing. "Wait till we tell Xavier that we've fixed his problem, and he'll be—"

Swish.

The doors opened and Xavier stumbled into the room, having been pushed by a suited man wearing a bunny mask.

Evan made eye contact with Xavier, who sported a pained and aggrieved look on his face.

"What the fuck?"

"Evan! Don't tell them anyth—"

"—Shut the fuck up," Dog said, before punching Xavier across the face. "Be a good little doggy and close your mouth before I knock it off your head."

Before Evan could figure out what was happening, a suited Ram walked into the room and pulled a shotgun from his suitcase.

"Oh, fuck."

Evan backed up and held out his arms. "Xavier? What the fuck is happening?"

Bobby peered his head around the end of the bank of machines and gasped. "Evan?"

"Yeah."

"Who are they?"

"I dunno."

Bunny dropped his suitcase on the floor and kicked it toward Evan's feet. "I'll keep this *brief*."

"Ha. Funny," Dog quipped as he clutched the back of Xavier's collar and dragged him along the path that led to The Grid.

"Pick up the suitcase, and get your girlfriend to step out with you. I don't want her to think we haven't seen her, and get brave and try to attack us, or anything."

Careful to carry out the man's demand, Evan collected the suitcase from the floor. "Bobby, get out here. They're serious."

"I am, I am."

Bobby stepped out from behind the serves with his arms out.

"Hello, sweetheart," Bunny said in his mangled, electro-infused voice. "Is it just you two in here right now?"

"Yeah."

"Good."

Bunny stopped a few feet in front of Evan and sized him up. "You're new here, aren't you?"

"Yeah, I am."

"Lead programmer?"

A quizzical expression fell across Evan's face. "Yeah."

"Not surprised," Bunny snorted. "This company gets through dozens of LPs every week. They all end up committing suicide or murdered," he said, nonchalantly, and then sized Bobby up and down. "Ain't that right, girlfriend?"

Bobby had no choice but to nod, quickly, and hope not to get executed. "Yeah."

"Yeah," Bunny said. "Working here is a cunt's job, and only a cunt would wanna do it. Profiteering out of other's misery and broken families, all for the sake of a quick blowjob. But, hey, who am I to judge, right? We just want the cheat codes."

"The cheat codes?" Evan asked.

Xavier tried to fight back, but Dog tightened his grip on his shirt. "Evan, no—"

"—Ignore your boss," Bunny said. "We want the hard drive with the Rubicon mark on it."

"But that's *InstaBate*'s central data core," Evan said.

"That's precisely why we want it," Bunny said. "Take it out, place it in the briefcase, and then hand it back to me. Do it careful."

"Goddamn it," Xavier said.

"Do it, or my friend, Dog, will execute your boss, and this fucked-up piece of shit rabbit to my left will execute your girlfriend. If you're lucky, he won't hump her corpse after he does it, but I can't guarantee he won't."

The Ram and Bobby exchanged glances.

"Okay, okay," Evan said. "I'll do it."

Xavier squeezed his eyes shut, far from wanting to see the offense take place. Evan stepped up to The Grid and traced his index finger cross the multitude of house hard drives.

Finally, he landed on a device named TR, with a small sticker displaying a neon blue cube underneath it.

Clip-clip.

Bobby watched Evan remove the medium-sized drive from the machine and pass it to the man with the bunny mask. "Here."

"Put it in the case."

"Okay, okay."

Carefully, Evan slid the device into the suitcase and waved the passing heat away from his palms.

The Bunny snapped the case shut and lowered his head to Evan's hand. "What are you doing?"

"It's hot."

"Hot?"

"Yeah," Evan said, and threw a glance at Bobby. "*Duck.*"

"Duck?"

The Dog aimed his shotgun at Evan's chest. "He ain't no duck, he's a—"

Evan launched forward, extended his pinkie finger, and stabbed Bunny in the shoulder.

"Gah!"

Xavier and Bobby immediately hit the deck. Dog yanked on the trigger and fired a shot at Evan.

Blam-spatch.

Evan's ribcage exploded in a shower of blood and flesh. The shell tore through his liver, stomach and spinal column with such force that his body sprang into the air and crashed back-first against The Grid.

"Evan!"

Bunny snatched the shotgun from Dog's hand and swung it around, focusing the end of Xavier's face.

"Don't shoot."

Both Bunny's and Xavier's eyes met for a brief moment, before the former roared at the top of his lungs. "You wanna die, too?"

"N-No," Xavier begged. "You have what you want."

Bunny kicked the crouching Bobby in the stomach and tossed the suitcase at Ram. "Get up."

"Why do I have to carry this?" Ram said. "I'm already carrying my own case."

"Shut the fuck up and move."

Ram raced to the far end of the Blue Sky room and tore Leanne's lanyard from her neck. "Come on, let's go."

"Go, go, go."

Dog shoved the terrified Xavier forward. "Don't even think about raising the alarm, asshole."

Bunny took a final look at Evan's still-beating heart buried deep inside his smoking chest cavity. He turned to Bobby, who crawled to his new colleague in pain.

"I'll leave you to take care of your boyfriend. He may need a band aid for that wound," Bunny said, before racing off.

The door to the room slid open, and Ram, Bunny, and Dog exited with Xavier.

Bobby uncovered his eyes and spat a rope of drool onto the floor. He winced as he took to his knees and finally laid eyes on his friend.

"Guuuuh," Evan puked a fountain of thick, congealed blood down his chin and struggled to reach inside his busted jacket pocket.

Bobby gasped and scrambled over to the dying man. "Oh, fuck. Evan. We need to call you an ambulance—"

"—Nuh-nuh," he wheezed and spluttered.

Bobby pulled his cell phone from out of his pants pocket and flicked it to life. "It's okay, stay still. Keep your eyes open."

"Nugh," Evan struggled. "Nugh—"

"—Shh. It's okay, it's not too bad."

Bobby was fucking *lying* - Evan was lucky to have survived this long. His beating organ slowed in an instant, and Evan slumped against The Grid with his tablet in his hand.

He closed his eyes and roared with pain, his nostrils filling with blood. "Uck-uck-uck—ngggg."

"What, what?"

"G-get—th-them—"

"—Get them?"

"L-Leave, g-go," Evan groaned as he lifted his metal pinkie to the far door. "G-Get—"

Bobby turned to the door, and back to Evan. "I can't get them. They're armed."

"G-Gunna—k-kill—"

Evan rammed his pinkie into the socket on the side of his tablet just as Bobby climbed to his feet. The final actions of a dying young man perplexed him.

Just what in the hell was he doing?

"I, uh—"

"—Guh—g-go—"

A torrent of white-and-red goop blasted down his neck from his mouth as the screen on his tablet flicked to life.

A connection had been made.

Bobby stepped back and accidentally hit one of the servers. "Oh, Jesus Christ."

"Yaaaaarrrgggggggghhhhh."

Sptich-spatch-ch-ch.

Evan passed away screaming at the top of his busted lungs as his body flipped up and around. To Bobby, it seemed Evan's very lifeblood was being sucked out of what little remained of him - and into his device.

"Evan?"

The man's right hand dropped the tablet, finally releasing his pinkie.

***

Bunny led the charge through the main office area with Ram and Dog following behind.

Xavier kept up the pretense of all being well, but as the cubicles of concerned eyeballs whizzed past, he knew that they knew something was wrong.

For one thing, they *surely* would have heard the commotion in the reception area.

The three animals appeared to escort him past his subordinates, which was altogether very strange.

"Get back to work," Xavier barked at the workforce. "Stop staring at me."

Each worker duly obliged and returned to their screens, but kept a stern eye-out for what might happen next as the men returned to the reception area.

Bunny closed the glass door and surveyed the smoke-filled reception area. He turned to Xavier and slapped him across the face.

"Ow."

"Thanks for giving us what we wanted," Bunny said, before turning to his two colleagues. "Let's go."

"Fuck yeah."

Dog and Ram ran over to the elevators with their suitcases, leaving Bunny to impart his final instruction to his victim.

"Call me sometime, eh?"

Xavier didn't have words for his captive's particular brand of sarcasm, and just stared through the eye holes in the mask.

A pair of powder green eyes seemed to smile back at him.

"Fuck you," Xavier said.

"Obviously, it goes without saying that you won't raise the alarm. Or go to the police. I know you have a dead kid back in the server room, but I trust you'll take care of it."

"I'll take care of *you*, you fucking asshole."

Bunny giggled and tapped Xavier on the shoulder. "That's the spirit."

Before he raced off to the elevators and joined his two colleagues, he stopped to throw a final message to Xavier. "Oh, and that PA girl of yours, wherever she is. Give her one from me, okay?"

Dog hollered down the hallway by the elevators. "It's here. Come on, stop molesting him. We need to go."

"I gotta go, Manning. See ya."

Bunny spun around on the spot and ran out of view, leaving a thoroughly disheveled and angry Xavier to return to the office and face the music.

A million courses of actions - and resulting consequences - rushed through his mind as he entered the office area.

Everyone looked back at him, demanding answers.

"What? Get back to work. Everything's cool."

Just then, Xavier arrived at a conclusion. The corpse in the Blue Sky Room was definitely the first thing to attend to before anything else.

Chapter 4

Bobby crouched over Evan's dead body, trying his best to ignore the incessant whirring and beeping coming from the labyrinth of servers.

The bloodletting was so bad that much of it had caked into the carpet.

"Shit, Evan."

Bzzzz.

Bobby's tablet came to life in his hand. The neon case sparked up and illuminated the wrinkles in his palm. Confused, Bobby made the mistake of glancing at the screen.

"Huh?"

"G-Get them—"

"—What the fuck?" Bobby screamed and dropped the tablet onto the blood-soaked floor.

Looking up at him from the screen was a chattering, neon contour skull. "B-Bobby."

"Evan?"

The Skull's jaw lifted up and down like an evil cartoon as it struggled to speak. "Get them. T-Take me with y-you."

"Get who?"

The Skull grunted and moved its forehead to the screen as if it was trying to head butt its way out. "Fuck. Take me with you. Go."

"Evan?"

Bobby slid his hand under the tablet and lifted it up. "Evan, is that *you*?"

The Skull rammed its blue-striped bony forehead to the screen from the other side of the tempered glass. "*Get them*. Run."

"Okay, okay."

Bobby went to race for the door, but immediately stopped in his tracks. He pointed to the decimated corpse leaning against The Grid. "But, your body?"

Roar.

The Skull gnashed its misshapen teeth, causing Bobby to shriek like a little girl.

"Jesus fucking Christ."

The Skull grunted for what Bobby felt would be the last time. "Go."

Bobby squeezed his eyes shut and took a deep breath.

Just then, Xavier ran into the Blue Sky Room with his ID Card in his hand. He spotted Bobby shaking his head and preparing to run.

"Chariot?"

"Manning?"

Bobby made a dash down the corridor and headed for Xavier, who raced up to him.

"We need to do something about Evan—"

"—Sorry, man, I gotta go."

Roar.

The tablet in Bobby's hand vibrated. The Skull grunted at Xavier on its way past his hips.

"Where are you going?"

Bobby twisted around and ran backwards, feeling his way for the door. "I, uh—no, there's no time to explain. Evan's not dead."

Xavier double-took and glanced at his corpse, and then back at Bobby.

"What? What do you mean he's not—"

"—I gotta go," Bobby yelped. "We need to catch these fuckers."

He slid through the door and ran off, leaving a thoroughly confused Xavier wondering what to do next.

***

The basement button on the elevator panel glowed orange.

Bunny, Dog, and Ram stood in a triangle formation as the lights pinged their way down from the seventh floor.

"Well, that was easy," Dog said.

Ram scratched his exposed neck with his fingernails. "When can we take these fucking masks off?"

Bunny faced forwards. "Not yet. The second these doors open, get in the van. No messing around."

Bobby dashed past the elevators with his tablet in his hand. The Skull floated around on screen and knocked its nose against the left-hand side of the device.

"Use the stairs. They're taking the fourth elevator—" it said, before vanishing from the screen.

"Where are they going?"

Bobby pushed a man out of his way and slid across the floor on his heels.

"Hey, watch we're you're going."

"Sorry!"

The Skull blinked back to life as Bobby hit the top step and jumped down two a time, using the handrail to steady his balance.

"Basement," The Skull said. "They're headed for the basement."

"Jesus Christ, I can't outrun an elevator."

"I'm hacking into the building's security, keep running—"

Schwipp-blip.

The Skull tumbled into the oblique darkness on the tablet as Bobby pushed forward, turned the corner, and descended the next set of stairs.

He glanced at the glassed walls that offered a view of the road a hundred feet below. A build-up of traffic had formed at the parking lot entrance, which inspired him to run faster.

"God, I'm so outta shape."

"Quit whining and keep running."

The Skull spun around inside the tablet and slammed its jaws together, scaring the shit out of his human friend.

"Stop doing that."

"Second floor, get a move on," The Skull said. "I can't hold them forever."

"I'm going, I'm going."

Shunt.

The elevator cage stopped just before the second floor, as evidenced by the two lights flashing on the panel.

"What the fuck?" Dog barked. "Why have we stopped?"

"Shit, not now. Not now."

Bunny looked up and around for any sign of life. Frantic, he stepped to the panel and punched the buttons. "Come on, you piece of shit."

Ring-ring-ring.

"Please be advised, the elevator is currently experiencing technical issues. Please remain standing."

Ram looked up at the strip lights on the ceiling and unclipped the lock on his suitcase. "Maybe we'll go low-tech on this motherfucker."

He wrenched the shotgun from out of the suitcase and prepared to open fire.

"What are you doing?"

"I'm going old school on this motherfucker."

Bunny slapped Ram so hard that his mask nearly flew off. "Imbecile. You open fire and we'll have five-oh swarming this place like flies around shit."

Dog extended his finger and went for the alarm button. "I'll take care of this."

"What are *you* doing?" Bunny snapped.

"We're sitting ducks, here."

Ram cocked his shotgun and pushed Bunny out of his way. "Fuck this. Stand back."

"Ah, shit."

Bunny and Dog turned away and pressed their fingers to their ears.

Bang.

The panel on the wall blasted apart, shooting tiny shards of plastic and metal in all directions.

Whump.

The cage shunted around on its descent.

Relieved, Bunny and Dog exhaled and chuckled. "Well, well, well, turns out you really are user friendly."

"I ain't getting caught trapped in this fucking elevator," Ram said. "Fuck, I'm sweating so bad in this godforsaken mask."

Bunny gripped the handle on the elevator wall and prepared to kick the doors open. "Never mind that now. Get ready to get outta here."

The second button flashed, and then the first. It seemed that someone on the first floor might have called the elevator.

"Shit. If we stop on level one, let the fucker in, and then execute them when the doors are closed."

Ram steadied himself and swung the shotgun at the doors. "You got it."

"Ready…"

Ping.

The cage stopped, and the doors opened. A young woman raised her eyes at the three animals in suits. She gasped at the Ram, who aimed his shotgun at her head.

"Good afternoon," Bunny said.

The woman bit her lip and almost soiled her underwear. "Oh, umm—"

"—You'll take the next one?" Bunny asked, sternly.

"Sure."

"Yeah, good idea."

Ping.

The door swiped shut, cutting the three men off from the astonished lady.

All three exhaled once again and looked at the floor.

"Shit, that was close," Ram said. "I was about ready to blast her pretty face off her neck."

"Shame, she was hot," Dog offered. "We shoulda taken her with us."

Bunny thumped Dog on the back and pointed at the doors. "Be a good doggy, and get the keys for the van ready. Here we go."

Ping.

"Basement Level. We hope you have a very nice day."

Bunny raced out of the elevator and waved Dog and Ram over with him. "We will, thanks."

Dog ran at speed past several rows of cars and hollered over his shoulder. "Come on, come on." He pointed his car key at a large, silver van.

Beep-boop.

The alarm echoed across the concrete blocks as the man approached the back of the vehicle.

"Load up the back, go."

Dog wrenched the driver's side door open and climbed inside. He inspected the rear view mirror and coughed inside his mask. "Ugh. It's so fuckin' hot in here."

The back of the van slumped up and down.

When Dog peered into the rear view mirror, he noticed two things.

The first were his colleagues in the back of the van.

The second was the door to the stairwell flying open and producing a sweaty, out-of-breath man in spectacles wearing a white shirt with the *InstaBate* logo.

Dog started the engine and leaned into the mirror for a better view.

"Oh, shit. It's him. *It's him.*"

"Who... him?" Bunny snapped from the back of the van.

"The geek with the fucking glasses and two-week-old body odor. From the server room."

"The one we didn't kill?"

Ram reached for his shotgun and kicked the back doors open.

Whump.

Bobby ran across the tarmac and clapped eyes on the Ram pointing his gun at his face from fifty feet away.

"Oh, shit."

Bunny pointed at him. "Fuckin' shoot him."

"Shoulda done it earlier, upstairs."

Blam.

Bobby ducked just in time for the cement pillar behind his head to burst apart from the bullet hit.

"Go, go, go, *fuckin' drive*."

Dog slammed on the gas, flicked the shift to drive, and gripped the steering wheel.

"You got it."

Screeeech.

The van's tires spun across the ground, causing its back end - and Ram and Bunny - to fly around one-hundred-and-eighty degrees, before bolting off towards the parking lot ramp.

"Woof, woof!"

Ram reloaded his shot gun and blasted at Bobby again. "Eat lead, you cocksucking millenial *fuck*."

Bam.

Bobby jumped out of the line of fire and ran alongside the parked vehicles. The bullet crashed into the trunk of a black Bugatti.

The hood burst open and smashed against the ceiling as Bobby raced towards a gray Ford X706.

"Bobby?" came a grunt from his tablet.

"Yeah?"

"Stop admiring the fucking paintwork and get in your car."

Bobby reached into his pocket with his free hand and grabbed his keys.

"Get in and follow them."

Breathless, Bobby picked up the pace and aimed his car key sensor at the back of the gray Ford.

Biddip-boop.

The back of the car seemed to bounce as the vehicle unlocked.

"Get in," The Skull said. "Put me on the passenger seat."

As Bobby neared the car, the driver's side door lifted up like a giant bat wing. He slid his ass onto the seat, reached up, grabbed the handle, and yanked the door down.

Flump.

He dropped his tablet onto the passenger seat and spoke up at the ceiling.

"Ignition initiated, auto start."

Vroom-vroom.

The car's engine burst to life, along with the lights and buttons on the car's dashboard.

"Ford X706, huh?" The Skull cackled from the tablet resting on the seat. "Please tell me you got the Dynamique version with autopilot installed?"

Bobby strapped his seatbelt across his chest and fastened it into the socket. "Of course I did. I'm not an idiot."

"Good. Get driving," The Skull said. "I'm gonna try and patch into the traffic system and find out where the fuckers are going."

"You can do that?!"

"Dunno. But we're about to find out."

Bobby grabbed the steering wheel and slammed on the gas. The car tires screeched before catapulting the car towards the exit ramp.

Bobby yelled as the back of the car bounced off the dent at the foot of the ramp and flung up a shower of orange sparks. "Ah, shit. My fender."

"Fuck your fender," The Skull said. "Just step on it."

Vroooom.

The Ford X706's tires slid across the road as Bobby hit the brake and spun the steering wheel. He applied the gas again and dug his heel to the floor.

Two oncoming cars swerved out of his path as he straightened up into the right-hand lane.

"You see 'em?" The Skull asked.

Bobby leaned forward and squinted. "Yeah, back of that silver van. They've closed the doors."

"Follow them."

"But they're armed?"

"Yeah," The Skull said. "With bullets."

"Uh, isn't that enough?"

"Nah, they're not armed with what we've got, hehe," The Skull said.

"What are we armed with?"

"Knowledge and power."

"Oh, *great*."

Bobby rammed his foot to the floor and forced his vehicle to speed up. The silver van shot ahead and threatened to disappear from view for good.

Suddenly, it jutted to the right, and veered toward the slip road.

"They're taking the exit onto the freeway."

The Skull tumbled around the screen like an epileptic ghost, before freezing for a second in the middle of the screen. "I know, hold on."

Bip-bip-bip.

Bobby shook his head and turned into the right-hand lane. "What do I do, Evan? Evan?"

A friendly voice from his car's speakers, *"Please standby."*

"Standby?" Bobby yelped.

The Skull enlarged on the screen and opened its jaw. "Okay, I'm in.

"In? In *what?*"

"The traffic system, motherfucker."

"What traffic system? What the fuck are you talking about—"

One by one, the traffic lights on the slip road flicked from green to red, causing the silver van to slow down behind three vehicles.

"Got 'em," The Skull said. "God, I love WiFi."

"WiFi?"

"Yeah, good ol' Ford X706. You can't fault their routers. But I can't hold these lights forever."

"What do you mean you're—"

"—Godamnit you speccy fuck, stop asking questions and catch up to them. I'm out of range."

"Out of range?"

"Fuck me, there's an echo in the car," The Skull snapped. "Yes, dickhead. Get me in range. Ride up alongside 'em."

Bobby pursued his lips and spun the steering wheel to the right, feeling sorry for himself.

"Aww, why me?"

"Hey, asshole," The Skull said. "You're not the one who got their guts blown out by the fuckers. Now drive, before I upload my foot in your ass."

"Fine."

It was at this moment that Bobby decided he might die today, and violently. The events playing out had started normally enough, but as of half an hour ago, shit, as he'd usually say, had gotten very real.

Bobby's vehicle bounced along the tarmac and screamed through the grass verge, bypassing the cars in line for the exit.

"They're gonna turn green any… second… now…"

The red bulb on the traffic light died and the green light blinked to life.

"Ah, fuck," Bobby said as he stepped on the gas.

The cars in line bounded past the side of the Ford one by one, to a series of angry, blaring horns.

"Sorry, sorry, sorry," Bobby said with a helpless look on his face to many, many middle fingers being flipped from behind the various car windows.

"Never mind those fuckers, drive."

"What do you think I'm doing, ordering a pizza?"

"Shut your mouth and join the freeway."

Screeeech.

Six cars shot past on the freeway as the gray Ford X706 swerved around and joined the fast lane.

Dead ahead, the two doors on the back of the silver van seemed to rattle back and forth.

The Skull rammed its head against the glass and squealed. "Ah, fuck, you know I can't see shit from here. All I can see is your upholstery."

"I can't put you on the dash, you'll slide off," Bobby snapped as he concentrated on the road.

"You're gonna have to be my eyes and ears—"

Neeeaaawwww.

Bobby pushed the steering wheel forward and tilted it to the right, narrowly avoiding a collision with a yellow car driving alongside him.

"Shit."

"Fuck," The Skull spat. "Drive nice."

"I'm trying my best."

"Now I can see why Manning hired you. You can only do one thing at a time—"

"—Fuck you—"

"—And badly, at that."

"Again, fuck you—"

Bobby stopped mid-sentence when the back doors of the silver van burst open to reveal Bunny and Ram standing with their guns aimed right at his windshield.

"Oh dear."

"What?"

"I don't think they like us following them."

The Skull bolted around the screen in fury. "What makes you say that?"

"Let's just say *you're* safe hiding down there."

"What—?"

Bang-smash.

Ram fired off a shot. The bullet chewed through the roof of the car, sending it off course and slamming into the side of the yellow car in the next lane.

Blaaare.

"I'm sorry," Bobby yelped. "Evan?"

"Yeah, hi."

"They're shooting at me. I don't think I want to do this anymore."

"You fucking fairy, speed up—" his voice whirled out from the device, then changed to that of an automated female's, *"Initiating WiFi scan. Please standby."*

"Who's in there with you?"

"Your mom," The Skull joked angrily, before returning to the business at hand. "Just get me close to the van. Alongside it. I need to get within ten feet of the dashboard."

"Ugh, fuck."

Vroooom.

Ram reloaded his shotgun and stomped his foot on the floor. "Where the fuck does he think he's going?"

Bunny lifted his shotgun and aimed it at Bobby in the driver's side. "Here he comes. Here, little piggy—"

"—Stop teasing him and blow his fuckin' head off!" Ram screamed.

"Fuck yeah," Bunny said before pulling the trigger.

Blam.

The bullet smashed the windshield, and burnt a hole in the passenger seat.

"Aww, shit."

Bunny and Ram watched as the Ford X706 sped up and out of sight, driving alongside the van.

Dog turned to his left and raised his eyebrows. "Here, he's up here. He's driving next to us."

Bunny and Ram yanked the back doors to the van shut and raced to up the front seats.

"Where?"

"There, look."

Back in the X706, The Skull examined the bullet hole in the back passenger seat and frowned. "What was that?"

"One of their shells."

"Shit, that could've blown your head clean off."

"Gee, you think?"

"Yeah, look at it."

Bobby began to cry for his life. "The next fucking bullet just might."

"Stop crying like a little bitch and concentrate on the road."

The Skull said as it moved around and spotted a wire coming from the dashboard.

"Plug me in. USB port.

"Wh-what?"

"Wh-what?" The Skull mocked, evilly. "The *fucking cable* coming from the port on your dash. Plug me in."

Bobby yanked the end of the cable and tried to plug it into the socket on his tablet.

"Oooh, you little devil," The Skull joked. "Aren't you gonna buy my dinner first?"

Blam-smash.

The driver's side window on the x706 exploded, vomiting thousands of tiny shards of glass all over Bobby's head and shoulders.

"Gahhhh."

He looked to his right to see Dog had shot at him with his firearm, and followed it up with a nasty throat-slit motion.

"Woof-woof!"

"Oh, God," Bobby said. "I'm so dead."

"Okay," The Skull said from within the screen on Bobby's device. "I'm about to transfer myself now. Keep alongside them."

"And what? Get my head blown off?"

"If I can't get in, they get away, and that's it. They win. Step on it."

Bobby couldn't help but notice the free stretch of road up ahead, but found the sight of Dog reloading his shotgun to be much more of a concern.

"Oh, fuck—Evan, I dunno what you got planned, but do it quickly."

"WiFi transfer Initiated. Loading…"

"I'm in," The Skull said. "Keep alongside them."

"Evan?"

"Yeah?"

Bobby chanced the inevitable through his incessant wailing. "If they kill me, can you bring me back to life like you?"

"Uh, no."

"What?"

Bobby saw Bunny lean forward next to Dog and aim his shotgun at the car.

"WiFi Port: 202-505… transfer started."

"It doesn't work like that," The Skull said. "I just need five more seconds."

"Are you WiFiing into the van?"

"Yeah, keep up with them—"

Bang-schplatt.

Bobby's temple burst open and splattered the dashboard, and his tablet, with blood.

"Shit, Bobby!" The Skull cried.

Bobby's mostly-decapitated corpse slammed against the steering wheel, causing it to veer away from the van.

Swerve.

The X706 entered the left lane.

"You motherfucking *bastards*," The Skull said.

"Transfer complete."

"Ah, c'mon, c'mon."

Suddenly, The Skull's image elongated and whipped off the screen, causing the dashboard to spark up like a firework.

"I'm in."

The X706 smashed against the side of a red Chevrolet, pushing against the bodywork - and off the lane.

Smash.

The two vehicles careened into the metal railings on the side verge, causing both vehicles to rocket into the air and explode as they crashed back down to the road.

The cars behind slammed on their brakes and blared their horns as the carnage built up in front of them.

The first two cars darted into the back of the X706.

Ka-blaaam.

A huge gulf of fire rocketed into the air. Whatever was left of Bobby roasted into the sky, as more and more cars plowed into the vehicular bonfire several feet behind the speeding silver van.

"Fuck yeah," Bunny said. "We got the fucker."

Dog yelled over his shoulder. "Pull the doors shut. We're nearly there."

Bunny and Ram wasted no time in doing as Dog instructed.

Whum-bump.

The doors slammed shut.

"You see that?" Bunny giggled. "I shot the fucking virgin in all four eyes."

Bunny pinched the left ear on his head and tugged at the mask.

"I guess that'll be a closed casket for his mom at the funeral, huh?" Ram asked.

"Fuck yeah, although the ugly prick woulda needed a closed casket without the bullets, anyhow."

Bunny pulled the silly rubber covering from his head and slammed it to the ground.

The man underneath had sweat profusely, and dampened his gray mustache.

The man's name was George Gilbertson, deputy director at Manning Inc.

"I guess we can take 'em off now," George said.

Ram grabbed the horns on his mask and tore it off his head to reveal an African-American face. When he licked his lips, the chrome-plated spear daggered through the middle of his tongue nearly cut his bottom lip.

"Be careful."

"Hey, George," the man said. "I dunno how I kept that piece of shit mask on my head for so long. How do I look?"

"Do you really wanna know?"

"Nah, man."

Dog still had his mask on. He didn't want to take it off due to the visibility people might have of him from outside. "Okay, Exit 11A. We're nearly there."

George flicked open the suitcase and grabbed the hard drive. "Try and get us there in one piece. We don't wanna fuck this next part up."

"Sure, Bunny. You got it."

"You can stop calling me that, now. We can use our real names."

"Yeah, George."

Little did the three men know that, somewhere buried deep within their electronic dashboard, The Skull could hear everything.

Evan's voice whirled around the circuitry behind the sat nav screen. He kept away from it.

"George?"

"ETA five minutes," Dog said.

George giggled to himself and slapped his black friend on his shoulder. "Bang on time."

"Man, don't fuckin' touch me."

"Ah, Oxide," George said. "What's a little touching between rich friends, huh?"

"Man, get your pasty fuckin' digits away from me, ya hear? Shit. I ain't on InstaBate, and I don't appreciate you molestin' me."

Evan's voice shimmied through the console, quietly. "George. Oxide?"

"I'm sure they're gonna *love* what we've brought for them."

The silver van took Exit 11A in relative peace and tranquility, and made for Chrome Valley's industrial estate.

Chapter 5

Chrome Valley Industrial Estate
~Unit 118~

A dirtier and less charismatic area of the valley would be hard to find. The industrial estate's permanent gray buildings signaled the end of the world. Fences as far as the eye could see were interrupted by the occasional puddle that reflected the overcast skies.

The silver van rolled to a stop in one of the ample parking spaces by the sliding door to the building.

George peered over the front seat and tapped Dog on the shoulder. "Tarin, take that stupid fucking mask off. We're good."

"Thank fuck for that," he said. "I could hardly breathe in that thing."

Dog removed his sweltering mask and flung beads of sweat onto his lap. He took a deep breath and sighed.

"Let them know we're here."

"I think they'll have heard us."

Oxide hopped out of the back of the van with his two suitcases and ran over to the building.

"Okay, open up. C'mon."

Tarin switched off the ignition and pulled the key card from the slot under the wheel.

Little did the three gentlemen know that Evan was somewhere inside the dashboard…

A whirlwind of pixels circled the darkness to form the shape of a lengthy corridor. Blues, whites, yellows, the color list was endless as the small squares whooshed past.

"Where the hell am I?" Evan's voice bounced from side to side as the heady haze of pixels twisted away. One by one, they formed the outline of a human head without skin, ultimately resembling a badly-drawn skull like something out of a vintage video game.

"Scanning... scanning... c'mon... *scan*."

From the top of the darkness, a blinding white light tongued to the bottom. A giant tomb of electronic nodes pulsed to produce a yoyo of an ellipsis...

Scanning.
Scanning..
Scanning...

Black text crunched down the white light, offering a selection of bizarre names.

"C'mon," The Skull said. "Before the battery loses its j-juice."

The hundreds of unit numbers flashed before The Skull.

"Unit 118, they said Unit 118."

Hundreds of thousands of searched numbers rolled down at a million miles per minute. Eventually, the one The Skull was looking for slowed before his face.

Unit 118. Please login.

"I gotcha."

The Skull's jaw slammed up and down violently as the number 118 enlarged to such an extent that it enveloped the darkness, and blocked-out.

Access granted.

Seconds later, The Skull was in.

***

Rumble.

The giant warehouse door rolled up to reveal three suited men, silhouetted by the hazy sunshine burning into the ground behind them.

A young black woman with long hair turned to the folding light as it crept along the ground and illuminated the interior of the warehouse.

"Hey, is that you?"

The light from outside rolled up her blouse and past the patch covering her left eye.

"It's them, all right."

She turned to her friend, a muscle-bound male with a neck that matched the thickness of his arms.

The folding warehouse door squeaked across the ceiling before slamming open at the end of the rails.

George moved in with his bunny mask in his right hand. "Fuck me, we gotta get that door oiled. I think there was someone in SiliChrome Valley that must have heard all the squeaking."

"Not exactly inconspicuous, huh?" the muscled man asked.

"Here, Elmer. Take this."

Elmer snatched the flying mask from the air and pulled it out. The fluid from George's face melted into the pores of his skin. "Yuck."

George threw the bunny mask at him and smiled at the dark-skinned woman. "Hey, Alyssa."

"George?"

"How you doing?"

"Fine," she said, suspiciously. "Did you get the thing?"

"Of course we got the thing."

George turned to Oxide and clicked his fingers. "Suitcase."

Oxide made his way through the middle of the warehouse. Four ultra-high definition cameras stood on tripods, facing a cold-looking metallic table at waist height to all involved.

Two vises were clamped at each end.

A double-thick sheet of cloth lay underneath, pinned to the concrete by the table legs.

Absentmindedly, Oxide stopped to take in the view and shuddered before speaking. "Shit's fucked up. Is this where the thing happens?"

"Uh-huh," George said. "Don't get too familiar. You're not staying to watch. You're nearly done."

Tarin and Oxide didn't look especially happy with their new location. The latter placed the suitcase on the metal table, but couldn't help noticing a few strands of very fine blonde hairs trapped in the jaws of the vice closest to him.

"I feel sick."

"Fuck how you feel," Elmer said. "Just give Alyssa the case."

"Okay big fella, cool."

"My name is Elmer, you dirty fuckin' slave."

George held out his hands and chuckled with familiarity. "Hey, hey, play nice. We're all friends here, right? No need for the racism or dick-swinging. We can certainly do the latter when we've retrieved all the data and start selling to the highest bidder."

Oxide retrieved the Rubicon drive from the suitcase and lifted it up for all to see.

"We have the technology."

Alyssa raised both eyebrows, but only her right eye demonstrated just how impressed she was. "Please tell me everything went smoothly."

"As smooth as a baby's ass," George said. "If you'll pardon the pun."

Carefully, Alyssa took the drive from Oxide's hands and returned to her computer at the far end of the room.

Oxide and Elmer took a moment to stare at each other and wonder if breaking out into a fistfight might alleviate any tension in the room.

"The fuck you looking at?" Oxide asked.

Elmer looked the man up and down, and landed his eyes on the chrome plated spear through his tongue. "You kiss your mother with that mouth?"

"No, I lick yo momma's fuckin' pussy with it."

Elmer chuckled so hard his lungs nearly burst. "Ha. Boy, I tell ya, you keep that shit up and I'll crush your fuckin' head in my bare hand."

Elmer meant what he'd said. When he lifted his palm, everyone gasped at how deadly it looked. It had the strength of a thousand men, judging by the muscles sardined across his forearm and wrist.

He clenched his fist in a split-second, enabling his muscles and veins to protrude through the skin.

"Crush. Your. Fucking. Head."

"Okay, man," Oxide said. "You win."

Alyssa made a concerted decision to ignore the immaturity taking place at the table. She slotted the hard drive into the computer at her desk, and began typing on the keyboard.

"How long will it take to get the data off?"

"Shouldn't take too long to fire up on an H-SSD," she said. "Depends on how much data there is."

"There's tens of millions of user profiles on it," George said.

"Maybe half an hour, then?"

Elmer slammed the metal table. "You wanna see how I do 'em?" he asked Oxide.

"No."

"I'll show you, anyway."

Elmer spun the first of the two vise handles around and around and opened the jaws. "Depending on their size, we usually put their hair here, and close it up. Nice and tight. They ain't going nowhere without the hair on their head."

A quick search under the table with his right hand was all he needed for the next explanation. A collection of plastic zip ties.

"Once they're secured and can't move, we bend their ankles up and back. If they're supple enough, we close their feet behind their head, and tie their ankles together. The force bends their legs back, and gets their holes nice and wide."

Tarin couldn't help but satisfy his curiosity. "You tie them up with plastic ties?"

Elmer slammed the ties on the table and gesticulated what the result might look like with his bare hands. "Uh-huh. Head up this end, ass down the other end, all balled up like a store-bought chicken."

Oxide and Tarin's eyes followed Elmer to the corner of the table to switch on a megawatt power lamp. The shiny metal surface burst to life.

"Then, it's showtime," Elmer explained, and pointed to the four cameras. "Alyssa starts the live feed and we do our thing. Me, George, and the spiders."

"The spiders?" Oxide asked. "The fuck's that?"

"Some of the users like to join in, take a load off," Elmer grunted in all seriousness and lifted his arm. A blue, faded spider with electric thunderbolts sat over the veins in his wrist. "Male, female, don't matter to them. We do our thing."

"Do your thing?" Tarin dared ask, fearing the worst answer imaginable. "What do you mean?"

Elmer took five steps back and reached for the shutter on the wall behind him. He grabbed the handle with tremendous force and pushed it sideways.

Tarin and Oxide's jaws dropped when they saw the tools hanging on the wall.

"Man, fuck me."

Elmer chuckled and reached for a large power drill with the bit missing at the end. "This one's my favorite. Runs ninety minutes on a full charge, and the beauty of it is that you can attach anything on the end. Whatever they want."

"They?" Oxide asked.

"The viewers."

Elmer reached for a twelve-inch vibrator and screwed it on the front. As he returned to the table, he flicked the side switch and armed the device.

"Now, imagine she's on the table, yeah? And here's me at the end," he said without a trace of emotion or empathy. "And I start this and shove this motherfucker right up in her. Hit the pelvic floor, make 'em scream like a banshee. Then, you break through. Puncture right in, and bury the fucker deep in her guts."

The power drill roared to life, sending the gelatin vibrator bouncing around like a horse on steroids.

"Last one we did this to fuckin' expired right here on this table before we unloaded—"

"—I think I'm gonna be sick," Tarin said. "I don't wanna know, no more."

Elmer aimed the machine at Tarin. "You're gonna be sick? Wait till you see how much we get paid per view, per session, per subject. *Then* you'll be sick."

Oxide shook his head with dismay. "This ain't right, man."

"Yeah, I get it," Elmer growled. "You're just like everyone else, ain't ya? You can look away and bury your head in the sand for the right price."

Oxide knew the guy was right. It was precisely the reason he had involved himself in this nastiness. Hearing the rumors was one thing, but seeing where it all took place was quite another.

"Listen, man," Oxide chanced. "If I wanna go to the butchers and buy some beef, I don't wanna know how it ended up on the slab. Ya feel me?"

"Sure," Elmer said. "But not everyone wants to be the butcher. Enough people wanna be the one who's a step further up the food chain."

Elmer slammed a hacksaw on the table, followed by a hammer, and a giant blowtorch.

"Sure, we have 'em all. Doctors, teachers, senators, you name it. But everyone's a decent, upstanding member of society. Until they ain't."

CCTV#1
Southern Wall.

"C'mon, c'mon," Evan's voice bounced around the plastic from inside the darkness. "Give me the fucking picture. Tell me where I am."

A rectangular black-and-white image sizzled to life, showing the metal table in the middle of the warehouse.

Elmer's image leaned over the table and spoke in a tinny rendition of his usual voice. A replay of what happened seconds before.

"Sure, we have 'em all. Doctors, teachers, senators, you name it. But everyone's a decent, upstanding member of society. Until they ain't."

The image froze, then flipped around one-hundred-and-eighty degrees. Floating behind the transparent, monochrome image was a colored skull eying the participants.

"Enlarge image," The Skull said.
Bwup-bwup-bwup.

Three bumps into the side of Oxide's head revealed his mouth and the chrome spear through his tongue.

"Oxide?" The Skull said. "Ugh. You're one *ugly* motherfucker. Shift right."

The image blew up larger and scrolled right. The Skull ghosted forward and examined the man's face.

"Tarin? The guy opposite you must be Elmer. Zoom in."

The picture enlarged once again, dampening the HD image into a series of fine, oblique pixels.

A tattoo of a spider with thunderbolts shooting out either side of the man's wrist. A big, hairy belly to match, which threatened to rest on the metal table.

"Scroll down," The Skull commanded, before regretting his decision.

The image revealed the sheer size of what Elmer was packing between his legs, forcing The Skull to tumble back and chatter its jaw.

"Jesus fucking Christ. No wonder he's *not* wearing pants."

The Skull rotated to face the darkness behind him. "Next camera."

Schwip.

He disappeared into the black algorithmic ocean…

Alyssa looked up from her computer terminal. "It's done. Transfer complete."

George peered over her shoulder and saw the command message. *Transfer Complete.*

"Are you sure it's done, done?"

"What does it say on the screen?"

"Okay, no need to be sarcastic. Seems we're done. Good work, little lady."

George arched his back and reached into his pocket for his phone.

"I'll call him now and let him know we're all set."

Before he unlocked his phone, he caught sight of the three men surrounding the metal table and lost his temper.

"Hey, assholes," George yelled. "Stop fucking around with the tools. Elmer?"

"Yeah?"

"They don't need to see the product, okay? Keep that shit to yourself."

CCTV#2
Northern Wall.

Evan's voice erupted into the darkness, "Let's see what we got here."

A dark-haired woman at the computer in the corner of the room, directly below the camera. She turned to the man standing behind her.

"What does it say on screen?"

"Okay," the fuzzy image of a man said. "No need to be sarcastic. Seems we're done. Good work, little lady."

The pixels formed the head of a skull and shimmied to life. "George? George Gilbertson?"

The playback showed George accosting the three men at the table. The Skull flew into the pixelated image and hovered above George, who held his phone to his ear.

"What the fuck is going on, here?"

The playback of George walked through The Skull's face and talked into his phone. "Yeah, it's me. We got it. Yeah, the whole thing. We're ready for the auction."

"An auction?" The Skull asked. "Shift right."

The image scanned right as Elmer moved away from the metal table and approached a single door at the west-side of the room. "I'll be back in a moment."

The Skull blinked off and on as the man opened the door and disappeared behind it.

"There must be another fucking camera, here."

Whump.

Elmer closed the door behind him and yanked on the elastic on his underwear. "Goddamn idiots."

A quiet and muffled cry came from the corner of the darkened room, followed by a shuffling of skin-on-concrete.

Elmer grinned at the sight and rubbed his hands. "Now, now, not long to go, my pretty little thing."

A young teenage girl screamed into her bright red ball gag. Her bare heels had bled profusely from kicking across the ground.

Her hands were tied together above her head.

She tried to call out for help, but to no avail, "Mffgg."

Elmer stepped to her feet and crouched down in front of her. He took delight in her attempts to break free, knowing full well it was futile.

"Stop screaming."

The young woman's green eyes vanished in an instant when she lowered her eyelids.

"Now, listen. I wanna tell you something. Nod if you can hear me."

Reluctantly, the woman slumped against the wall and lifted her head up and down. The sight of a ghastly overweight man at least twice her size put the fear of God into her chest.

Elmer revealed the content of his right palm. His cell phone flickered to life under his fingers, and he showed her the screen.

"I dunno if you know this, but your mom has been a very, very bad girl. Look."

When he scrolled the screen to the right, the picture of a woman with shades slid into view.

A profile picture.

A woman named Ashley Richard.

"This *is* your mom, right?"

The young girl's eyebrows raised with fright. She nodded and squirmed, and struggled for freedom.

"Mffggh."

"It's too late for that, now, *Alex*."

He clenched his fist and socked her across the face, nearly knocking her out. A blotch of blood seeped from her mouth and flooded down her chin.

"You keep this squirming up, and I'll replace your gag with something much bigger. *Meatier*. Do you understand what I'm saying?"

All the girl could do was whimper and accept her fate.

"Now, see your mom? I told you she was a bad bitch. Your father doesn't know this, and I know you don't, but she signed up to this app called InstaBate. That's right, she's fed up with your father. Look at this."

As Elmer ran his thumb down the screen, a list of all the hookups Ashley had undertaken scrolled past.

Elmer read some of them aloud. "Robert Joseph, Daniel Buckley, Clive McCord, Mo McMillan, fuck, she got about a bit. Ugh. What a cunt."

Scroll-scroll-scroll.

Alex writhed in pain and burst into tears, her muffled wails echoing in Elmer's ears and encouraging him to bait her further.

"Heh," Elmer said. "Look at the filters your dirty-ass mother has put on. Mutual masturbation, face-sitting, watersports, giving and taking, *Wizard's Sleeving*. You do know what a Wizard's Sleeve is, dontcha?"

Alex shook her head, flinging her tears in all directions.

"That's InstaBate talk for *Anal*, Alex. Your mom takes it in the ass with these dirty pricks."

"Mfgghh."

The walls seem to close in and cocoon Alex. Her heart beat faster and faster the more the stranger spoke.

"What your mom doesn't know is the InstaBate app, uh, ain't exactly free. You know what I'm saying?"

Alex shuffled back and vomited against the ball gag. "Mffghh."

"There's a little saying in our game. If you don't pay for the product, then you *are* the product."

Alex blasted her lungs into the ball gag and kicked her feet into the air, desperate for freedom.

Elmer burst out laughing and followed up the perverse merriment by spitting on her face.

"That's right, Alex. *You* are gonna pay for your mom's sneaky little fuck-arounds. While she's out sucking dick, we take the good stuff. In other words, you. The good daughter. While mommy's back is turned, with AIDS-riddled nails scratching down it, you're gone, and the chance to make some serious bank presents itself."

Elmer swiped the screen to reveal a paused video.

A metal table.

Four power lamps at each corner.

A girl much like Alex writhed around on the table.

"How much is a human life worth?" Elmer asked, rhetorical though his question was. "I dunno about you, but I think it's worth nothing. The market is saturated with enough pricks using up oxygen, I gotta think it can't be worth more than the cost of the electricity used to download that piece of shit app."

Her long hair held in place within the jaws of a vice, and balled up like a store-bought chicken.

"You ever stared into the eyes of someone who's about to die, Alex? Look at her."

Alex's eyes lifted away from his spider-lightning tattoo on his wrist, and froze solid, and dry.

Fear set in as the sound of the video fired to life.

"This was yesterday's video. Why don't you have a little look-see?"

Elmer had seen the video many times before. He knew each gasp, hiccup, and cry for help. Every single pixel on the video burned into his retinas, much like the hundreds of others he'd filmed with his gang.

"I'm only showing you this because you're going to die. We can't let you go now. But we can let you off the planet in as much pain as I can figure out."

He watched the video play out in her eyeballs, reflected off her pupils. A single teardrop formed in the corner of her eye as the hideous wailing and squeals subsided into an intermittent clutch of snores and gargles.

"Look at that, Alex," Elmer whispered. "Can you see what we did to her? Let the picture sear into your pretty fucking head."

The figure in the reflection from Alex's eyes stopped moving, but whatever was happening on the outskirts didn't let up.

The snores and gargles from the woman in the playback turned to silence, but it didn't stop the others doing whatever they were doing to her.

All remnants of vibrancy drained from Alex's face.

When Elmer removed his phone from her head, she stared blankly into the ground.

"I wanna reassure you, but I won't insult your intelligence, Alex," Elmer said. "You've already had it bad. I want to say I'll make it quick, but I won't. I'm going to make it slow, and cause you so much hurt you'll beg for death. I'll prolong it so fucking hard, because I want to see you in pain, and so does everyone who'll be watching. I want to see it in your eyes as you slowly fade away."

Alex went limp in her restraints and closed her eyes. She'd stopped squealing, at least, which pleased her captor.

"No escape, Alex," Elmer said. "No hope, no future. I want to assure you that what's going to happen to you isn't your fault. It's your mom's. Remember that, while the intense pain becomes your new normal."

The Skull hadn't made it into a CCTV camera at all. Instead, it had suffered the same traumatic experience as Alex.

He'd found his way into Elmer's phone.

The WiFi symbol spat another bar as the man stood to his feet.

Evan's voice crept through the phone's speakers. "Jesus Christ. They're going to kill her."

Elmer returned from the stock room with a shit-eating grin on his face. He waved his phone in the air and caught everyone's attention.

"Hey, guys. How are we all doing?"

George pressed his index finger to his mouth and indicated that he was speaking to someone on his cell phone. "Shh. I'm talking to him."

Elmer hopped, skipped, and jumped over to Tarin and Oxide. "Well, guys, I just met our next movie star. Very pretty. A bit older than we usually like, but hey, a mouth's a mouth, ain't it?"

"We ain't staying around to watch your sick murder show, man," Oxide said. "As soon as we're finished up, we're outta here. And you best relocate, because I dunno if I can walk the streets of Chrome Valley knowing that this sick-fuck shit is going down around here."

"Ooo," Elmer giggled. "Touchy-touchy. Heh. You sure you don't wanna stick around and see me turn that bitch's womb into ground-up corn beef?"

Tarin grabbed Oxide by the shoulders before he launched himself at the big guy. "Man, I'mma shoot you in the face, you sick fuck."

"No, Oxide. Leave him alone. It isn't worth it. We're nearly done and paid."

Oxide made eyes at the towering mound of disgusting human staring back at him.

"See you in Hell, asshole."

"Not if I see you first," Elmer said.

"You know I'm packin' right? I got a gun in the case. I could take it out and blow your motherfuckin' head clean off. And I wouldn't lose a second of sleep."

George lowered his phone and hollered at the men. "Would you two faggots get a fucking room or shut the fuck up? Can't you see I'm talking to Chrome Valley's finest, here?"

"You talkin' to a cop?"

George covered his cell phone and nodded, quietly. "Shh."

Oxide shoved Tarin away and rolled his shoulders, refusing to back down from Elmer.

"Man, you're lucky we're nearly done, here."

Elmer grabbed the hammer and knocked the head against the metal table. "Shame. I'm just about to get started."

The Skull saw everything through the second CCTV camera in the room. Directly below, Alyssa made the mistake of looking up from her terminal and stared into the camera lens.

Her ears pricked up, somewhat startled. "There's something not right, here."

George cut the call and approached her from behind. "What?"

"I dunno," she said. "I just have a weird feeling."

Evan's voice blew from The Skull's jaw as it whipped around the featureless void. "You're Goddamn right about that, bitch. It's time to get inside your computer."

The Skull faced down to see an ocean of pixels waving around.

Whip.

The jagged oblong darted into the sea, forcing the squares to explode...

Alyssa returned to the screen and adjusted her eye patch. "Everyone, listen. This is serious."

"What is it?" George asked.

"Shut your cell phones off. There's some kind of interference going on. No more WiFi till I get this figured out. It's possible that we're being watched."

George tapped her on the shoulder. "We're being watched?"

She punched a command on the keyboard. "Configuring gateway. Until I reset the machine, I want no connectivity at all."

George turned to Tarin, Oxide, and Elmer. "Fellas? You heard the girl. Turn your phones off."

Tarin and Oxide pulled out their phone and cut the WiFi off. Elmer backed up from the table and swung the hammer around in his hand. "I don't got a phone."

He pointed to his bloodstained underwear.

"I left it in the stock room with the girl."

Whump-bump.

The loud bang came from somewhere up above. Everyone looked up, searching for the source of commotion.

Oxide freaked out and tried to shake off the sudden fear of God. "What the hell is that? Man, fuck this, I want out of here."

George held out his hands, expecting some rainfall. "No. No, it's the warehouse door. I'm sure of it."

"It can't be," Alyssa said. "I've shut it off."

Rumble.

The large slab of metal began to slide under the ceiling and curve down the gaping entrance to the building.

"What are you doing?" George asked.

"It's not me," Alyssa screamed.

"That's right, bitch," The Skull said from within the circuitry of the computer terminal. "It's *me*."

The Skull head enlarged and burst through the scrolling commands, headed straight for a rectangular slab of tempered glass.

Bop.

It's forehead rammed against its own reflection.

Orange sparks blew out from her computer terminal as the command prompt disappeared, only to be replaced by a black screen and a flashing skull face.

When its jaw opened to speak, its Evan-like voice blared through the speakers. "Alyssa."

"Fuck."

Startled, she pushed herself back on her chair and nearly had a heart attack.

"I'd stay away from the fucking door if I were you."
"Oh, Jesus."

The lights in the warehouse fizzled off and on, shrouding the entire area in a blanket of temporary darkness.

George turned around to the monitor to find a thoroughly shaken Alyssa. "Hey, what's going on?"

"Hey, Gilbertson," The Skull on screen said.

"What the *fuck* is that?"

The Skull tilted its head forward and offered him a sneaky retort. "I. See. You."

Oxide, Tarin, and Elmer witnessed the stand-off from the other end of the warehouse.

"Man, fuck this," Oxide said. "I'm outta here. Yo, Gilbertson?"

"What?"

"You can wire me my fuckin' money, man. I ain't staying here another fuckin' second."

George reached into his jacket. "You're going nowhere, asshole."

It was too late.

Oxide pushed Tarin out of his path and bolted for the exit, hoping he'd be able to slide to freedom before the sliding door shut.

"Hey," Tarin called out. "Don't do that."

"Fuck this!"

The Skull pressed the side of his bony face against the screen with such strength that the monitor bulged from within.

As the glass blew out, the cheekbone fizzled into a transparent static in the real world. "Goddamnit."

Alyssa jumped out of her chair as she witnessed the algorithmic apparition's jawline enter reality, followed by a long, bony arm.

"Oh my God."

"Get back," George screamed. "Jesus fucking Christ."

Tarin reached into his suitcase and pulled the shotgun out. "Stand back. I'm gonna put a hole in that motherfucker's head."

The Skull's elbow bent out first, pushing a shockwave of electricity through the air in the room. "C'mon. Give it to me."

The door slid around and continued its trajectory to the floor, just as Oxide leapt forward.

A spider-web of bony fingers extended in all directions as the first digit protruded and darted toward the *return key* on the keyboard.

"Eat this, you sick fuck."

Oxide propelled himself forward and slid on his chest along the floor.

The light from outside sliced down and out of sight. He was seconds away from freedom.

Press.

The Skull's skeletal index finger hit the return key, and sped up the closing door's speed.

Time seemed to slow as Oxide rolled through the last foot of space between the door's edge and the ground, when—

"Aggghhh!"

Crunch-Spitch.

The door slammed down on Oxide's screaming mouth, impaling his spinal cord against the ground, and severing his head clean in two.

"Oh dear," Tarin gasped, as he watched his friend's feet kick up and down.

Alyssa rose from her chair and covered her mouth in horror. "My God."

"For fuck's sake, someone open the fucking door," George said. "We can't leave him there like that."

A sniveling sound of death folded down the man's shoulders, coming from the other side of the door - and his head. "Gutch-gutch."

A thick jet of blood blasted around the man's writhing body from the lower half of his head.

"Alyssa," George yelped. "Open the door."

Frantic, she kept an eye on the screen as she tapped frantically on the keyboard. "I can't. It's shut off."

George waved Elmer over to Oxide's erupting legs.

"Oh for fuck's sake. Do I have to do everything around here?"

George fell to his knees and grabbed Oxide's left ankle. "Stop kicking, you asshole."

Whump-whump.

"Elmer, take his right leg. Fuck."

"Already ahead of you."

The big man took the right ankle, and both stood up and pulled back with all their might.

Elmer roared as he wrenched the leg back. "Pull, pull, pull."

"I am, you stupid ass."

Tarin blinked rapidly, trying to process the sight of two grown men trying to pull his colleague away from the door.

The skin on Oxide's neck split apart as the weight of the lower half of his body moved away.

"Oh God, I think I'm gonna be sick," Tarin said.

Grind-grüinnd.

The door continued to burrow into the ground through Oxide's gaping mouth.

"Gwesh-gnagh—"

"—Aw, stop complaining, you fucking moron," George winced as he kept pulling. "We're trying to set you free."

Elmer grabbed Oxide's right shin in both hands and bent it back. "Ngggg."

"What the fuck are you doing?"

"Shut up—"

Snap.

The shin bone snapped in half, sending Oxide into a muffled, bloodied screaming fit.

He grabbed the protruding bone and bent it back, forcing it out from the man's kicking leg. A fountain of blood splashed up Elmer's man breasts.

"Got it."

"What are you doing?"

Elmer dropped the leg from his hands and marched up to the door. "He's dead anyway."

The lower half of Oxide's head opened as he puked a mixture of mucus and blood up the door.

"Hold still, dickhead."

Elmer pushed his left hand onto Oxide's chest and stabbed Oxide's shinbone into his neck.

Tarin and Alyssa turned away and shook their heads with disapproval. "Fuck this."

Wrench-tear.

Elmer yanked the shinbone through Oxide's screaming throat. Clumps of flesh catapulted away from his neck as the sharp edge tore through it.

George relaxed his grip on Oxide's left leg and watched on as Elmer ran the bone out, having cut the right side of Oxide's throat away.

"Nearly got it," Elmer said. "Pull, pull."

George tightened his grip and yanked the leg back.

Oxide's body came with it, leaving the top half of his head on the other side of the door.

Several of Oxide's teeth scattered around the tornado of blood and mucus.

Clang—ting.

The chrome spear that once nestled in the dead man's tongue hit the floor.

George dropped the leg and carefully stood to his feet. Lying before him was *most of* his former associate.

Elmer chucked the shinbone onto Oxide's chest and rubbed his hands together. "So, *that* happened."

George rubbed his palms on his suit and pointed at the build-up of splattered remains of Oxide's head and neck. "What are we gonna do with the body?"

Elmer thought for a while, and then arrived at an idea.

Whump.

The door to the stockroom burst open and slammed against the inside wall.

The light from the main area filtered into the room and blasted Alex in the face.

Her eyes opened wide as she screamed into her ball gag for help.

"Mffghh."

Scooch-scooch.

The silhouette of a giant, sweating man folded into view in the doorway, ass-first, pulling something across the floor.

"Mffghh."

Elmer reached over and picked up the decapitated body in his arms. All he could do was offer a pathetic grin at the poor girl.

"Hello, Alex."

She squirmed around and pulled on the restraints on her wrists. "Ng, ng—"

"—Sorry about this, but you got company."

He threw Oxide's corpse across the room. It landed chest first against the wall and tumbled to the floor.

"We had a bit of an accident. Sorry about the smell. We'll get rid of him soon. Actually, we may have him in the show later on tonight."

The terror in Alex's eyes was palpable. "Aww, don't look at me like that. I said I'm sorry."

Alex shuffled her feet away from the headless corpse and groaned into her gag. If she could set herself free, the first thing she'd contemplate was suicide at this point.

"I wasn't meant to give you this till later, but here," Elmer said. "A little something to calm your nerves."

He stormed over to a desk in the darkened corner of the room, and picked up a tiny, bullet-shaped piece of plastic.

"You know Prizm, right? It'll help you chill out till the fun starts."

Alex shook her head and kicked her feet at the approaching man. "Nggg."

"Now, now, calm the fuck down."

He reached up with his huge doors-for-hands and grabbed her wrist. The tip of the plastic popped off, to produce a small syringe.

"Hold still, princess."

"Mffgh."

She fought back for all her worth, but to little avail. Elmer slid the syringe into her wrist and squeezed the capsule.

Two seconds later, her eyes rolled back into her head, and she went limp against the wall.

Elmer tapped her face and wiped the sweat off on his underwear. "Good girl. Take a nap. You're gonna need your energy pretty soon."

Chapter 6

Four walls of digitized code surrounded the floating Skull. Evan's temper had grown violent. Desperate for answers, he tried to navigate the mainframe via Alyssa's terminal.

Her hurried voice of concern waded into the system from the microphone attached to the monitor.

"Who the fuck was that?"

George's voice followed as The Skull whizzed around, searching through the infinite amount of green-on-black codes that cocooned it.

"I recognized that fucking voice," George's voice echoed. "Someone's definitely following us. Are you sure the data is secure?"

"As secure as it can be."

"Yeah," Evan's voice pummeled from the jaws of The Skull as it scanned the data. "I wouldn't be too sure about that, asshole."

"We've got over fifty million users' details up for grabs, now. It can't get out. Not yet, anyway."

"And here they all are," The Skull said. "I need to get outta here."

Tens of thousands of random names, along with their personal descriptions, job titles, and addresses, riffled up and down the four walls of data.

"Doctors? Lawyers? Jesus, even the police," Evan's voice grew louder and angrier. "They're all involved."

The Skull zoomed around them all, reading them as fast as it could.

"Stop!"

A blanket of names slid to a halt in front of The Skull's eye sockets. A dim glow appeared deep in each of them, confronted by a name - *Denton Rossco*.

Evan's voice flew out from The Skull's mouth. "Denton Rossco? You'll do."

The Skull leaned back and bolted through the text that made up the name, leaving the drifting voices of confusion in the warehouse to tumble into nothingness…

***

Name: Denton B. Rossco
Age: 35
Source Code: 090-780-020874

A flashing image of a two-year-old toddler on a beach blasted into view.

Evan's voice crept through the sand. "Oh, so this is you, huh? Cute kid."

The friendly grimace on the kids face shimmied left and right, producing the outlines of a skull. "Denton B. Rossco. Thirty-two-years ago. Devotion Beach. An old photograph."

Whip-whip-whip.

The image slammed down like a falling domino to reveal a slightly older child blowing out a birthday candle.

A young couple with party balloons smiled as they watched the kid blow out the candle opposite an older boy cheering him on.

The Skull beat the boy to it and huffed the flame on the candle out. "Fifth birthday party huh?"

Tag: Mom, Dad, James, older brother.

"Aww, how sweet."

The Skull rammed the top of the image with its head, smashing it to pieces.

Several images of a young Denton Rossco playing in the back yard with his dog drifted down in front of The Skull, accompanied by a text heading - *Fun in the Backyard*.

Shopping trip to the Kaleidoscope Mall, 2018.

Birthday party at Burger Face, 2019.

Multiple tags of his friends and family popped up on each image of everyone involved. Old, young, small, large, tall, short, of all colors, creeds, and nationalities.

"What happened to all these friends of yours, Denton B. Rossco?"

The Skull shifted around, finding itself in the man's *HeadBook* profile.

"Something more current. You're my way outta here." *Scroll, scroll, scroll…*

A video slowed to a halt on Denton's page. The still image showed the man in a white vest with a huge smile on his face.

The Skull eyed the man's face for a moment, suspecting something bad. "Play."

Denton spoke to the camera.

"Hey guys, so here I am. Keep this to yourself and everyone in the forum, but I found this really cool app. It's called *InstaBate*, look."

He lifted his cell phone to the camera and showed the *InstaBate* image to those who were watching.

"Check it out," he continued. "See all these profiles. I'm hearing the ratio of men to women is something like three-to-one. Better get in on it now before every horny dude with a dick hears about it."

The Skull shifted to the right of the giant IMAX-like screen. "Yeah, yeah, Denton. Good advice for a fuckin' pervert. Come on, where are you? Don't make me look for your address, asshole."

Denton stood up from his chair. Dressed only in his boxers, it seemed whatever was coming next was going to be troubling.

"Here, check this bitch out. She's married to some useless, no-good cripple. Pretty hot, huh? Her name's Kara. Kara Milton."

The Skull whipped forward and took in the image of the woman's striking face. Her flame-red hair stood-out like a sore thumb.

"Kara Milton?" The Skull asked, before shifting back and allowing the playback to continue.

"Man, when I'm done with her, I'll pass you her details," Denton giggled. "She's a fucking *demon* in the sack. Lets me fuck her in the mouth, the pussy, the ass, everything. Had to go out to the store earlier today to stock up on Plan C pills, just in case my seed gets her knocked up."

The Skull stopped speaking and continued watching.

"So, yeah, get this InstaBate app. It's free, and there's no in-app purchases. Get yourself some action now before the dicks outnumbers the pussy."

The Skull snapped. "Stop."

Denton's ugly image paused before The Skull's face. Evan's voice careened from the hanging jaw. "That's where you're wrong. *You* are the fucking product."

The Skull whizzed into the image.

The further it traveled, the more the individual pixels burst into strings of text.

"Come on, Denton," The Skull said on its journey into the algorithmic ocean of Denton's profile. "Show me the money."

Bzzz.

The sound of footsteps on a cold, hard floor in utter darkness.

A light snapped on the corner of the room, followed by a second, third, and finally a fourth.

An illuminated metal table with a naked teenager laying in the middle of it. The image only took up a small portion of the left-hand side of the screen.

On the right, Denton B. Rossco watched on, along with tens of thousands of others.

InstaBate User# 155770.

A giant man in a long, grubby overall appeared in the live feed. "Welcome to the Undernet. We hope you enjoy the show."

"Fuck yeah," Denton said, eager to get the party underway in the comfort of his own bedroom. "Do it."

Camera #2: on the other side of the table. The crisp and clean high definition provided a detailed look at the events about to unfurl.

Denton's voice bled across the screen. "Mmm. Nice."

The big man lifted his arm to reveal a spider tattoo with electric thunderbolts at the side of it.

Watching from the other side of the playback was Evan. The Skull.

"I swear to God you're all fucking dead."

Tap-tap.

Camera #3: A close-up on the girl's face.

On the adjacent end of the screen, Denton's head flew past as the image landed on the large man's hand tapping the teenager's face.

He spoke with a digitally altered voice. "Wake up."

The girl squeezed her eyelids and opened them, instantly shocked by where she was.

"Where am I?"

"The drugs are wearing off. Just relax. Every muscle in your body."

The man's hand reached between her legs, and began rubbing up and down.

"Especially *this* one."

The girl froze with fear as she stared up at the man's head, which was out of shot.

Denton's voice produced a visual wave across the events playing out. "Put your fat finger in her."

When the man shoved his arm forward, the girl screamed so loud that her vocal cords appeared to snap.

"Shut up."

Denton's voice elevated to a high-pitch excitement. "Do her, do her—"

The Skull hovered above the image of the girl screaming for dear life, only for the man to shove a ball gag between her lips.

"Shut the fuck up."

The rigid edge of the ball chipped her two front teeth as the straps fastened around her head.

"Be a good girl and lay down."

Whump.

The butt of the man's palm punched into her forehead, smashing the back of her head against the metal table.

"Like mother, like daughter, huh?"

The Skull couldn't squint, but the corresponding bones on its face lowered in anger. "I know you. I know your voice."

Whip.

The girl's shoulder shunted up the table, having been forced by the man's hand between her legs. Denton's face slid into view, watching the abuse unfold in real time.

"Cut her throat," he murmured as he rubbed himself. "Nice and slow."

The Skull began to shake like an out-of-control food mixer. "Motherfucker."

"Do it," Denton said. "I wanna see the look in her eyes—"

"—Gaahhhhh."

The Skull's jaw elongated and produced a deafening sound of evil.

Rumble-rumble-rumble.

The surrounding video images vibrated along with the perpetual scream of vengeance. The edges of The Skull blew out and enveloped the playback, before producing a God-shaped ray of fire shooting in every conceivable direction.

"Die, motherfucker, die!"

Bolt.

A series of blurred images whizzed past The Skull as it flew down endless connecting pathways.

"Come on," Evan said, as his Skull avatar negotiated the endless electronic tunnels via the WiFi.

A ghostly live image of Denton's face talking to someone erupted through a shaft of digitized light cracking through the darkness.

"Crazy to think you're just a couple miles away," he said. "So close, yet so far. Fuck, I'm going out of my mind without you here."

The InstaBate logo folded into view. Cupid stepped into the circle, ready to draw its arrow and fire at The Skull.

"Shit."

Ptchoo.

The synthetic arrow shot past The Skull's brow and daggered into a number: 155770.

Kara's voice shattered against the wall of data.

"Jesus Christ, Denton."

His voice bled through the speakers as he moved the lens on his phone closer. "I know, look at the effect you have on me."

"Stop it, Denton," Kara's voice softened and turned into a light moan of pleasure. "Jesus Christ, stop it."

"That no-good husband of yours in bed sleeping, is he?"

The Skull twisted to the side as the tunnel of communication burst to life, the verbal exchange between Denton and Kara imprinted in bright, white text.

"Yes, he is. Denton, please. Don't—"

"—Can't you sneak out for an hour?" Denton said. "Come to my place and let me destroy you."

The Skull turned left and vanished into a brilliant glass screen. "My pleasure, asshole."

Whump.

The remnants of The Skull's ghost smoked out as he disappeared into the void, and left Denton's proposal hanging in the air. "I want you to see what… you're… missing…"

***

Kara stood in the kitchen with her ass pressed against the stove. She moved her hand under the belt on her thighs and threatened to expose herself to the person on the other end of her cell phone.

Denton's hushed and excited tone crept through the speakers on her cell phone. "I gotta say, I really like what I'm seeing. I guess I was right."

Kara moved her finger between her legs faster. "You were right?"

"Uh-huh."

"Yeah, let me explain."

Spitch-spatch.

The kitchen lights blew out, blanketing the kitchen in darkness.

Illuminated by the light from her phone, Kara gulped and blinked. "What the fuck?"

Slam.

The electronic kitchen door rolled shut, and produced three flashing green lights, indicating that it had locked.

Bzzz. Bzzz. Zip.

Denton's voice heightened with fear from within her phone "Kara? H-Help m-me—"

His paused face split into a thousand tiny digital squares. The pure white walls of his bedroom snapped to black, producing a peculiar negative-effect.

"Denton?" Kara asked. "What's h-happening—"

His voice growled into an evil baritone. "K-Kara—I—I—"

"M-My God."

Just then, The Skull appeared in the vast, dark void on her cell phone screen, cackling like an evil clown.

"Kara Milton? Are you K-Kara M-Milton?"

"Huh?"

The Skull twisted around and zoomed so far into the screen, it nearly head-butted the phone out of her hand.

"Goddamn it, are you Kara fucking Milton? Answer me."

"Yes, I am, I am. Wh-who are you?"

The Skull shifted forward and appeared to grin with its bony, electronic jaw. "You *have* been a naughty fucking girl, haven't you?"

Kara hyperventilated and clutched her chest thinking she was suffering a stroke. "Whuh—whuh—"

"—Yeah, it's you all right," The Skull's jaw chattered in time to Evan's frustrated voice. "Hold your phone tight. Watch *this*."

Denton gripped his cell phone in his hand. He raced to the bed naked as the day he was born, terrified by the fear seeping into the room.

"Hello, Denton," The Skull said from within his phone. "Fuckhead."

Utterly astonished, Denton held his device to his face and stared into The Skull's lifeless eye sockets. "Wh-what?"

"I know what you did."

Slowly, The Skull's head seeped out from the screen. The second it hit the real world, it turned into a transparent static bunch of pixels.

"Eat this, motherfucker."

The Skull leaned back and slammed its forehead on Denton's nose.

"Gah!"

His two front teeth punctured through the glass and snapped away from his gums as his forehead slammed against the floor.

Kara's face appeared on his phone, shocked, as she watched The Skull attack her fuck buddy.

"Denton Rossco. This piece of shit is about to help me help you understand that I am not fucking around. Keep watching."

"No, don't," she squealed. "You're hurting him."

The Skull chattered its teeth and blasted out of the screen. "Come here, big boy."

Denton had dropped his phone, and the angle was slanted as it faced his TV screen atop his dresser.

The electronic skull burst onto the TV screen and grinned.

"Hey, Rossco. Stop lying around and get busy, asshole."

Kara watched on in horror as Denton rolled onto his back and used the edge of the bed to pull himself to his knees.

"My G-God," he shrieked at the image on the TV. "What the hell is that?"

The Skull's jaw moved up and down and flung back, encouraging the man to approach him.

Rossco. Come here.

Terrified, Denton glanced at his phone and staggered across the carpet. "Kara?"

"Denton!" she screamed.

"Hey! You two lovebirds shut the fuck up and watch. Come here, Rossco."

The man obliged the violent apparition and stepped towards the TV set.

"Denton Rossco, 108 Sears Road. Born October 14th."

"Y-Yes?" he said to The Skull.

InstaBate User# 155770.

"Wh-what do you want?" he asked the sneering, talking skull.

"You look like shit. You're missing your two front teeth."

Kara's live feed played on Denton's cell phone from the floor. "Denton, run!" she screamed at her phone.

"No. Don't you dare fucking run. Touch my face."

"No," Kara screamed. "Don't—"

As if possessed, Denton's fingers touched the screen and burned, his skin glued to the plastic.

"Aggghh."

The Skull roared with laughter as the barbecue effect tore through the man's forearm, past his elbow, and set his shoulder ablaze.

"Kara? Do you see what I'm doing to your well-endowed boyfriend?"

Kara screamed through her tears. "You're killing him."

Denton's entire naked body burst into flames, shooting a deathly smog of cooked flesh racing across the ceiling.

Whvoom.

The bed and carpet caught fire as the TV exploded, which had no effect on the laughing skull on screen.

"Die, motherfucker, die."

The jaw of The Skull expanded and bulged through the TV screen — when it left the contents of the television set, in the real world, the image turned to pixels.

The Skull enlarged and chomped on Denton's abdomen, cutting him clean in two. The top half of his body split apart between The Skull's pixelated teeth as the image slid into the television set.

The bottom half of Denton's corpse fell to its knees, expelling its distended organs around his ankles.

The Skull tumbled into the depths of the barbecuing television set… and buzzed to life on Kara's cell phone.

Kara stepped away from the stove in shock.

Her hand shook so much that it nearly released her phone.

"Have I got your attention now?"

Kara didn't dare move, breathe, or speak.

"Good."

The Skull's jaw opened to produce a video-game like rendition of Denton's battered corpse on the screen.

"Be careful. You don't want to get his guts on your fingers."

"Gah!"

The phone sprung from her clutches and into the air.

"Don't drop your phone, either. You're gonna need it."

Kara caught her phone on its descent and squealed into the screen. "What the hell is going on?"

"Listen carefully to me."

Kara froze still, disbelieving her own eyes, with The Skull staring right back at her.

Evan's voice seeped into the fury as The Skull spoke. "I'll take your silence as acceptance that you believe I am serious. I know you, Kara Milton. I know everything about you. Every dirty and unprotected detail. And if you want your secrets kept hidden, you're going to do exactly as I say…"

Kara hiccuped, unexpectedly, still staring at the screen. The Skull clearly meant business, and would wait forever and a day, simply looking at her, until she made the next move.

"Uh, uh—"

"—Uh, uh, uh," The Skull mocked. "Take all the time you need, Milton. I know this has come as a shock."

Kara half-chuckled in fright, "A shock? I, uh—I d-don't know what to say."

"You can zip your jeans back up for a start, you filthy woman."

Without tearing her eyes away from the screen, she reached down and tugged the golden zipper back up to her belt.

The Skull grinned, knowing he had the better of her. "With your husband and kid sleeping upstairs? You call yourself a decent wife, you son of a bitch?"

Kara felt her fear turn to mush, and then to fury. "How do you know about me? You don't know me."

"On the contrary. Wait."

The Skull vanished, and was replaced by a series of photos from Kara's social media.

At a restaurant hugging her mother.

At the beach with her son. Just beside them was a blanket with an empty wheelchair resting on it.

Evan's voice accompanied a veritable delicacy of hundreds of personal pictures. "You getting the picture, now, Kara?"

When the photos dropped from the screen, her InstaBate profile slid in their place. Kara's image was her at her very best - lipstick, carefully applied make-up, voluptuous, and with bountiful red hair.

"Or should I call you InstaBate User# 808118?"

The fear of God entered Kara's heart. "Oh, Jesus."

"Your husband and kid are just upstairs. It'll take me approximately one tenth of a second to appear on their phone with every single dirty hookup you've had. All the pictures. All the text chats. All the cocks you've sucked—"

"—*Fuck you.*"

Kara pressed her thumb onto the off button on her device and squirmed into the screen.

"No, Kara, don't you dare shut your phone off—"

Bzzz-ow.

The phone went dead, and she dropped it to the kitchen counter. "Oh, God. Oh, God."

She closed her eyes and calmed her volcanic breathing down as best she could.

"Please, wake up. Wake up," she muttered. "I c-can't. I can't."

A moment of respite had her calm down enough to stop her heart trying to climb up her throat and jump out of her mouth. She clutched her chest and opened her eyes to see her dead cell phone staring up at the ceiling.

"This must be some kind of joke—"

Ping! Brrrr.

Just as she spoke, the microwave pinged to life.

Kara jumped in shock as the digital counter read 01:00 and the light inside glowed as the central glass disc turned around.

"Oh, *fuck*."

Wvhooom.

All four discs on the oven top burst to life, causing Kara to jump away from the fierce heat.

"What the fuck—?"

The refrigerator rattled left and right, almost dancing on the spot. The violent action caused the door to swing out and slam against the wall.

"Agh!"

Blast.

The electronic device attached to the faucet on the wash basin blinked, beeped, and forced the water out at full speed.

Kara didn't know which way to turn.

The electronic numbers digital clock on the wall began to spin from zero to nine, through all four columns.

Kara screamed and ran for the kitchen door. She gripped the edge and tried to roll it back along the casters, but it was locked in place.

"Help! Help!" she screamed, but her call for help wasn't loud enough. The door wouldn't budge.

The telephone handset on the wall next to the refrigerator jumped in its housing.

Ring-ring. Ring-ring.

Kara launched out of her shoes in shock and raced over to the wash basin. She turned the caps on both the hot and cold taps to find that they were locked.

The water was about to fill up, tip over the edge, and splash to the floor.

The fires from the oven discs licked up, threatening to incinerate the cupboard a few feet above them.

The microwave roared louder and louder, just as the digital timer turned from 00:38 to KA:RA.

Kara could barely speak.

Trapped in her kitchen, it seemed the room was going to murder her.

Ring-ring. Ring-ring.

The spinning digits on the wall clock slowed down to read CA:LL.

She turned to the handset on the wall, reached out to grab it, and place it to her ear. "Help!"

"*Never* turn your phone off again."

"Who the fuck is this?"

The same voice that belonged to The Skull was now shooting into her ear from the handset. "Turn your cell phone back on."

"No!"

"You're standing in a coffin of your own making if you don't turn your fucking cell phone back on. Now turn it on."

"Oh, God," she squealed in terror. "Make it stop. Please, make it stop."

"Turn. Your. Cell. Phone. On."

The dial tone zipped out from the handset.

Kara didn't have much of a choice.

She slammed the handset back into the wall cradle and snatched her cell phone from the hearty flames erupting from the oven top.

She held her thumb against the *on* button and coughed the carbon monoxide from her lungs. "C'mon, c'mon, 'cmon—"

Brii-iing.

The screen fizzed to life.

"Come on," she screamed.

A background picture of her young son and husband was the first image to appear on her phone, followed by the icons along the top. Battery power percentage, WiFi signal, date, and time.

Just then, the rings on the stove died down.

The microwave lost its power.

The jet of water coming out of the faucet died down to nothing.

On her cell phone, several apps appeared one after the other.

"You made the right choice, Kara."

The Skull shivered to life in front of the apps and appeared to rest itself against them.

"What the fuck is going on, here?"

"I don't have time to explain," The Skull said. "You're going to do something for me."

Kara held her breath with her eyes wide open. "What?"

"Please tell me you have a gun somewhere in the house."

"No, I—"

"—Maybe, I dunno, in your safe—"

"—We don't have safe—"

"—Which is under your stairs, plugged into the router on a WiFi protection capacity code reading 1128."

"What?" Kara gasped. "How the *fuck* did you know that?"

The Skull sneered at her. "I didn't. Just a lucky guess. About the gun, I mean. What gun do you have?"

"It's a Glock 17. But I've never used it. We've never even taken it out of the safe before. Never needed to."

The Skull nodded at the kitchen door as it suddenly slid open and offered Kara a way out. "First time for everything."

Chapter 7

Kara slipped through her front door and closed it gently.

The warm evening breeze brushed past her red hair. As she traversed through her front yard, she couldn't help but think of her husband and son. Compelled to leave them sleeping in their beds, and now carrying a concealed weapon under her jacket, she knew that the night's events had taken a turn for the worst.

"Where are we going?" she asked.

Evan's voice escaped through her fingers from her cell phone as she passed the gate. "Get in your car, quietly."

Her purple Saab 101 was parked out front, sticking out like a bruised thumb, as usual - a symbol of relative wealth, in accordance with the road she lived on - 77 Sears Road, on Chrome Valley's east side.

Kara hit the button on her car key pad, opened the door, and slid into the driver's side.

"Close the door and listen carefully."

Kara pulled the door shut and set her cell phone on the dash behind the steering wheel.

The Skull flew across from the left-hand side of the screen and spoke directly to her. "You ready?"

"No."

"Doesn't matter," The Skull said. "You're going to help me."

"I want to know why you're blackmailing me. Why I'm in my car. And why I'm ducking out of my house with my family asleep in bed."

"You know I am deadly serious, don't you?"

"I know you're a fucking psychopath, or I must still be asleep. Or I'm in a coma. Or I've lost my fucking mind—"

"—Quit the dramatics, Milton. You're no Somnambulist, I can assure you. There's a woman a few doors down from you who sleepwalks, according to her medical records, but I'm not in the business of disclosing other people's data to strangers."

"You're not?"

"No," The Skull said.

"Who are you, anyway?"

"I'll explain later, And that leads us quite neatly, really, to why you're sitting in your beautiful 101 and talking to a ghost."

Kara closed her eyes and wiped a tear from her cheek. "I just want to know what to do."

"Take the gun out of your bra before your blow your nipples off."

Kara cleared her throat and pinched the butt of the gun. She held it up like a used rag, disgusted with herself, and dropped it to the passenger seat.

"I hate these things. I much prefer my kick-boxing classes."

"Yeah, let's see how well your hand-to-hand combat skills work out for you tonight."

"What?"

"Shut up and drop the gun in the glove box," The Skull said. "I don't want you getting us pulled up by the police and getting busted with a loaded firearm."

"Fine."

She reached over and punched the glove box open, which gave The Skull an incredible view of her cleavage.

"Yikes," he said. "I can see why he didn't swipe-left."

"Get fucked."

"That's very kind of you. Maybe later."

Angered, Kara closed the glove box, sat up straight and snorted with disdain. "Done. Now what?"

"I'll make this quick. That secret lover of yours. Denton something."

"Rossco. His name was Denton Rossco."

"Like it matters," The Skull snapped. "Do you know what he was doing when he *wasn't* telling all his friends about how dirty you are?"

"No—What? What are you talking about?"

"I wanna show you something," The Skull said. "Let's have a little look at how he amused himself when he wasn't balls-deep in your guts."

The Skull tumbled back like a kicked football into the obliqueness of Kara's cell phone, and was replaced with playback footage of Denton masturbating at his computer desk.

"So, here's your knight in shining fucking armor, jerking his little nub of a prick off to this—"

A crash of wails and cries from a youngster rattled the interior of Kara's vehicle. At first, she struggled to comprehend what she saw on screen.

She recognized the man on the right in his own window watching the events on the other side of the screen.

Then, an undeniable feeling of sickness pervaded her stomach.

"Keep watching, Kara."

"Oh, my God."

"Watch what they do to her," Evan's voice trickled out of her cell phone's speakers with a cool solemnity.

Kara lowered her head and bit her lip. "I've seen enough."

"Look at the way your late fuck buddy watches what's happening."

Kara braved another return to the screen. Denton's face beamed with delight as he pleasured himself to the ghastly events taking place on his own screen.

The cries from the footage turned to a bizarre, prolonged snorkeling, the sound of liquid escaping a cavity from a hole burrowed in someone's face.

Kara's soul melted away and seeped into the fabric of the driver's seat. The inescapable feeling of despair and guilt pressed their hands around her body, reducing her to a quivering wreck.

Her voice turned to stone as the sound from the video playback continued. "Turn it off."

"Okay."

The playback evaporated, enabling the colorful contours of The Skull to beam with life as it floated in the middle of her screen.

"My name is Evan Cole. I was killed about six hours ago. First day on the job, and they ransacked the place. They gunned me down, and left me for dead. But I uploaded myself, don't ask me how, into the ether. The motherfuckers responsible for my death are the same ones producing this shit for the Undernet."

"The Undernet?"

"The InstaBate app is a front," Evan said via The Skull. "Over fifty million users and counting. If you don't pay for a product, then you are the product."

"We are?"

"You, your family, your friends, whoever they want to ruin. Everybody's fair game in their eyes."

Kara shook her head and spotted her teary reflection in the driver's window. "I don't understand."

"What don't you understand? The girl in the video was the daughter of an InstaBate user who lives thirteen doors down from you. In that house over there. The one with the red door."

Kara leaned forward and gripped the steering wheel. Evan was right, there was a red door with no sign of life coming from the windows at the front of the dwelling. "My God. They must be out of their minds with worry."

"That's how they do it, Kara. Millions of adults wanting a fling, and giving up their privacy in order to do it. It's ironic. They know everything. They know your interests, your movements, hell, they even track your whereabouts."

"They know every single damn thing?" Kara asked.

"You have a son, don't you? His name is Rex. He's eight-years-old."

"What?" she asked, concerned.

"Cute kid. Beautiful blue eyes."

"What the—How do you know that?"

"I'm in the system, Kara. I know everything. I have access to your social media history. "I can snatch the data in seconds."

Kara felt her hand go for the car door and pull it open. "Shit, shit, shit—"

"—No, Kara. Don't."

She rested her hand on the door and obeyed the command coming from the screen. "Why are you telling me this?"

"Because you're going to help me stop it. I need your help. No point going back in to protect your son, Kara, because if you don't help me, then they'll keep on doing it. And they won't fucking stop."

Kara licked her lips and swallowed hard. "Tell me what you want me to do."

"I, uh—they got something from Manning Inc. A hard drive containing each and every users' details. The CFO there fucked over the company, and I want to stop them. If we don't, everyone's lives are compromised. And I want those fuckers dead."

"Where are they?"

"Chrome Valley Industrial Estate," The Skull said. "They have a warehouse there. It's where they filmed the stuff I've seen, and they're still there, preparing to do something. I don't know what it is, but it's not going to be good."

"Why don't we call the police?"

"Because the chief of police is in on it. We can't trust anyone. We have to do this ourselves."

"Why do you need me?"

"Because I'm only as good as the network. I can turn on a faucet. I can move from device to device, but I can't physically do anything. I need someone to act with me, in the real world, and that's where you and the gun come in."

"You want me to kill them?"

"No," The Skull said, slowly. "You leave that to me. I want you to help. Think of your involvement as an added compliance assurer."

Kara squeezed the steering wheel and turned on the ignition. "If I do this, do you promise to keep everything with me a secret?"

"If we don't succeed, everyone is going to find out. All your nasty, dark secrets will become public information. Innocent people will be abused and killed."

"I'll help you, Evan," Kara said with concern. "But I need to know that my family will never know what happened. I don't care about myself anymore."

"What we're about to do is very dangerous. I can't guarantee a damn thing."

The news was devastating for Kara. A dilemma to end all dilemmas stared her right in the face - in the form of an electronic skull, practically pleading with her to help.

"But I can guarantee you this," The Skull chanced. "If we succeed and bring these evil fucks down, you're in the clear. Your call."

Kara slammed her foot on the gas and lifted the handbrake. She took a final glance at the glove box and grunted in anger. "Fuck it. Take me to 'em."

"That's my girl."

The car shot off down the road and turned the corner.

Chapter 8

Chrome Valley Industrial Estate
Unit 118

The sun disappeared behind the murky gray building complex an hour ago, leaving the haze of a cooked concrete ground shimmering against the fences.

Kara's Saab 101 turned around the corner and splashed through a puddle. Her cell phone slid across the passenger seat with The Skull floating on screen.

She leaned over the steering wheel as she applied the brake.

"What can you see?" Evan asked.

"It's empty," she said. "Just a silver van parked up by the entrance."

"That's theirs. Okay, they're still there. Stop the car."

"Right."

The skies wouldn't be clear for much longer. A sense of foreboding hung in the air, caused by a smothering of darkness in the distance.

"It's gonna rain soon," Kara said as she applied the handbrake.

"We're gonna rain on them. Take the gun and get out of the car. Take me with you."

Kara looked at her cell phone and grabbed it in her hand. "Please tell me what I'm going to find in there."

"You're not going to like it. At all."

"I figured you might say that."

"When I was last there, there were four of them. Two of them are armed, but we'll wait till they're at their most vulnerable. Get me close to the building and into their WiFi range."

Kara stepped out of the car and felt a rush of warm air blast across her face. She attached the gun to her belt and pulled the flap of her jacket down to conceal it.

"How close do you need to be?" she said as she approached the fenced-off parking lot.

"Closer. I'm scanning for available networks. Once I'm in, I'm in. Switching views now, take a look."

The Skull fizzled away to produce a snapshot of the CCTV image he'd taken earlier. The metal table took up most of the image.

George and Alyssa hung in the bottom-right corner by the computer desk.

"Zooming in."

"What's this?

The Rubicon hard drive lay on the table next to Alyssa's keyboard.

"Okay, you see that hard drive? They call it the Rubicon. It's what they raided the offices for, a sixteen-teraflop box that we need to take with us. It contains all the details of each and every InstaBate user. Next to the woman is the terminal they're using. We're gonna need to destroy it."

"What? How am I meant to do that?"

"We're gonna have to get creative, or persuasive. Probably a little bit of both. I'll be working with you from within the network. I'm your eyes and ears on the inside, and you're my eyes and ears on the ground."

The Skull fluttered to life behind the tempered glass on her cell phone. "We can go new or old school when we destroy it. I'm in favor of doing both just to make sure."

Scanning for WiFi...

Kara lowered her cell phone and took in the enormity of the warehouse. "That video you showed me. Is this where it was filmed?"

"Yeah. Nobody's ever gonna check the industrial estate. It's perfect. Until now, that is."

"Sick bastards."

"Keep moving, I need a better signal strength."

Kara took a single, cautious step to both the warehouse door - and her fate.

"When the garage door opens up, that's your cue to introduce yourself. Catch them unawares. You'll see a big guy by the table. He's the one you need to point your gun at. Get ready."

Kara felt her heart stop beating as she passed her phone from her right hand and into her left. She reached into her belt, retrieved the Glock 17.

"Safety catch off."

"Yeah, I *do* know how to use my own firearm, thanks."

Click.

The catch slid across to the left.

"You *do* know how to shoot, don't you?"

"It's been a while since we visited the range. I'm hoping pointing and pulling the trigger will work?"

"It usually does. If anyone tries anything, you have my permission to blow their fucking heads off. But be careful who you aim that thing at."

Kara took another step closer to the warehouse door. The silver van loomed to her right - big and imposing, and pushing the fear of God further into her chest.

"Are you ready?"

Kara steeled herself and tightened her grip on the gun. "I'm ready."

"Put your phone in your pocket. When the doors open, we're on."

Biddip-beep.

"Transferring now. See you on the inside."

The Skull flew into the vanishing point within the phone, rendering the device lifeless in her palm.

She whispered as she slid it into her jeans pocket and held her gun with both hands. A moment of madness pounding at her temple. "Shit, Kara," she asked herself. "What the fuck are you doing?"

A sudden *whump* sound came from the back of the van. Kara averted her eyes to the back doors and noticed the back tires bounce back and forth.

A man's voice came from around the corner, and out of Kara's vision. "Come on, get out."

Once the command had been given, a series of muffled cries followed. Kara lowered her head to see a pair of bare feet covered by a white sheet skirt across the bumpy, graveled ground.

"What the—?"

Then, everything went silent.

Kara held her breath when she saw a pair of shoes next to the bare feet.

"Shhh," came an angry male voice from behind the van doors. "Be quiet," he said in broken English before the muffled cries died down.

Kara dared to step forward with her gun drawn, ready to open fire on whatever was taking place behind the vehicle.

"Who's there?"

No response.

Kara moved forward and kept her eyes trained on the back of the van as she walked up the side of it. "Who's there?"

Just then, a gnarly, dampened cry of help whirled around from the end of the van. "Mfgghh."

Kara raced forward and aimed her gun. "Oh, shit," she gasped as she laid eyes on a suited man with a dog mask for a head, and a shotgun in his hand.

"Stop."

The Dog turned his head, slowly, and glanced at Kara. "Who the fuck are you?"

"Who the fuck are *you*?"

The Dog sneered and yanked on a white piece of material. When his arm bent back, it pulled a scared and gagged teenage girl with him.

The girl had cuts and bruises all over her face. A devastating wave of terror welled in her eyes as she screamed into the ball gag strapped to her head.

"Mffghh."

Kara clutched her gun in both hands and threatened the man. "Let her go. Do it."

Dog wrenched the squealing girl up to him and jammed the barrel of his shotgun under her jaw. "No. You drop your gun, bitch, or this little doggy's gonna lose her head."

Kara kept her gun aimed at the man's head. "I mean it. Let her go."

The Dog leaned into the girl's face and sniffed around. "Mmm. You know what they say, don't you. If it looks pretty, and smells pretty, then what's between her legs is gonna be *damn* tasty."

To both Kara and Dog's surprise, the girl rammed her knee between his legs without warning.

Dog squirmed and yanked on the trigger. "Ooof—"

Bam-schplatt.

The top of the girl's head exploded into a messy firework of flesh and gore. She tumbled back and hit the ground dead, just as Kara opened fire.

"Oops. Bad doggy," the man joked.

"You sick *fuck*," Kara screamed as she shot Dog in the shoulder. The shotgun pinged from his hand, flew into the air and crashed by Kara's left foot.

Dog clutched his bullet wound and fell to his knees. Blood seeped through his fingers as he coughed up a storm inside his rubberized mask. "Nggg."

"Get the fuck up, Fido. We're going walkies."

Thud-thud-thud.

The back of the silver van sprang to life, creating a series of heated and overexcited thumps.

Dog tried to look at his wound through the holes in his mask. "You f-fuckin' shot m-me."

Kara kicked the shotgun over to the van and gripped the back of his mask.

She tore it off his head and saw a sweating, white man puking down his front. It was Tarin, who was in severe danger of passing out.

"Get up or I'll blow your fucking head off."

Tarin climbed to his feet and spat a mound of blood onto the tarmac.

Thud-thud-thud.

The back of the van shifted from side to side. Evidently, there were a bunch of people in there desperate to get out.

"Open the fucking door," Kara said. "Do it, or you're a dead man."

"Fuck."

Kara stood back and aimed her gun at his head as he moved forward and pulled the back doors open.

"You're never gonna get away with this," Tarin said.

"We'll see about that, fuck face."

Kara turned to the back of the van, astonished to see what was inside. "Jesus fucking Christ."

A van full of young girls climbed out one by one, and fled into the parking lot. Most of them were covered in white sheets.

All of them were barefoot.

"Run, run, run!" Kara yelled. "Go, get out of here."

Tarin misunderstood her command and began to run after them.

Kara fired a shot at him, forcing him to freeze on the spot. "Not you. Stay right where you are."

Glitch

Dozens of girls and boys surrounded the man on their escape, running around him like a giant stone in a babbling brook.

"You're never g-gonna get away with this," Tarin said. "You do know who you're fucking with."

"No, I don't," Kara said. "But whoever they are, they have no idea who *they're* fucking with."

Tarin pushed his palm onto the bullet wound on his shoulder. The rush of screams and curdled cries from the escapees thundered into the air.

A young boy, no older than nine years old, climbed out the back of the van, crying for dear life. Kara stared at him as his sheet covering got caught in the van door.

The kid hopped onto the ground in tears.

Kara stared at him and felt her heart turn to stone. "Hey, kid."

"Please don't shoot me."

"I'm not gonna shoot you," Kara said. "Do you know where you are?"

The boy shook his head and covered his bare chest.

"Follow the others. Someone will find you and take you home. It's okay. Go on. *Run.*"

Tarin scoffed and made evil eyes at the youngster as he ran out of the parking lot. Kara made sure the kid turned the corner and vanished into the deadened, dark night - and far away from the hellhole the van had delivered him to.

Kara took a moment to think about her actions, and the event she'd become involved in. The concrete beneath her feet seemed to bleach around her feet and pull her into the Earth's core.

"You sick fucks," she whispered.

As she lifted her head to Tarin, a teardrop rolled down her cheek. "Gimme a good reason I shouldn't blow your goddamn fucking head off right *now.*"

Tarin displayed little in the way of empathy. "I got nothing."

Kara lifted her head to the warehouse door. "The door's about to open any second now. Tell me who's in there."

"Fuck you."

Kara fired a shot in the air and screamed. "Tell me."

"There's loads of 'em, man," Tarin said. "They're all armed, and ready to fuck."

"Get up."

Tarin arched his back and waited for the next order.

Kara spat on the ground and kept her gun pointed at his face. "You're gonna help me take down whatever the fuck is going on in there."

Whirrr.

As if on cue, the gears on the mechanical door fired up. The bottom part shunted away from the rails and began to lift up at what felt like one millimeter-per-hour.

Kara grabbed Tarin's collar and pulled him in front of her chest, and then buried the barrel of her gun into his temple.

"Stay here nice and quiet."

The warehouse door lifted further.

The legs of the metal table were the first thing she saw, followed by a series of deathly chokes.

An excited male's voice crept under the cries, followed by a series of chants and cheers. "Go on, fuck her."

"Damn it," Tarin said. "You don't wanna see this—"

"—Shut the fuck up," Kara whispered into his ear. "Be a good little insurance doggy, okay?"

The light from the parking lot lamps stretched under the door as it continued to rise up and fold across the ceiling.

Kara's tongue fell out of her mouth when she saw a dozen naked men surrounding the metal table, goading each other to take turns.

"Jesus Christ."

A naked man in a Bunny mask held out his arms to the main camera at the far end of the room. "Ladies and Gentleman, welcome to the greatest motherfucking show on Earth!"

A serrated dagger flew into his hand, which he waved around in a state of sexual frenzy. "Pay no attention to the slab of meat on the fucking table."

He turned around, having not seen Kara and Tarin standing by the opening door.

The Bunny spoke with George's voice. "Just like all the others. When we prepare meat, we need to hose it down first. Then, we tenderize it."

The Bunny pushed the naked men out of his way and reached the far end of the table.

It wasn't until he'd reached the table that Kara realized each of the naked men were wearing a mask of their own; cats and dogs of all breeds and colors, as well as a Ram's mask that had once belonged to Oxide.

The Ram's body was much larger than the others. Both he and the Bunny sported electric spider tattos on their wrists.

"Hold her up, boys," Bunny said. "Let the fine people of the Undernet see her scared, little face."

As the men moved out, a girl with dark hair screamed into a ball gag. Kicking and pushing proved to be futile, outnumbered as she was with her would-be abusers.

Bunny grabbed a fistful of her long, black hair and angled her head at the high definition camera at the foot of the table.

Bunny pushed her head back and forth, play-acting as perverse ventriloquist for the gagged girl. "Hello," Bunny mocked through her squirms for freedom. "My name is Alex Richard. My mommy is a slut. She cheats on my daddy with perverts, some of whom are watching right now. But she doesn't know any of this because she's a dumb broad who's only good for one thing."

Bunny stared at the girl's gagged mouth and grunted.

"Okay, maybe *two* things."

Kara gulped, unable to process the vision of utter hell playing out before her.

The Ram clenched his fist and thumped down on Alex's nose. The cartilage on the bridge of her nose busted apart. Several teeth cracked from her gum as she choked on her own blood.

"Ugh," Ram said in Elmer's voice. "I got her dick lube on my hand."

"Dick lube?" Bunny asked.

"Saliva. Nasty fucker."

The naked men slapped themselves between their legs and fist-bumped one another.

Bunny clapped his hands together and ushered the first man to the edge of the table, between Alex's opened knees. "Help yourselves, boys. Form an orderly line."

Kara felt her heart turn to fire and suppress the urge to pull on the trigger and execute Tarin. She glanced at the far corner of the room to see a young woman with an eye patch.

She didn't know her name was Alyssa, and couldn't have known the disgust the woman felt at being party to the proceedings.

Behind Alyssa, a dark monitor played the filmed events on the table in staggeringly crystal clear and close-up precision.

The first masked man bent Alex's thighs out like an open book and rode up against her.

"Wow, that slipped in easily, didn't it?" George said from under the Bunny costume. "Take your time, nice and slow."

Tarin ducked his chin and whispered. "I told you you didn't wanna see this."

Alex stopped squealing and closed her eyelids, close to passing out, as the man had his violent and wicked way with her.

The Skull appeared on Alyssa's monitor. The glare caught Kara's attention from the other end of the room, forcing her eyes to jump out of their sockets. "Evan?"

Ja-ja-ja.

It shifted up and down, left and right, seeming to send a message to Kara.

She took in a lungful of air and rammed the gun into Tarin's temple.

"*Stop,*" she shouted at the top of her voice. "Get away from the fucking table."

The Ram, Bunny, and the naked men looked up, wondering where the voice came from.

It was instantly clear to them that they'd missed the warehouse door opening, especially over all the shouting and screaming coming from their victim on the table.

"Do as she says, man," Tarin shouted. "Please."

"I swear to God I'm gonna blow this cocksucker's head off," Kara said. "Get on your knees. *Do it.*"

Bunny pushed one of the undressed abusers out of his path and stood before Kara, naked. He turned to Alyssa and pointed at the monitor. "Cut the feed."

"Okay."

Just as her finger hit the button on the keyboard, a digitized Skull smiled back at her from inside the monitor. "Hello, Alyssa."

"Huh?"

"Keep the feed going," The Skull said. "There's been a change of programming."

George ripped off his Bunny mask and threw it to the floor. "Alyssa, cut the feed."

The woman didn't know what to do, suffering contradicting instructions from a naked man and a Skull on her monitor.

Ultimately, she made her mind up - and hit the button on the keyboard.

"Bad idea," The Skull said.

George wiped the sweat from his brow and braved the woman holding her Glock 17 to his accomplice's head. "Tarin?"

"Aw, fuck, man. Why'd you have to say my name?"

"She's not gonna shoot you."

Kara threw her left arm around Tarin's front and held his back to her chest with the gun buried in his temple. "Don't fucking try me, asshole."

"So, you blow my associate's head off, and then what?"

Kara didn't have an answer. It seemed there was no way out of this stand-off.

The Ram reached under the table and pulled out a shotgun. He cocked it and aimed it directly at Kara's face. The action provided some relief to the masked men, all of whom lowered their hands, and considered joining in the attack.

"Tarin?" Elmer asked.

"Uh, yeah?" came the response from the terrified man with the gun to his head.

"Please tell me the goods in the van are secure."

Tarin squirms turned into a pathetic blubbing. "No, man. She released them."

George could barely contain his anger. He held out his arms and grinned evilly at Kara. "Was that your doing?"

"You're damn right, fuckface."

"What's your name?"

Kara threatened to pull the trigger and take Tarin out of the game for good. "*Fuck you*, that's my name. Stay back."

"Well, *Fuck You*, I think you've made the biggest mistake of your life. Under any ordinary circumstances, I'd suggest you drop the gun and walk away, and pretend this never happened."

George reached down and slapped his rigid penis for effect.

"But this isn't any ordinary circumstance," he explained. "You've seen my face. You know everything, now. So, I'm going to give you a choice."

Kara inhaled and threatened Tarin further with her gun. "Stay back, or I'll put your nasty bitch-dog to sleep."

"Option one. Give it up, and we'll make it nice and quick for you. Or, there's option two. But you're not gonna like it. Is she, fellas?"

The masked men punched their fists together with excitement.

"Hello, no, she ain't."

The Ram focused his right eye down the sight of the shotgun and cleared his throat. "Fuck that, George. Let me blow her pretty little head off right now and fuck the neck hole."

"Now, now, Elmer," George giggled. "Don't spoil option number two."

Alex lifted her head and began to hyperventilate. A sudden gush of blood blasted out from between her legs and splattered up the floor.

"My God," Kara screamed. "What did you sick fuckers do to her?"

Her voice was the only sound audible in the warehouse at this point in time, which further antagonized all involved.

Practically helpless, Kara looked up at the ceiling and screamed for a miracle. "Evan? Where are you?"

"Evan?" George said, confused. "Evan... *Cole*?"

Kara continued her cry for help. "Evan, please. If you can hear me, do something—"

"—Ha, Evan can't help you. We killed that nerdy prick already," George said as he moved a step closer with unerring confidence. "So, release my associate, and let's get on with the killing."

The standoff occurred behind Alyssa, who stared into the black void in the monitor. She lifted her right hand up to her face and wiggled her fingers.

A whiff of smoke came from the keyboard, traveling behind her fingers. "I'm in," she muttered.

She clenched her fist hard, and then expanded her fingers once again. A blob of blood peeled out from her right nostril and fell into her palm.

When she turned around, she momentarily lost her balance. "George?"

"What the fuck do you want now?"

"I—uh," Alyssa said, trying to acclimatize herself to her own voice. "I—I d-don't want t-to work for you, anymore."

Confused, Kara stammered at the woman. "Wha—what the fuck—"

Alyssa tilted her head to the side and produced an evil, angry smirk across her face. A final wink was all it took to reassure Kara that Evan was working his magic.

"Oh m-my God."

George punched his fists together and screamed at the woman. "Alyssa? What's gotten into you, you stupid cunt?"

She swung her head to the left and widened her eyes. "Evan Cole has."

"What—?"

Alyssa jumped forward. "Kara, *now*."

"What?" George squealed. "Elmer, show this bitch who's boss."

"You got it."

Blam.

He fired a shot at Kara, but the bullet caught Tarin square between the eyes. His head exploded like a busted watermelon and splattered Kara's face.

"Agh!"

Alyssa launched herself at George.

Kara kicked Tarin's corpse in the back, sending him crashing into the naked men at the table. The shotgun wound puked the contents of his neck across the table, flooded past Alex's legs and splashed to the floor.

"Goddamn it," Elmer screamed as he fired a second shot at Kara. She dived behind a stack of crates by the wall, just as the top one exploded.

"Damn it, you fucking bitch," he roared as he reloaded the shot gun. "Get her."

Kara squealed as fragments of wood showered down around her shoulders. What seemed like a thousand bare feet ran across the ground in her direction.

"Shit."

She hopped out from behind the crates and fired three shots at the approaching horde of naked men.

The first bullet missed and crashed into the metal table.

The second and third bullets hit the first man in the face, shattering his forehead and cheekbones from his skull. A mound of blood shot out and splashed onto the gloved man behind him.

"Ugghh."

He slid the side of his glove across his eyes and smeared the blood away. He kicked the middle crate, sending the stack over and onto its side. "C'mere, bitch."

Kara kicked the wall and fell to her ass as she pointed the gun at him and opened fire.

Bam-bam-spatch.

Two successive shots blasted into his thighs, punching the flesh into his groin. The third bullet clipped the tip of his penis, thundered between his thighs, and smashed against the door.

The gloved man dropped to his knees, the force of which busted his thigh bone in two, and planted his face on the floor. He reached out and groaned, firing a jet of thick, black blood out of his anus.

"Fuck me."

Kara kicked herself back and waved her gun at the next two men. "Get back or I'll shoot."

Elmer reached above his head, grabbed the horns on his mask, and whipped it off his head. He hurled it at Alyssa, as she staggered towards George.

The rubber mask bopped off her head as George bolted towards her. "You fuckin' asshole."

"Aggghh."

Alyssa jumped into the air and screeched. "Come here for a killing."

Clutch.

She planted her palms on George's head and pressed her thumbs into his eyes.

"Agghhh—"

"—I know everything," Alyssa's voice croaked as Evan's pushed through. "Every name. Every address. Every goddamn motherfucker."

Elmer swung his shotgun at Alyssa's head. "George, stop fucking around with the broad and get outta my way."

"Gah—"

Elmer yanked on the trigger.

Blam.

A bullet fired out of the barrel, rocketed across the metal table, and caught Alyssa's right forearm. Her limbs pinged back, sending her somersaulting into the air, and crashing head-first into the monitor.

The device wobbled back and forth as she jumped to her feet.

Ptchoo-ptchoo.

She spat out two of her teeth and grinned at George as she used her sleeve to wipe the blood from her mouth. "Hey, big boy."

Elmer cocked the shot gun and aimed it at her. "Fuck me."

"Nah," she said with a twinge of Evan's voice. "You first."

Blam-blam-blam.

Alyssa slid to her knees as the monitor suffered the onslaught of bullets. The screen exploded in a puff of smoke as the case twisted around and hit the wall.

"Shit, the Rubicon," Alyssa screamed at Kara, who slid back across the floor. "Get it."

Kara was far too busy fighting the naked, masked man looming over her. "Uh, I can't—"

"—I'm gonna tear out your eyes and fuck the sockets," the man grunted. "Come here."

"Ugh, shit."

Whump.

She booted the man between the legs. He groaned and buckled over, holding his thighs. Kara scrambled to her feet and grabbed the smoking, shattered monitor from the computer desk and slammed it on his head.

Whump.

She tossed it at the metal table and booted her assailant in the side of the head. "Fucking *die*."

Whup-whup-crunch.

A final stomp to the back of his head crushed his forehead into the ground. She lifted her heel from the cavity and kicked the fragments of skull and brains across the floor.

When she looked up, she saw four naked men reach for the compartment on the wall behind the table.

Elmer grabbed a hammer and chucked it at one of the men. "Some bastard take that bitch *down*."

"Got it."

He passed a machete, a power drill, and a buzz saw to the three others. "Reloading. Kill her."

"Fuck yeah," they screamed.

"And when you've killed her, drag the body over here so I can fuck the corpse."

Chapter 9

Alyssa grabbed Kara's Glock 17 and swung it at George's head. "Get back, you murdering piece of shit."

"You're not gonna shoot me."

"Think again, asshole. You killed me. I think you owe me a murdering."

She lifted the gun at George's face and pulled on the trigger.

Click-click-click.

The gun was empty. Quick-thinking, she tossed it aside and threw her arms out in front of her.

"Evan Cole?" George asked.

The burning red pupils in Alyssa's eyes seemed to expand with rage. "Just wait till Xavier Manning finds out who fucked him over."

George gripped his penis in his hand and moved it up and down. "What?" he chuckled. "Evan, who do you think is in charge of all of this?"

"What?"

"Who do you think organized the raid? Who do you think stands to profit from blaming *you* for failing to protect everyone's data."

The fatal revelation caused Evan to stop within Alyssa's body. Everything made sense to him, now.

"You hired me to blame me?"

"Uh-huh," George grinned at Alyssa's stunned face. "Your body's bundled in The Grid. Nobody will find you, and everyone thinks you're to blame. You're nothing but an unfortunate anomaly. A *glitch*, if you will. *Cunt.*"

Alyssa scowled at the man as Evan's murderous voice fell from her mouth. "You're all dead."

"Night night, little girl."

Blam.

She threw herself forward and grabbed the metal table with her fingers. Alex's feet kicked up and down so hard she almost kicked herself in the head.

"Fuck's sake, Elmer," George screamed. "How hard is it to shoot a non-moving target, you asshole?"

Alex screamed into her ball gag and wiggled her toes right in front of Alyssa's face. "Nggghh."

She grabbed the girl's foot and pulled herself to her feet, only to be met by Elmer's shotgun once again.

Alyssa gasped and froze solid, as Elmer twisted the gun in his arms and dug the barrel into Alex's forehead. "Wanna watch a murder show, motherfucker?"

"Don't do it—"

"—Heh," Elmer shouted over Alex's screams of turmoil. "You ever see the damage a twelve gauge does to a kid's face? It's fuckin' horrible. Here, lemme show you—"

"No—"

Alyssa launched over the table and scrambled towards Elmer's shotgun.

"Sayonara, motherfucker."

Elmer yanked on the trigger just as Alyssa grabbed the barrel and pushed it away.

Ker-blamm.

The shotgun cartridge blew one of the table legs away, causing it to topple the end of the table to the floor.

Clang.

Alyssa slid down the diagonal surface, as the lower half of Alex's body twisted around and hung down the shiny tabletop surface, her hair hanging from the vise.

The seams of her bangs carried the weight of her body and began to tear apart.

Rii-ii-iipp.

"Aghhhh," Alex squealed at the scalping effect the vise was having on her.

Alyssa scrambled to her elbows and climbed up the squealing girl and reached for Elmer's gun. "Gimme that."

"Get the fuck off me," Elmer screamed as he yanked on the trigger.

Blam-spatch.

The bullet hit the outer part of Alyssa's left thigh. Her hip crashed onto Alex's chest, forcing her to heave and puke into her ball gag.

Schplattt.

"Gaaaahhh," Alyssa screamed as she socked Elmer across the face. "Come to mommy."

Alyssa punched her tiny fist into Elmer's mouth and grabbed onto his jaw as he bit down in agony. His head bent down to the table as she applied her strength and used his face to pull herself up the table.

Her feet kicked off the shiny surface, further compounding the weight onto Alex's shoulders.

Teaaarrrr.

Alex's scalp bled as it opened up across the front of her face. "Gaaoow."

Alyssa dug her heels into the woman's shoulders and jumped onto Elmer. The man spun around and around with the woman on his back. "Get off me."

Slam.

He pressed himself against the compartment on the wall and grabbed the last remaining weapon on the wall — a pair of scissors.

Whip—whip—whip.

He spun the plastic around his chunky finger, catching Alyssa's face with several swipes.

Lines of blood burst up her cheeks and across her neck as she ducked to avoid the flying sharp ends of the scissor.

"Nagghhh."

Alyssa sank her teeth into Elmer's neck. He screamed as ropes of blood splashed on her face.

The man tumbled back and fell over the diagonal surface of the metal table, knocking Alex's ball gag clean away from her mouth.

The half-scalped girl's cries of agony shattered through the room as she gripped the higher end of the table to prevent her own body weight from scalping her further.

Her heels kicked off the ground, pushing her legs in all directions.

Kara moved to the table and went for the Rubicon hard drive.

It smoldered and burned, having been hit by a bullet.

"Shit."

She regretted facing the other way when she saw three naked men, each with a weapon, headed her way.

The first sported an orange tabby cat mask. In his hand was a fully rotating power drill with a gelatin vibrator attached to the end of it.

"Come here for a fucking."

Without warning, she gripped the Rubicon hard drive and kicked herself away from the computer desk. She lifted her arm and went to strike the man across the mask.

Whump.

She punched the man in the mask with the hard drive. On the rebound, the jellied vibrator smacked Kara in the face and landed on the floor, hopping around like a desperate fish out of water.

The man groaned and felt around his mask's plastic whiskers as Kara bent over and picked up the still-running power drill.

"Get back, fuckheads."

The next man in line wore a cartoon dog mask, and carried a machete.

Swish-swish.

He threatened her with the fifteen-inch blade. "Now, now. Let's not get too *cut up* about this, huh?" he said. "I'll carve your tits off and give myself a nice lipstick makeover."

Kara kicked the first man in the chest and stood her ground. "You wanna end up like your friend, here?"

"I wanna end up *in you*, honey."

The man raised the machete above his head and went to swipe, but skidded in the build-up of blood that had collected on the floor.

He fell forward just as Kara rammed the power drill into the air.

The whirring drill bit caught his fall under his chin, and pushed through his lower palate, shattering the jawbone.

The full weight of his body planted the rest of his head onto the spinning drill as Kara roared and lifted her arms.

Crunch-crunch-splitt.

"Aggghhh," she screamed as the drill burrowed through the middle of his head - through his brain, and split through the crown of his skull, and out through the mask.

The cartoon dog face jerked around, slowly at first, and then faster and faster as the drill killed the man.

Kara lifted her legs and kicked the corpse in the chest, flinging a mound of bodily detritus, blood, and bile from his head.

Splash-crash.

An ocean of gore splashed onto the ground, hitting the other two men in the chest and thighs.

"Who's next?"

When Kara waved the power drill around, the spinning flesh and bits of bone shot in all directions.

The next two naked men watched as she grabbed the drill with two hands and rammed it down into the first man's screaming mouth.

Grind.

The drill pinned the back of the man's throat to the concrete ground. The fragments of rubber from the cat mask picked away, causing a furious mountain of blood and teeth to fountain into the air.

Wrench.

She lifted the drill out of the mask and swung it at the next man, who approached her with a hammer.

"You killed him," his muffled voice bled from out of his giraffe's mask.

"And you're next," Kara said, before directing her eyes between his legs. "You always carry around something *that small* with you?"

The man stepped forward and chuckled within his mask. "I'm gonna tear your fucking heart out."

"I'm gonna tear your fucking balls off."

The man hurled the hammer at her with all his might. Kara sidestepped and flung her head to the side.

Clang.

The hammerhead smashed against the wall and hit the floor.

"Oops," Kara said as she picked the hammer up from the floor and smashed him across the face with it.

The man's giraffe mask flew off his head, revealing a broken eye socket with a distended eyeball hanging out of the bloodied socket.

"Gnesh-Gwuck-uck," he squirmed as he held his face in his hands.

Kara smashed him across the face with the hammer again, catching his wrist and shattering the bone.

"Ugh."

She swiped again, this time catching him in the neck. The hammer head wouldn't budge, cocooned inside the flesh on his neck.

She barged into him and whipped the hammer from the cavity, taking out a clump of flesh with it.

Splat.

The man's giraffe mask filled with his own blood like a balloon attached to a water hose.

Kara yelped and smashed the hammer across his face. It knocked the mask off his head and sent it hurtling through the air, leaving her to swing it around and smash him in the face once again.

He fell forward into Kara's arms. "I gotcha, big boy."

Whump.

She chucked the hammer in the air, caught the handle, and performed an upper-cut — right between his legs.

The hammerhead jammed inside his anus, as she tightened her grip on the handle and swung her arms around.

As the man slammed chest-first to the floor, his tail bone snapped through his skin as she ripped the metal head from out of his rectum.

An ocean of red guts gushed across the floor. Kara wiped the hammerhead on her jeans and threatened the last man in front of her.

"I never knew I had this in me," she said. "But if you want some more, come and get some."

Skid-skid-slip.

As she backed up, her heels screeched and squeaked across the ocean of blood and gore that built up on the ground.

Alyssa grabbed George around the neck and screamed into his face.

"G-Get off m-me—"

"—N-Nooo," Alyssa's voice intertwined with Evan's as she strangled the man with all her might. "I c-can't g-get—"

Fitch-spitch-spark.

She dropped to her knees, taking George down with her. Her fingers sizzled against the skin on his neck.

Static erupted up her arms and torso as she screamed. Blood fired out of her nostrils

"What the f-fuck is g-going on?" George yelped and kicked the woman away. She tumbled ass-over-tit across the blood-drenched floor, looking like a video game sprite, flashing on and off at a rapid pace.

"Gwuck-gwuck."

Alyssa rose to her knees and yelled as hard as she could, but it only made her new-found transparency worsen.

"Don't just stand there, you fat fuck," George said to Elmer. "Shoot her."

"My pleasure."

Elmer turned the shotgun at Alyssa and pulled the trigger.

Blam.

The bullet shot through the air, straight through Alyssa's static-thunderstorm of a face, and crashed into the wall behind her.

George shook his head, confused. "What? It went right through her. Shoot her again—"

"—No," Kara shouted from behind the crates. "Stop."

Fizz-schpit-spatch.

Alyssa writhed in agony on the floor in a futile attempt to fight off her bizarre algorithmic death.

"Whup-whup-gwuck," she spurted as her body tumbled back and forth. In a few seconds, it seemed she'd disappear entirely.

The back wall and broken computer could be seen through her translucent body as she rolled back and forth.

"K-Kara, h-help m-me."

Kara reached into her blood-caked jeans pocket and pulled out her phone. "Here, Evan. Take this."

George and Elmer watched in stunned silence as the cell phone bounced through the sea of blood and guts and landed next to Alyssa's face.

She groaned, and slammed her forehead onto the black mirror.

"What the fuck?" George said over the heightened squeals coming from Alex.

Now face down, Alyssa's buckled up and down like a hiccuping donkey as her head burst into flames and produced a dirty stench of burnt hair and skin.

Her chin crunched into her nose, and forced her eyeballs from their sockets, which turned into a series of pixels as they melted into the screen.

"Fuck me," Elmer said. "Your phone is *eating* her."

Her shoulders broke and folded over her spine as the cell phone continued to chew and swallow her whole.

Kara spotted her opportunity as the two men watched the carnage. She backed up behind the remaining crates and cowered behind them, safely out of sight.

Gwump-crunch.

"Yaaooooww," Alyssa's voice traveled down her ribcage as, one by one, the bones snapped out like a budding flower and vacuumed into the screen.

Fizzz.

Her hip bones, pelvis, thighs, knees, shins, and heels folded like a rolled-up cigarette paper, crunching and splintering, before the device had sucked her in whole…

… The Skull burst to life on the cell phone screen and zipped around, ostensibly caged within the four corners of the screen.

George held his hands out in front of him as he dared to step forward. "Evan?"

The Skull pushed forward and rammed its head against the screen. "George. George Gilbertson."

"What happened to Alyssa?"

The Skull's eye sockets beamed red for a split second, before Evan's voice burst through the speakers. "Dead."

"And… what happened to you?"

"Dead," The Skull said.

Kara covered her mouth as George took another step toward her cell phone in the swamp of human remains.

As she moved back, her elbow knocked the second crate. Something inside shifted around.

"Huh?"

Peering in, she saw several mounds of plasticine, off-white in color. The name "C4" etched in black across each one.

"Oh, sh-shit—"

"—Agggghhhh," came a girl's scream from behind the crate, which caused Kara to cover her mouth again.

Elmer's voice followed after it. "Yo, bitch. Behind the crate, you fucking slut. Come on out and see what you did," he said, before launching into a furious tirade. "I said get the fuck out and see what you made me do, you sick bitch."

She turned back to the naked George a few feet away from her. Fascinated by The Skull's presence on her cell phone, he crouched down and reached for the screen.

"How did you do this?"

The Skull shuddered, angrily. "I could tell you, but then I'd have to kill you. Do me a favor."

"What's that?"

Evan's voice slowed to a creepy demonic halt as he gave his next instruction. "Touch. My. *Face*."

George gulped as he extended his index finger and went to touch it.

"Don't touch it, man," Elmer shouted. "Fuck. You saw what he did to Alyssa, man. Don't touch it."

Evan's voice crashed to a halt as the eye sockets grew to twice their size on the cell phone screen. "Touch me, Gilbertson. You can touch all those innocent girls you abducted, right? So you can touch me."

"Don't do it," Elmer said.

Transfixed, George pushed his finger forward and lowered his fingertip to the screen.

Half an inch before the fibers of his skin hit the screen, a warm, orange glow of death plumed from the glass.

Zzzzzz-ii-ipp.

"Agh."

George whipped his finger away and covered it with his other hand. "Fuck."

"Touch me, asshole."

George shook his head like an infant and nearly burst into tears.

"You chicken piece of shit," The Skull roared. "Touch me. Put your finger on the screen and touch me."

"No."

The fear of God etched its way down George's spine. He went to move to the table and turned around to face Elmer.

"Give me that fucking shotgun—oh, Jesus fucking Christ."

Elmer smiled and cocked the shotgun. "You like?"

George's jaw dropped in fear when he saw what he'd done. "Elmer?"

"Uh-huh?"

"Easy, now," George said. "Take the gun out of her and pass it to me."

"Aww."

Kara peered through the slits in the crates and held her breath. A blurry vision of a pair of girl's legs shuddered back and forth.

"Ngggg," the girl squealed through her snapped vocal cords.

She moved her eyes up to the next slit and was just about able to make out half a length of long hair clamped in the vise.

A puddle of blood collected around the heels of the girl's feet.

George's voice could be heard bouncing off the walls in a quiet and concerned fashion. "Elmer, please. Take your finger off the trigger. She's been through enough. We need her alive."

"Nah," Elmer grunted, out of Kara's view. "We kill her, then we kill the cunt behind the crate, then we kill that Skull thing, then we get outta here."

"Ignoramus! We need this girl alive, not blown apart all over the fuckin' valley."

Kara gripped the crate and moved her left eye into a hole blown into the wood by a stray bullet. "Huh?"

Once the image focused in her eyes, she gulped and heaved. "Oh, God."

George stepped forward and hushed the weeping girl in a peculiar move of reassurance. "Hey, Alex? It's gonna be okay. Elmer is going to do as I say, okay?"

The girl squirmed in a state of sheer catatonia.

Elmer had inserted half the length of the shotgun inside Alex's vulva.

"Elmer, take the gun out."

Instead of complying, he turned to the crates. "Yo, bitch. Stand the fuck up or I'll blow this bitch's pussy out the top of her skull."

The lack of a response angered the man. He yanked the end of the gun up so hard that Alex fainted onto it.

"You hear me? Stand the fuck up."

Kara slowly rose to her feet with her hands outstretched. "Okay, okay. Just don't hurt her."

Half of Alex's scalp had torn from her head, and taken much of the slick dura mater that once covered her brain.

Her eyes shuddered underneath the gloopy, cranial membrane roping down her nose and cheekbones.

"H-Help m-me—" Alex croaked.

"Let her go," Kara said. "Please."

"Get on your fucking knees," Elmer said, threatening to blow the girl away.

"Okay, okay."

A million names and addresses whizzed past The Skull as it flew down a series of electronic ports.

"Goddamn it, where is it? Where is it?"

The Skull flaked into a bunch of pixelated blocks as it zoomed towards a circular hole in the algorithmic vortex of ones and zeros.

"Camera one, camera one."

A gray and white light shone from the far end of the cylindrical tunnel of lights and data.

"There it is," Evan's voice blew out from The Skull's jaws.

The phrase *Get on your fucking knees, Cinderella* thundered past The Skull as it whooshed past a blocky rendition of Elmer's hand attached to the shotgun, leaving a ghostly smoke wake behind it.

An IMAX-sized wall showed Kara dropping to her knees.

Okay, okay.

The light at the end of the spinning barrel of circuits and data blew out and screamed towards The speeding Skull.

"Camera one, asshole," Evan said. "Wait till you get a load of *me*."

Kara placed her hands behind her head and remained on her knees.

George grinned and rubbed his bloodied hands together. He pointed at the unconscious, snoring Alex with the gun between her legs, and then back at Kara.

"What can I say? Everyone gets fucked eventually."

"Why are you doing this?"

George burst out laughing and grabbed his penis in triumph. "Because, my sweet little thing, we have the power. And you? Them? They're nothing."

"Yeah," Elmer said with pride. "Born to fuck."

George nodded. "Amen, my nasty little friend. What do you get the man who has everything? I'll tell you. You get him the thing nobody can have."

"We'll find you," Kara said. "And we'll take you fucking down."

Elmer lifted his right arm and hooked his finger over the trigger. "Wanna see what happens if you try to find us?"

George turned to his accomplice and licked his lips at the gory sight caused by the barrel of the gun. "Show her."

"Stand back," Elmer said. "It's gonna get messy."

He poised himself to yank on the trigger, but before he could, the camera to his right exploded, pushing tiny shards of glass over his shoulder.

"Wha—?"

George jumped in shock as a six-foot ghost-like skeleton dived head-first out of the camera lens and wrapped its bare arms around Elmer's neck.

Both men crashed to the floor, forcing the shotgun to slam against the table between Alex's legs. The impact caused her to open her eyes and wake up, screaming for her life.

"Fuck," George yelped and scrambled to safety on the lower end of the table. He grabbed the shotgun and rammed it between Alex's legs.

She screamed in pain as the skin around her vulva fused around the intense heat of the freshly-fired barrel.

George held his breath to avoid the stench of burning skin and flesh as he shoved it further inside Alex.

"God, that fuckin' stinks."

As he looked away, he caught The Skeleton wrestling with Elmer.

"Get off me, you fuck—"

"—Aggghhh."

The Skeleton's body sparked up like a firework show all around its see-through body.

Kara stood up with her hands behind her head. "Evan?"

Elmer threw a punch, but his fist went through Evan's skull like a bulldozer swinging into a cloud of smoke.

"Motherfucker," Evan screamed as he clutched Elmer's neck and swung him to the side and smashed his face against the wall. "Why don't you be a good little pervert and die?"

"Wugghhh—"

Smash-smash-crack.

Evan slammed Elmer's face against the weaponry cabinet three times, each one more forceful than the last. Bits of teeth and jawbone pinged in all directions as Evan grabbed the back of the man's head and crunched the back of his skull.

Cratch.

Evan flung the back of Elmer's head to the table, slung his right arm between his legs and performed a number of breaks up his body.

The top of his spine broke in two in Evan's fingers, before the lower half of his back pulverized and burst out above his ass.

"Nice and neat, motherfucker."

Crunch-snap.

Evan spun the mound of half-breathing flesh around on its feet, gripped the back of his head, and stared into Elmer's eyes.

"When you see *The Skull...* you're dead."

With no time to think, George raced over to the table, wound the vise handle open, and released Alex's hair.

"Shhh," he said. "Come with me."

He clenched the shotgun handle in his right hand and, with his left, held the back of her head.

When he pulled her away from the table, the rest of her scalp tore from her head and splatted against the surface.

"Sorry about this," he said, now with her body draped in his arms. He kept his finger on the trigger and sploshed through the sea of blood and gore, headed for the door.

"We can't stay here anymore."

Elmer's head hung, broken, in Evan's arms.

"How you feeling, you sick fuck?"

The man vomited a torrent of puke and blood through The Skull's face and splashed across the floor behind it.

Evan didn't take the sentiment too well. "Ugh, you sick fuck." He tightened his grip on Elmer's throat with his transparent left hand, and reached between the man's thighs with his right.

Clench.

"Look at me in the face, you fuck. *Look at me.*"

Elmer's final glance into the face of the apocalypse would be his last.

"When you dance with the devil, you better make sure you get your cocksucking *footwork* right."

Stomp—crunch.

Elmer's right foot crunched, splintering the bones out the sides

The Skull screamed like a banshee as it thumped the back of the man's neck with such force that it shattered his collar bone.

Snap-break.

Elmer's chin slammed down to his stomach, pushing his distended spine out through his liver.

Crunch-crunch-snap.

Evan folded Elmer over again so that his face slapped into his thigh. Evan squeezed Elmer's hard penis in his right hand so hard that the end ballooned out and turned purple.

"You goddamn, red collar cocksucker—"

"Aggghhhh—"

Evan rammed Elmer's screaming mouth down onto his own erect penis.

Schlump-schplatt.

The end of his penis burst up his windpipe and out through the back of his neck, causing a flood of puke to burst out of his nostrils. Elmer's dead, limp body fluttered as the force of his own appendage cut off his oxygen supply for good.

His nostrils blasted the contents of his stomach so violently that it forced his eyeballs to roll back into his skull, reducing him to a balled-up pile of gore-drenched human flesh with his thighs pressing against his ears.

Elmer's body went limp in the skeleton's arms. "Ugh, get off me."

He dropped the freshly impaled corpse to the ground and turned to face George, who carried Alex in his arms.

"Very inventive, Evan," he said, knowing full well that he had the upper hand. "You really should've worked with us on the videos we were making."

"Fuck you. You're next."

"Ah, not quite. I think you're gonna open the door and let me and Alex outta here."

The Skeleton began to fizz and break apart, causing Evan to groan in pain.

"What's the matter, Evan? Whatever fucked up voodoo you're into, you can't stay in the real world too long, huh?"

"Ugh," Evan gargled and staggered around, looking for an available electronic gadget to rescue him.

He spotted Kara's cell phone at the far end of the warehouse and scraped the spilled organs and human gore across the floor as he made for it.

Pleased, George chuckled to himself and teased the trigger on the shotgun. "That's right, you bony fuck head. Open the fucking door."

The second Evan fell to his knees, his body flicked into a static light show. "Ugghhh."

"Do it," George said, teasing on the trigger. "Get in, go everywhere, kill everyone. But first, open the fucking door, or Alex's chances of having children of her own look very, very dim."

Evan roared in pain at the ceiling before smashing his blinking head into the cell phone. "Gwaaaarrrr—"

Schwip.

He vanished into thin air in a split second.

George hoisted Alex up in his arms and grimaced at Kara. "What the fuck are you looking at?"

"I dunno?" she spat with anger. "A filthy fucking pervert who's about to die?"

"Very funny. Get your boyfriend to open the door. We're gonna leave, and if you try to follow us I'll pull the trigger."

Whirrrrrr.

To Kara and George's surprise, the mechanism on the wall fired to life and rolled the door up the railings.

"Good, good."

George bent over and slipped through the opening. His bare heel caught something on the floor which sliced into the sole of his right foot.

"Owww."

He looked down to find a chrome plated spear, and chuckled. "Oxide. Seems so fucking long ago, now."

The door shunted to a halt as George smiled at Kara. "See ya later."

The woman did nothing but inhale and exhale and try to fight the murder from her heart. She watched on as George opened the van door and stepped inside with Alex attached to the shotgun.

Whump.

The door slammed shut just as the engine sprang to life.

"You let him go," Kara said, knowing Evan was listening, somewhere.

His voice blew out of the speakers in the room. "I had to. He was going to execute that girl."

Kara suddenly realized where she was. A field of murdered bodies littered the floor. She couldn't see the gray concrete for the amount of blood, guts, and human remains.

The stench made her want to puke, but the air drifting in from the open door held her back.

The van's lights blinked red.

The back tires twisted to the left.

Evan's voice blew around the room. "Pick up your phone."

She splashed through the bloodied floor, slid her hand under her cell phone and picked it up. "Got it."

The Skull appeared on screen as a chattering bunch of pixels. "It's okay, Kara. We'll get him. We'll get them all."

"You know who they are, don't you? Please tell me you know every single piece of shit involved."

"Every single one," The Skull said as he knocked his head to the right of the screen. "And pretty soon, the whole world will know."

Clink-clink.

"There."

Kara averted her eyes to the crates. "Are you serious?"

"Fuck yeah. Take one with you—"

Kara and The Skull turned to the parking lot to investigate the sound of two successive gunshots. The interior of the van lit up twice.

Blam-blam.

George had pulled on the trigger and apparently executed Alex.

"Oh, shit," she said. "Oh, no."

George's hearty laugh pounded out of the driver's side window.

"Please, no."

The van's tires skidded on the ground before propelling the vehicle out of the parking lot. On its way out, the passenger door flung open and released Alex's freshly-executed corpse to the concrete below.

Kara moved forward and kept her eyes on the dead body lying in the dust rising from the cold, concrete ground.

A few drops of rain fell from the sky and bulleted into the pool of blood escaping Alex's wounds.

Kara stopped a few feet away from the corpse.

"Alex," she whispered, close to tears and vomiting. "I c-can't—"

"—Let me see. Show me."

Evan's voice rifled up her forearm from her cell phone.

Carefully, shocked, she lifted her screen to face the corpse on the ground.

"I think I'm going to be s-sick."

The damage done between her legs expelled her organs. What looked like a thick snake had burned through her groin and abdomen, past her torso, and up her neck to the only part of her head that remained. The result was complicated mound of ex-human that fired a stench of rancid death into the night air.

Neither Kara nor Evan could speak at the sight of the executed girl. Alex had been thoroughly executed.

"We're gonna get him," The Skull said. "We're gonna get them all. I promise."

Kara burst into tears as the rain fell harder around her. "You promise me we'll do ten times worse to that fucker than he did to this poor girl, right?"

"I swear to God," Evan said. "Don't look at her. Get back to the car. Our next move is something we definitely don't want to fuck up."

Murder was in the air, and revenge wasn't far away.

Kara's tears turned to rage as she looked away from the ground and raced out of the parking lot.

Chapter 10

The city lights rolled up the windshield. Kara was at the wheel, at least physically. Mentally, she was a million miles away.

The only thing that kept her anywhere near being in the moment was the sight of something rocking back and forth on the passenger seat, right by her cell phone. It was covered in plasticine.

"Why did you make me take it?"

The Skull remained steady on her cell phone screen and took a moment to answer. "It's C4. We have a use for it. I need to get to The Grid and destroy it. Just that one stick is enough to take them off the map for good."

"Shouldn't we just call the police?"

"Kara, I've seen tens of thousands of names of those involved. Some of them are high profile at the CVPD. Lawyers, politicians, anyone worth a damn who's in charge of anything serious in the valley. Enough of them were watching the live feed, too. If I told you all the names, you'd turn the car around and leave *the planet*, much less the valley, for good."

Kara found the news astonishing. "The chief of police at the Chrome Valley Police Department is in on it?"

"Yeah, his name is Raymond Banshade," Evan revealed. "Gilbertson put a call into him earlier, and he was watching the feed , back there. Calls himself Princess12 online."

"Princess12? Weird name for an old dude."

"You have to ask yourself something, Kara. Why would a guy in his fifties pose as a young girl like that?"

In her infinite naivety, she didn't know the answer. "I don't know?"

"It's probably better you keep it that way, then," Evan said. "He's only been with the valley force a month. His predecessor was murdered. There's a widespread epidemic of that happening all over the place."

The freeway wasn't busy at this time of night. Only a smattering of cars joined her on the freeway en route to Evan's apartment, which added to Kara's feeling of helplessness.

Kara had spent much of her time crying when she got into the car. Her blood-soaked clothes clung to her skin when they didn't stitch into the fabric covering the car seat.

It would only be a matter of time before someone would happen upon the carnage they'd left in their wake.

Kara's eyes focused on the road ahead. Somehow, her car felt bigger now that she was inside, as if she'd shrunk in size.

"Where's your apartment?"

"Next turn," The Skull said. "The second tower."

The Freeway Five Estate
~Chrome Valley West~

The seedier, uncared-for side of the valley was a place Kara wasn't used to. The night had been more than she could handle, and going home wasn't an option.

Her Saab 101 rolled to a stop by the playground.

When Kara climbed out, a cool breeze hit her face like a vicious slap from a smog-laden hand.

"Take the C4 with you," Evan said from her cell phone. "We'll get you a change of clothes."

***

Apartment 238 on the second floor of the second tower. When Kara walked in, she was greeted with a hallway that led to the front room.

"Nice digs," she said to her cell phone.

"Yeah, I live alone, or at least I *used* to. It was, or is, something of a bachelor pad," Evan said before chuckling in anger. "You know, I didn't even know what tense to use, anymore."

"You're not technically dead, I guess."

"If I don't get into The Grid and access the international mainframe, I will be."

Evan's assessment of his life was scarily accurate.

The front room had long, black drapes covering the windows. A chalk pentangle had been drawn on the left flap.

Thousands of items of electrical equipment in boxes lined the far wall.

"I refuse to be stuck in Chrome Valley's network, scaring the shit out of small-timers," Evan said. "And if I can only survive a matter of minutes inside a human, then I want out. I want to go viral. Put myself to use, period."

"I hear you."

"And I can't do it without you, Kara."

"If it means causing misery and pain to those motherfuckers, then you know I have your back, Cole."

Kara could barely see the couch from the door to the room, and used it as an excuse to change the subject.

"My God. This place is a mess."

"Much like my life was," he said. "Take a seat. Plug me into my laptop."

Kara looked down at the coffee table as she lowered her ass onto the couch. A bunch of cables and connectors needed moving before she sat down properly.

She reached over to the laptop and took the cable in her fingers. "Okay, plugging in now."

The Skull froze on screen and prepared for the connection.

Click.

The laptop screen lit up to reveal a screen saver of a young boy of around eight years of age with an older woman and man smiling either side of him.

"Who's this?" Kara asked.

"My mom and dad."

The Skull's image flickered away from the phone and reappeared on the laptop screen. Kara's eyes traced the journey, now unsurprised at her new friend's ability to travel between devices.

The Skull floated over the picture of his father and scanned Kara's face from behind the screen.

"Something weird happened back at the industrial estate. Something I wasn't expecting."

"Evan, a lot of weird shit happened back there."

"Yeah, you acting all Bruce Lee, for one. Where did you learn to fight like that? Oh, let me guess. Kick-boxing classes?"

"What we did back there?" Kara said. "We were never taught *that*. But I had no choice but to smash those fuckers to pieces."

A lightning bolt appeared over the battery icon on her phone. The Skull seemed to produce a glow and provide her device with the energy replenishment it so badly needed.

She stared The Skull in the face and wondered aloud. "You mentioned something weird went down at the warehouse. What happened?"

"I think it's better that I show you."

"Okay."

"The corporation hired me the same day they killed me. I don't think it's an accident. I think they needed new blood there as insurance."

"How did you die?"

"They shot me dead. They killed Bobby, the guy who was working with me when we chased after them."

"Jesus."

"Yup. Widowed his wife, and his kid is without a father, now."

Kara squinted and shook her head in disbelief. "But—how? How did you get into the system?"

The Skull inched up to the screen. "That's what I was saying about something strange. It happened to that girl in the warehouse. She touched the screen. I got in, and then I got out."

"What are you talking about?"

"I want to try something," he said. "Touch my face. Gently."

Kara pressed her fingers together and frowned. "I don't want to."

"It's okay," he said. "I won't do anything weird. Do it for me."

Her right arm shook upon hearing the command. There was simply no way she wouldn't test the water with the ghost on screen.

"Okay."

Her index finger peeled away from her palm and traveled the ten inches from her chest to the laptop screen.

An inch away, an intense heat blew between her fingertip and the laptop screen, creating a warbled heat that forced the glass to ripple to the sides.

"Ahhhh," The Skull groaned. "I can feel it. *I can feel it.*"

"Feel what?"

"You."

Spitch-spatch.

Electric sparks burst in all directions as she kept pushing. Before she realized it, her fingertip had slid inside the screen and formed a part of The Skull's pixelated make-up.

The tiny blocks rumbled together and raced up her arm, forming a bizarre amalgam of computerized sprite and human being.

"Let… me… show… you…"

The light bulb in the ceiling lamp blew out.

Darkness fell around them…

***

Kara, can you hear me?

"Yes," she said. "Where am I?"

Do you feel any discomfort?

"No."

Good. Now, watch.

Several lights snapped on from all directions, firing an intense bright, white light into her retinas.

"Agh."

When she opened her eyes, she saw a young, fair-haired boy sitting in front of an old television set. The square screen displayed a black-and-white cartoon.

"Ladies and gentlemen, Channel Widowmaker is proud to present our latest animation series that's fun for the whole family. Star Jelly, and her amazing orchestra!"

The boy sat on his knees and marveled at the five-pronged star fish strutting its stuff along a theater stage.

"Hello boys and girls, my name is Star Jelly!"

Suddenly, the five pointed limbs went limp, and the character fell to the stage to howls of cartoonish laughter.

"Oh dear, Star Jelly. You have no bones, so you can't walk."

The young boy held his hands to his cheeks and laughed along with the program.

Kara found herself standing in the corner of the room watching the merriment, but it was soon cut short by the presence of an angry man waiting by the door.

"Evan?"

The boy looked over his shoulder to see who had called for him. He knew the voice, but the nasty-looking man reduced the child to that of a frightened lamb.

"Dad?"

"What have I told you about watching TV before you finish your fuckin' homework?"

The boy climbed up from his knees and began to cry. "I'm sorry."

"I'll show you sorry, you little shit."

His father kicked the coffee table out of his path, wound the belt taut, and went to whip him.

As the whip of leather cracked forward, the image ground to a halt and the weapon paused in mid-flight.

Evan's voice seemed to bleed from his father's skin as he explained what was playing

This went on for years. He hated me.

Kara moved through the 3D image and stepped in front of the still image of the crying boy. "Evan?"

Yeah, that's me.

Ziippp.

The still illusion flickered and rumbled, before snapping to an entirely different location. Kara yelped and jumped back, looking around for an answer to what was happening. "Evan? I don't like this."

You don't like it? Try carrying around these memories with you wherever you go…

A black line etched itself past Kara's thigh, and drew out to form a fully-formed single bed. "Wow."

The line created a pillow, and a sleeping teen-aged Evan resting on it. Kara moved back a few steps, and was shocked to see a fully-grown man walk right through her like a screen door.

"Huh?"

She remained perfectly still as the man stood over the side of the bed wearing nothing but his underwear.

"What's your father doing now?" Kara whispered.

Watch.

The man crouched to his knees and tapped the boy on the face. "Wake up. Fuckin' wake up, you little shit."

The boy's eyelids lifted, pushing him out of his slumber. "Dad?"

His giant, stubby fingers brushed over the boy's forehead in a vague attempt to reassure him everything was okay.

"Mom's asleep."

Kara knew what might be coming next, and turned to face the desk in the corner of the room. To her astonishment, it was littered with bits of computer equipment.

A white panel desktop casing, with several drives stacked inside it.

A black joystick.

And a battered, old office chair with the stuffing protruding from the end of the arm rests.

Can you see, Kara?

She moved to the desk with caution. "Yes, I can. Why?"

It kept me in my room. And away from him. A chance to escape. A chance to become an expert in something.

A gentle, throaty sucking sound came from behind Kara's shoulder, emanating from the bed. She closed her eyes and bit her lip, fighting off the urge to turn around and explode.

"Is that what I think it is?" she asked, quietly.

Yes, it is. Don't watch. Close your eyes.

Kara couldn't oblige the instruction fast enough and burst into tears.

It's okay, Kara. You'll see what happens when the helpless fight back...

The choking sounds stopped just as the room fell dark, leaving an echo of dread and horror tumbling away from her ears.

"I can't see," she said.

Yes. You can. It seems when I enter someone's body they can see my memories, and I can see theirs. Open your eyes.

Blink-blink.

A white corridor with fluorescent strip lights built itself around Kara when she opened her eyes.

Sniff-sniff.

"What's that smell?"

Probably disinfectant. This was the time I rectified the situation. At the Kaleidoscope shopping mall.

Kara turned around and looked up the far end of the corridor. Hundreds of shoppers whizzed past each other at speed a few feet behind a child's elephant ride.

Evan's father walked right through her. Stunned, Kara followed him past her body and watched as he made his way to the male restroom.

Go on, follow him.

She made her way past the vending machine and cautiously pushed the door open…

… and stepped inside the bathroom. Wash basins lined the wall to her right and provided her with a reflection of nobody.

Her reflection didn't appear in the mirror.

"Am I a vampire, or something?"

No. You're not really here. These are all just my memories. Watch.

An elderly black man mopped a patch of yellow liquid on the floor. He paused for a moment to watch Evan's father stand before a urinal and unzip his pants.

"Afternoon," the janitor said.

"Yeah, whatever," came the terse response over the sound of urine splashing against the porcelain. "Fuckin' coon. Stop perving over me and get cleaning."

"Well, now, there's no need for that language."

Kara wondered if either of the two men would see her, but it was as if she wasn't there.

Look at the door, Kara.

She moved her head to the door and saw it creak open. A tall lad with fair hair shuffled in, slowly, and held his index finger to his lips.

"Shhh," he said to the janitor.

"Is that you?" Kara whispered.

The fair-haired teenager clenched his fist and revealed his black, fingerless gloves. "Yeah, it's me."

"What are you going to do?"

Evan, now speaking through the mouth of the young man who'd walked in, nodded at his unaware father at the urinal.

"Watch."

"What—?"

Evan raced up behind the man, grabbed his shoulders, and slammed his forehead against the tiles on the wall. The stream of urine splashed up the walls and bits of broken tiles burst from the wall.

Slam-slam-slam.

The janitor's eyes opened in shock as Evan rammed his father's face into the wall, over and over again.

"How'd you like me now, you fucking bastard?"

He yanked on his father's shoulders and held him up on his feet. "I've been following you, Dad. Nobody's gonna save you, now."

"Hey—" the janitor interrupted.

"You shut the fuck up, and stay back. This don't concern you."

Evan pushed his father into the third wash basin.

"If you're in *my* convenience then it concerns me. Take this outside—"

Smash.

His father's top lip hit the edge of the basin, and cracked his nose open. "Gwurgh."

"Get the fuck up, rapist."

Glitch

Evan barged the janitor out of his way and went for his father, just as a punch hurtled towards him.

Clomp.

His father punched him in the face, sending him spinning around on his feet, enough time for him to grab his neck and shove the boy's head into the mirror.

Smash.

A shower of blood ran down Evan's face, the busted part of his skull bleeding profusely.

"You think you can just sneak up on me unannounced?" his father groaned in pain.

"Just like you did every night," came the response. "Like father, like son, eh?"

"You little prick."

His father grabbed Evan's hand in his own, and bent his pinkie finger back with all his might.

"Nngggggg."

Snap.

Evan's pinkie bone broke in half and hung over the top of his hand. "Aggghhh."

Quick-thinking, Evan snatched the mop from the janitor's hand, and whacked his father in the stomach. The force of the attack pushed the man back-first over the basin, facing the ceiling, and squealing in pain.

Evan lifted the mop above his head and went to stab down into his father's face.

"I fucking hate you. Die, motherfucker, die."

He slammed the top end of the mop into his father's screaming mouth and skewered him to the plughole via the back of his neck.

"Gnershh," his father's mouth spat a blob of blood as his body rattled around, pinned to the washbasin.

Kara watched on, soaking up the blood violence and, for the first time, it didn't affect her.

"You killed him."

Evan wiped his hands and glanced at the janitor. He had his phone in his hands, and had just called someone. "Yeah. I killed him. He killed a piece of me."

Just then, the restroom doors blew open and several security guards ran into the room. "Hey, you."

Evan grinned and threw a cheeky wink at Kara. "It was worth every second of the time the judge handed me."

The burly security guards bundled onto the laughing Evan as he gave himself up.

In the commotion, the bulbs blew out, one-by-one.

Flick-flick-burst.

They gave me seven years. Willy Gee, the black janitor guy you saw, said I acted in self defense. Got my charge brought down from murder to manslaughter.

Kara paced along the darkness in a spotlight. She reached up to her head with her hands and felt under her ears.

"Evan?"

Yeah?

"My head hurts. It feels like I have a migraine coming on."

It's not a migraine. It's electric interference. Just relax and keep your eyes closed.

She squeezed her eyes shut with such force that a light illuminated under her flowing, red hair. Several electronic pulses ran up and down her arm as her muscles defined themselves under the skin.

Open your eyes.

A second later, she lifted her head and opened her eyelids to find herself standing in the middle of a small library.

This is Waddling Gate Correctional Facility.

"Prison?"

Sort of. Look, there's me in the corner.

Sparks and flashing lights emitted from the corner of the room in front of a man in a yellow prisoner suit.

Spitch-spritch-tch.

The sparks flew higher and higher the closer Kara walked toward it. When she peered around the man, she saw him fuse a mechanical gadget into the end of his pinkie.

They put a plate in my head to replace the section of skull that was damaged. I just took it a step further.

Kara leaned in to watch Evan's hand as he welded the tiny connectors into the veins and bone sticking out from the wound.

A graphic of a freaky-looking skull bounced around on the monitor.

You won't believe how it happened. Just know that I am a genius, and able pull shit like this off.

Evan raised his arm and bent out his newly-acquired computerized pinkie. Kara's eyeballs followed the tip, as he planted it right between her eyes.

"Agh!"

Kara opened her eyes, and found that she was sitting on Evan's couch in his apartment.

The Skull had been waiting for her to return to the room, but she felt something very weird happening to her body when she glanced at her lap.

Her legs resembled televisual static, and she was able to see right through them to the couch.

"You're inside me," she whispered.

It's like I said, earlier. Something happened. When someone touched me, I could escape into them.

"The synapses in the brain?"

Tiny, electric signals the brain uses to operate the body.

Kara wiggled her foot, quite to her surprise.

See?

"You're controlling me."

You touched The Skull. But I feel like I'm losing control. Like I don't have much time left before whatever I took over from dies.

Kara leaned forward and grabbed a magazine next to the laptop on the coffee table. "Evan, p-please, this doesn't feel right."

Look.

She raised the magazine in front of her face. The title, *Big Six*, plastered across the top, featuring a handsome and suited billionaire on the front cover adjusting his cufflinks — *Xavier Manning, and the Rise of Synethetica. A new, improved Simple Machine. The Future is history in the making.*

"Why are you showing me this?"

He's the bastard responsible. My employer. They robbed their own headquarters, and needed someone to act as an alibi, or someone to blame.

A trickle of blood rolled out of Kara's nose and splashed through her legs and onto the couch.

"Oh."

It's started already. Everyone's in on it, including the police.

Kara dropped the magazine onto the seat beside her thigh. "My nose is bleeding."

I can't stay inside your body for too long. If I do, you'll bleed out and die in a matter of minutes.

"Why?"

Because the human body can't cope with me the way I am.

"Then get out of m-me," she pleaded, quietly.

Help me Kara. Together we can beat them.

The rush of blood turned to a jet. The static around her face fizzled faster as her entire body began to disappear. "I'll help you."

Touch the screen.

"Okay."

She leaned forward, closed her fist and pressed her knuckles to the laptop screen.

Evan's voice snaked through the speakers in pain. "Agggghhhhh."

Whump.

The force of the energy transference forced her back into the seat, unconscious.

Chapter 11

"Hold still, ma'am. We're gonna get you out of here."

A thunderous sound of sirens whipped around Kara's head and into her ears. The stench of burning rubber and devastated metal wafted up her nostrils and forced her eyelids to lift.

"Wha—?"

The blurry man leaned forward, surrounded by a bright yellow glow. "She's alive. I need a stretcher."

"Where—where am I?"

Her field of vision focused into view, providing her with a pin-sharp assessment of the situation she found herself in.

A derelict road.

A smashed windshield.

The dashboard had broken in two and narrowly avoided her stomach.

The man reached forward. "Take my hand if you can. But make no sudden movements."

She grabbed the stranger's hand before turning to her left and casting an eye on the passenger seat.

Her husband lay unconscious, pinned to his seat by a lamppost that had shattered through and pinned his waist and thighs to the seat.

Kara let out an ear-piercing shriek. "Ian!"

"Ma'am, please," the man in the hi-viz jacket said. "It's okay. We're going to get him out of there, too. But we need to get you out."

Ian's eyelids fluttered. At least he was alive and in little pain.

Kara batted the man's hand away from her arm and stepped out of the car. She didn't know how the crash had happened, but it might have been so much worse.

Rex waited at the curb in tears, clutching his stuffed elephant toy.

"Hey, sweetie."

A paramedic approached her before she reached her son. "Ma'am, we're going to need you to come with us. We need to take a look at you."

"Mommy!"

"My son," Kara asked in a daze. "Is he okay?"

"He's fine—"

Whirrr.

The deadening sound from the jaws of life machine fired up, as several firemen began cutting into her car's hood and surrounding bodywork.

"What—what happened?" Kara asked.

"That's what we're trying to find out," the paramedic said. "We think there was a glitch in your auto-dash which ran you off the road. We need to attend to your husband, and yourself, and make sure you're okay, first."

Kara raced over to the curb and hugged her son as tight as she could. "It's okay, honey. Mommy's okay."

"I thought you were dead," Rex said. "The car lost control."

She pressed her thumbs above his eyes and assessed his face. Apart from the sporadic cuts and bruises, he appeared to be shaken, but mostly unharmed.

"I'm so sorry, honey."

A few seconds passed, which was more than enough time for the guilt to tug away at her throat.

"Are you okay?"

Rex stared into his mother's eyes. Both his powder blue pupils morphed into fiery-red pins. "Mommy?"

"Yes?"

Evan's voice wove into Rex's intonation as he spoke. "Is… daddy… gonna… be… okay?"

"Huh?"

Rex's jawline lit up against the flashing blue sirens coming from the emergency vehicles. On closer inspection, Kara noticed that the pulsing flashes occurred *under* her son's skin.

"Rex?"

"Kara?" he snapped. "It's time to go."

"What? What do you mean it's time?"

From out of the blue, Rex's head enlarged like a barrage balloon. The skin on his face melted away to reveal a giant skull that rose above her.

She looked up and held her breath, and was about to scream when—

"Wake up."

Kara's eyelids opened, forcing her awake. "Agh!"

She looked around and acclimatized herself to her surroundings.

A semi-familiar place greeted her.

Black curtains with white chalk scrawled all over them. The coffee table she vaguely recalled hours before.

A laptop with a blacked-out screen sitting on top of it, inches from her knees.

"Wakey, wakey, Milton," Evan said from within the laptop. "Take my green bag. We got a corporation to take down."

***

Back on the freeway, Kara now sported one of Evan's old sweaters with *Public Enemy* written on the front of it. The hood hung down the back of her neck and collected the ends of her flame-red hair.

The sun began to rise in the rear view mirror, and cast dozens of long shadows across the road. To her, they resembled long, black daggers of death that threatened to burst the tires on her car.

Kara turned to the cup holder by her left knee. Her cell phone was plugged into the USB socket underneath the car stereo.

Evan's voice drifted out of the speakers. He gave her a command that was so quiet under the rumbling of the road that she couldn't hear it.

"What? Oh."

She reached out and turned the dial on the volume up a few notches.

"Can you hear me, now?"

"Yes, I hear you," she said. "How long was I out?"

"A few hours. You slept like a baby."

Kara gripped the steering wheel and pulled at her new sweater. "Where did I get this?"

"I took the liberty of changing you out of your clothes," Evan said. "They were all bloody and stank the place out."

She took in the view of the Freeway Five to her left. "I don't remember a thing."

"You don't remember me inside you? Walking to the wardrobe, and trying my clothes on?"

"No," she quivered. "And I don't appreciate you using my body without my permission."

"Oh, quit your whining. You've spent months cheating on your husband and letting strangers inside you, so how's this any different?"

Kara didn't know where to look to make her point. "Hey!"

"What?"

"How *dare* you judge me," she said. "How dare you. What, you think you're better than I am? Yeah, right. You're Mr. Goody-two-shoes who does no wrong. I accept I'm not perfect, but at least I have the guts to admit it."

"Are you sure about that, Milton?"

"And *stop* with the surnames," she snapped into the side mirror. "I dunno where you're fucking hiding, but I won't stand for your shit. *I'm* the one in the wrong, am I? Fuck you."

"Huh?"

"How *fucking* dare you."

Kara stepped on the gas and grunted. "Got me doing your dirty work, blackmailing me, and putting me through this fucking nightmare? I had nothing to do with this. Nothing."

"You were the first person I found—"

"—I've seen and done shit I should never have had to see, ever," she snapped as she roared the engine with her foot. "You son of a bitch."

"Well, shit, *Kara*. Knowing what you know now, would you go back and change it? Keep your head in the sand? Continue to be the product of abuse? Go ahead, tell me. And be prepared for your husband to receive bad news."

Kara spun the steering wheel and made for the next exit, which surprised Evan.

"What are you doing now?"

"Don't talk to me about bad news, you fucking asshole. Goddamn it, you wanna tell me about bad news? Fuck you. You don't know *me*. You know details, and you may have got into my head. But you don't know *me*."

The industrial estate hung in the far distance as Kara drifted towards the upcoming exit.

"Where are you taking us now?" Evan asked.

"Home. *My* home."

"What? Why?"

"I can't do this anymore, Evan," Kara said. "Not without taking care of business first. I can't have you hold your power over me like this."

"Goddamn it, get back on the road and ahead for Manning HQ like we agreed."

She gripped the green bag from the passenger seat and punched the ends open. A stick of C4 nestled inside next to a digital timer.

"How about I set the timer, jump out of the car, and let you roast into the night sky, asshole?"

"You wouldn't. You know how important what we're about to do really is."

She slapped the bag against the backrest and frowned. "You're right, I wouldn't. But I *would* do this."

The car turned right at the end of the slip road, and headed for the east side of the valley.

***

Kara parked outside her house, having said nothing to Evan on the journey from the freeway.

She grabbed her phone from the dashboard and took a final look at The Skull on the screen.

"Don't do anything stupid," Evan said.

"I won't be long."

"You can take me with you. As back up?"

She pressed the power button with her thumb and watched the skeletal avatar fade away. "No. I need to do this on my own."

"Kara, no—"

The screen went blank, and she opened the driver's door.

The walk to her house felt like an age.

The sun hung just above the roof and blinded her view of the front door as she traipsed up the garden path. A benevolent force kept her from moving quicker than she ordinarily would have, before she reached the front door and opened it…

Nobody was awake inside her house.

As she stood in the kitchen, she surveyed the phone on the wall, and the microwave in the corner underneath the wall shelves.

It was only a matter of a few hours ago when the room damn near killed her. Now, it lay dormant, and ready for whatever action she chose to take.

She walked over to the half-filled kettle and switched the stove on.

Click.

Next, she pulled out two small chairs from under the table. The water in the kettle started to rumble, forcing the device to shake at the end of the electric cable.

"No," she whispered. "Not anymore."

The stairs to the first floor landing felt softer than usual. Kara gripped the handrail as she took each step, one after the other, at half the speed she was used to.

The diagonal metal railings etched into the wall shot up to the final step, which contained a folding, plastic seat.

Kara reached the top, and folded the seat compartment down. A shudder ran up her spine, as she neared the inevitable.

When she leaned to the left, she saw Rex's bedroom door ajar. She breathed a sigh of relief when she saw him in his pajamas, sound asleep.

The master bedroom sat at the adjacent end of the landing.

"Here goes nothing."

Kara took a deep breath and crept along the carpet with the deftness of a feline about to pounce on its prey.

The closer she got to the door, the louder the voices from behind it grew.

"Huh?"

She pushed the door open, slowly, and saw a glimmer of light bounce around the wall, above the headrest of the double bed.

"Hey, where have you been?"

Relieved that her husband was in bed, she made up a vague excuse for her absence. "I just went out for a while. Couldn't sleep."

Ian lay in bed with the remote control in his hands, watching a news report, not that Kara had noticed what was on screen.

Ian muted the volume and smiled at her. "Did you go to your mother's?"

Kara shook her head, no, and then glanced at the wheelchair by his side of the bed. A stark reminder of the vivid dream she'd had a couple of hours ago and, ultimately, the reason she was in the bedroom.

"It's fucked up what's happening in the valley, these days," Ian said.

"What?"

He pointed to the TV with his remote. "Morning news. Not exactly pleasant stuff to wake up to in the morning."

Confused, Kara turned her head to the TV.

Dana Doubleday spoke into her microphone from the side of main street. The message at the bottom of the screen made her want to puke.

Breaking News:
Dozens of missing children found outside Kaleidoscope Shopping Mall.

A large service vehicle loomed in the distance behind her, surrounded by youngsters covered in silver foil heat sheets.

"Turn the volume up," Kara said.

Surprised at his wife's insistence, he did as instructed. "Okay, okay—"

"—As you can probably see behind me," Dana said into the camera, "the police presence here is vast, as a search is underway to find out how this all happened. One victim, aged ten, said they were abducted from the street yesterday afternoon and taken to an as-yet unknown location."

Kara watched the news report in a state of catatonia.

"Stay tuned for all the latest developments here at the Kaleidoscope. For SNN Sense Nation News, I'm Dana Doubleday—"

"—Ugh, I don't wanna see that shit," Kara snapped. "Turn it off."

Ian hit the power button and dropped the remote control onto Kara's pillow. "What's with you, lately?"

"Huh?"

She turned back to her husband and immediately raced for his wheelchair. "I've fixed some coffee. I need to tell you about something."

"Is Rex awake?"

"No, not yet," she said. "Come on, I'll help you down."

***

Ian hadn't touched his coffee.

He couldn't even look at his wife, who leaned against the wall with a forlorn look of disgust in her face. If she'd been any further into her state of repulsion, she'd let her coffee mug slip from her hand and hit the floor.

Devastated, Ian mustered the courage to break the silence. "How long has this been going on for?"

"I dunno, a few months, now."

"How many guys did you see?"

Kara sniffed and stared at her feet. She had no metaphorical cards to hold, and not much of a chest to hold them against. "Do I have to tell you?"

Finally, he looked up at her with tears in his eyes, forcing a response.

Kara cleared her throat hard and downplayed the number. "Two or three."

"Which is it?" he asked, not that the volume truly mattered.

"Three."

"Three," he said to himself, and let out a pathetic chuckle. "And I guess it was pretty easy to sneak around, right? What with my crippled legs, and all. I wasn't exactly gonna catch you at it, was I?"

Kara closed her eyes and swallowed what felt like a lump of volcanic ash down her throat and into the pit of her stomach.

"I'm sorry."

"*You're* sorry?" Ian said. "Yeah, right. You're sorry. We're all fucking sorry."

"It won't happen again, believe me."

Ian gripped the edge of the table and wheeled himself two inches away. "How am I meant to believe that?"

Her husband had a point. Could he ever trust her again, she wondered? If she'd have been in the same situation, she'd have been gutted just as bad.

"I don't know, Ian," Kara said. "What can I say? What can I say to make it better?"

"There's nothing you can *say* to make it better."

"No?"

Ian thumped his leg with his fist and felt nothing. "If you could build a fucking time machine, then maybe I could forgive—Oh, I don't know, Kara," he said through his trembling lips. "I just don't know, anymore."

"Honey, it meant nothing, I promise—"

"—I get it," Ian whispered. "I'm a fucking cripple who can't satisfy you."

"Ian?"

"Shut up and let me talk for a second."

Kara nodded and took her punishment like a genuine hard-boiled warrior.

"I don't mind you sleeping with other guys, I get it. It's no fun for me, either. Two years, and the whole fucking situation has been tumbling around my head like a tennis ball in a blender, just—" he stopped, and then got angry, "it just—you know, ugh, the whole fucking *thing* just never left my head. There's me, okay, sitting, literally, wondering when the subject was gonna get brought up, but it never did. I should've seen it coming. I should've known this was going to happen, but I didn't even—"

"—It's my fault."

"No," Ian yelled, angered with himself. "It's my fault. I never should've let you drive that night. I never should have allowed you—"

Ian burst into tears and sobbed into his hands. "Look at me, honey. I'm a no-good fucking cripple."

Kara snorted and let her husband grieve for their marriage. Deep inside her heart, and knowing her husband as well as she did, there seemed to be a little light at the end of their trouble tunnel.

She sat on the chair next to him and took his wrist in her hands. "Hey, hey."

"I just w-wished you'd told me, that's all," he sniffed. "Just, you know, g-given me the heads up that it's something you needed."

She held his hands in hers and stared him dead in his bleary eyes.

"I tried. Believe me, there were a few times I mustered up the courage. I was like, *"Right, now's the time, I'll go in there and just come out with it"*, and then, I dunno, I stopped myself. It was just easier to do what I did, honey, and I fucking hate myself. I hate myself for doing it, but you were gonna find out—" Kara held her mouth and halted her speech before any more came out.

Ian raised his eyebrows with suspicion. "What?"

"Nothing, nothing. I'm just a bit—"

"—No, no," he sniffed, and kept a careful eye on his wife's reaction for any sign of untruth. "Kara? You said I was going to find out? How?"

"Ugh."

She looked at her knees - anywhere but in his direction, heaven help her.

"Tell me," Ian said. "You might as well."

"The app I used. The data was compromised. Any minute, or hour, or day now, everyone would've found out about everyone involved. Everyone."

Ian considered what she'd just said. "So you wanted to get in first?"

Kara wiped a tear from her eye. "I wanted you to hear it from *me*."

"From you."

She nodded and half-chuckled like a busted schoolgirl. "Yeah. From me. *Fuck*," she croaked and then cleared her throat, braving the moral release once and for all. "It's the very fucking least you deserve after what I did. You deserve to hear anything that affects us directly from me, and no other motherfucker, I swear to God."

She thumped the tabletop hard, and felt a wave of release lift from her arm.

"Sweetie?" Ian asked.

Relieved that he'd used their sweet moniker, Kara produced a heavenly grin and squeezed his hand. "Yes, sweetie?"

"Thank you."

She could have pretended to be shocked, but the moment simply didn't call for it. Instead, she held his hand to her face and enjoyed the moment. "You're welcome."

A light shuffling sound came from the kitchen door. Both Kara and Ian turned to see what had caused it.

"Oh, hey honey," Kara smiled through her tears as Rex watched on, innocently.

"Mommy? Why are you crying?"

"Oh, honey, I'm not crying."

She stood up from the chair and crouched down before him. "Come on, give me a hug."

Rex grinned and ran into her arms. "Oh, my baby."

"Mommy, you're squeezing too tight."

"Yeah," she said with her eyes closed. "And don't you ever forget it."

As she absorbed her son's warmth, the vision of the young boy she'd saved at the industrial estate crashed through the darkness in her mind. The deep-rooted fear in his eyes forced her arms to tighten and grip Rex's body even harder.

"Mommy, you're hurting me."

She opened her eyes and released him in a split-second. "I'm sorry."

Without a thought for her actions, Kara rose to her feet and made for the door with a red mist in her eyes.

"Sweetie?" Ian called after her. "Where are you going?"

Rex chimed in, concerned. "Mommy. Don't go."

Kara reached the door and slid her hand into her pants pocket. "I have to go. There's something I need to take care of."

"Are you taking the car?" Ian asked.

Kara nodded and moved out of the kitchen. "I'll be back soon."

Ian turned to his Rex and held out his arms. "C'mere. Give me a hug."

Just then, Kara peered around the corner and caught their attention. "Oh, before I forget."

"Yeah?"

"This is gonna sound stupid, but, if you see a Skull appear on the TV, or on your phone, whatever you do, *do not touch it*. Okay?"

Confused, Ian smirked. "Uh, sure?"

"Good."

Kara slammed the front door shut and paced up the front yard, headed for her car. With her cell phone in her palm, she hit the power button and scanned the screen.

The first thing to appear in the black void was The Skull, who wasted no time in airing his displeasure.

"I don't appreciate you turning me off, Kara."

She thumbed the complaining image off the screen and scrolled through the app sheet. "Shut up for a second, will you. I just need to—"

Flick-flick-flick.

Finally, the InstaBate app slid into view. She gritted her teeth and sneered at the cupid icon, before holding it down and dragging up the screen towards the "uninstall" block.

"Good fucking riddance."

She released the icon, and it sank into the void of destruction - forever.

"Whoa, hold on," Evan's voice said. "What are you doing?"

"Erasing the past," she snapped as she opened the door to her car. "My family knows everything."

"You told them?"

"Uh-huh."

Evan sounded genuinely shocked by the revelation. "Oh. What did they say?"

"None of your fucking business, *Cole*," she spat with unreserved confidence. "And I'll tell you something else."

"What's that?"

"You better be careful what you say to me, or I'll uninstall your ass, too."

The Skull hopped around the screen and laughed. "Damn, you're hot when you're on top. No pun intended."

"Oh, you son of a bitch, you have *no* idea."

"I gotta say, you got balls turning me off like you did. But I confess, I do love it when you turn me *on*."

Kara dropped the phone next to the green bag on the passenger seat. "Fuck you."

"I bet that's not the first time a guy has told you that, huh, philanderer?"

"Fuck you."

"Or the last."

She grabbed the green bag with the C4 in it and threatened him. "You *do* remember what's in this fucking bag, don't you?"

The Skull whipped to the left and buried its bony nose cavity at the side of the screen. "Yeah."

"I could chuck you in there, set the timer, zip it up, and send you to fucksville."

"Uh, no, please don't do that."

Kara smiled, knowing she finally had the upper hand. "Then just remember who's in charge, now. Okay?"

For the first time ever, The Skull appeared contrite and apologetic. Not that a basic computer game visual of this detail was able to visualize its remorse, it somehow communicated it all the same.

"Sorry," Evan said.

Kara switched on the engine. "I don't give a rat's ass about your apology. Just shut the fuck up and punch in the coordinates to your former employer."

Chapter 12

Kara stared at the imposing and gray Manning Inc. skyscraper on the other side of the road. The windshield had seen better days, given what it had gone through during the night.

Fragments of blood and bone refused to budge when she flicked the wipers. The long plastic wands just bumped over the gore and smeared the effluence further onto the glass.

Not even the downpour of rain showering the vehicle could clean it.

"That's the main entrance," Evan said. "It's gonna be swarming with people attending the Synthetica launch."

Kara focused her eyes on the car's dashboard. The sat nav map had formed a bony jaw from the weaving streets.

"I admire you for what you did. It took guts."

Anxiety set in as Kara glanced at the green bag and grabbed the car door handle.

"Don't talk to me, Evan. Let's just get this over with."

She clutched the strap in her hand and wrenched it onto her lap.

"Heavy, huh?" Evan asked.

"Yeah."

"Don't worry about security. I'll take care of them. Just get them to touch the screen."

Kara kicked the driver's side door open and moved out of the car.

The road that separated her vehicle and the building wasn't very wide, but to Kara, it felt like an age to cross. The rain splashed down her face and dampened her hair across her brow.

"Keep your phone on."

Instead of providing affirmation, she focused her eyes at the front of the building and felt the fire rumble in her belly.

The six double doors to the Manning Inc. building grew in size as she stepped onto the sidewalk.

Determined for justice, she clutched the green bag strap over her left breast and ignored the crowd of well-dressed visitors gathering under the vast canopy that sheltered the doors from the rain.

Her cell vibrated in her free hand, which Kara kept face-down to the ground as she walked.

"Nice day for a killing."

She ignored Evan's well-meaning platitude but turned the phone up to her chest, grabbing a brief eyeful of the chattering skull.

"How the hell am I going to get past security? Look at all these people. There must be a hundred of them."

"The more the merrier, and don't worry about security. Just make sure you hand them the phone."

Kara was right - there were at least a hundred people gathered outside with the media. One of them was instantly recognizable to all - the svelte, sharp-suited Dana Doubleday, whose wet hair and soaking shoulders from the rain didn't prevent her from getting up in people's faces.

Dana and Kara exchanged glances as the latter double-timed it up the concrete steps and attempted to push past the crowd.

"Hey," Dana called out with her microphone in hand. "Do you work here?"

Kara kept walking with Dana in tow. "Uh, yeah. Excuse me, I'm busy."

Her cell vibrated in her hand. "Tell her to fuck off."

Kara stopped in her tracks and shot Dana an evil look. "Are you with SNN?"

Dana pointed to her cameraman and smiled. "Uh-huh, we're covering the launch, Stuart. We're looking for an exclusive before the show starts."

"I can give you an exclusive."

Kara threw her middle finger up at the woman.

"How's this for an exclusive? You don't know shit. Now fuck off."

Stunned, Dana watched the woman disappear through the first set of double doors, and played down the event in front of the perplexed crowd. Doing her best to keep face, she turned to her cameraman and grinned. "Stu, did you catch that?"

"Uh, yeah," he said.

"Goddamn white collar bitches."

Kara looked around the vast reception area as she strode towards the reception desk. The outside congregation had provided a sneak preview of just how busy today was at the company. It seemed the world and its cousin wanted in on the action.

The 150-foot screen hanging in the middle of the area advertised the launch of Synthetica, complete with annotated diagrams of the model in question.

Kara stopped to take in the epic effort undertaken by the company to excite its visitors.

"Jesus, I knew they were a big company, but I wasn't expecting *this*."

The image of the android model rippled in the air and transformed into a good-looking, chisel-jawed man in shades and smart suit.

His name flashed under his chest as he addressed whoever stood to watch - Xavier Manning: CEO Manning Inc.

"Welcome to Synthetica," the holographic representation said. "Where the future is history in the making."

"You know who that is, don't you?"

"Yeah," Kara whispered, taking in the enormity of the image. "It has his name just underneath."

"It's who we're here to see. And whose shit we're about to fuck up."

Kara blinked three times and shook the wonder from her head. Just then, the commotion coming from the line outside filtered into the reception area and brought her crashing back down to reality - and the task at hand.

"Kara?"

She did a double-take and lifted her cell to her chest. "Yeah?"

"We don't have time to stand around. Bypass the reception desk and go straight to the gate. Do it nice and calm, or we'll get kicked out."

***

Xavier stared through the window in his office and took a deep breath. He tried his best to ignore his reflection and instead focus on the sprawling cityscape looming before him.

"It's now or never," he muttered to himself.

The door to the room swished open and allowed Leanne into the room. "Xavier?"

He turned around with a pained expression on his face. "What is it?"

"It's time. They're waiting for you at the Arena."

Xavier rolled his cuff up his wrist and made his way to his desk. "How many are out there?"

"Several hundred. They're making their way up in the elevators, now. Mr. Gilbertson is waiting for you."

"Tell George I'll be there in five minutes."

"Okay."

Before moving off, Leanne felt a desire to get something off her chest. "Xavier?"

"What is it?"

"I just wanted to say good luck for this morning. I know how important it is for you, what with everything that's happened."

Xavier produced a smirk and pulled the desk drawer open. "Thanks, Leanne. You've been really helpful, too. I don't know if I could have done it without you."

Leanne felt her employer was acting strangely this morning, and she was right. Platitudes were rarely fired around the office, let alone back and forth between colleagues. The way he handled himself, cautious and slow, concerned her.

"Are you sure we're going to be okay?" she asked, quizzically.

"We hid the fucker's body in The Grid. Nobody will ever find him," Xavier said, sympathizing with her concern. "Once we're done, we'll get it removed, and nobody will ever know."

"It's just that I—"

"—Leanne?"

The woman stared at the man, ready to cry.

"Shut the fuck up," he said. "You helped me bury this, and I'll help you bury him. For good. Now, go and help welcome everyone to the Arena."

"Yes, sir."

Leanne quickly left the room in a state of paranoia.

Xavier watched the door slide shut behind her and breathed a sigh of relief. The watercolor painting of his father seemed to command his attention for the first time in a long time.

It was a moment of obligation.

A lifetime's worth of work his father wasn't around to appreciate any longer.

"Dad," Xavier said to the lifeless picture. "I don't believe in all this spiritual bullshit, but if you're out there, I just want you to know. I'm doing this for you."

The picture just smiled back at him as it always had, had he ever cared to notice. It was never going to acknowledge the sentiment.

Xavier frowned, somewhat angered by the fact the picture hadn't taken the message on board.

"Not that you were ever around to say *well done*, or anything. Asshole. I'm glad you're fucking dead."

***

One sneaker after another squelched across the shiny floor, bleeding rainwater out from the torn rubber sides.

A pair of darkened, damp jeans caked onto the skin of the legs inside them.

A green bag with black straps bounced back and forth above the right hip.

Kara had arrived at the security gate right next to reception, phone in hand, and smiled at the man who never returned the sentiment.

"I'm sorry, ma'am," the security guard said. "If you don't have a pass, I'm going to need you to sign in at the desk."

"Oh, no. I have a pass."

"Let me see it, please."

Kara looked up at the guard with a put-upon angelic face and held her phone at him. "Here. Take it."

Confused, the security guard took her cell in his hand and inspected the blank, dark screen.

"Ma'am?"

"Uh-huh?"

"This is a skull," he said, confused. "You're not that skinny—"

Bzzz. Schwip.

The screen fizzed to life, producing a blue-and-white contour of a shimmering skull bursting to life. Kara smirked and hoisted her rucksack over her shoulder, before catching the guard's name on his lapel badge.

"Ben?"

Stunned by the colorful picture show on her phone, he looked up at her and wondered why she was so cheery. "What?"

"Hello, Big Boy."

Ben almost dropped the phone to the floor as the fizzled skull appeared on screen and addressed him directly.

"What the fuck is this?" Ben asked.

"It's my pass."

The Skull enlarged on the screen and tilted the top of its skull in Ben's direction. "Yeah. Eat this, big boy."

The USB socket at the bottom of the phone blew dozens of orange sparks as The Skull slunk off the bottom of the screen, through the plastic, and seeped into the skin of Ben's wrist.

He stomped back with the phone in his hand and trembled as he stepped past the turnstile. "Whug-whug-whug," he spluttered, before his eyeballs rolled into the back of his head.

Kara moved after him. "Evan?"

"Whug-g-g—God—Goddamn it," Ben spluttered.

She snatched her phone out of the man's hand as his eyes snapped back into their sockets. A final, shit-eating grin from Ben signaled that Evan was now in control of his body.

"Fuck," he said in Ben's voice. "This guy is huge."

"Are you in?" she whispered.

"Yeah, but this fucker's heavy."

Kara looked over her shoulder in haste. Nobody had seen the bizarre event take place, but it'd only be a matter of moments before someone else came running to assist.

"Quick, get back. Into the hall."

"Yeah."

Evan struggled to control Ben's legs as he moved forward. He coughed into his hand and cleared his throat.

Ben patted himself down and felt for the man's ID card. "I can't stay inside this bloated sack of shit for too long. Here, I got it."

Kara held out her hand. "Quick, give it to me."

He dumped the ID card in her hand next to her cell phone, and reached into his belt. "It m-must be here, somewhere."

"What?"

"His—"

A knock of metal hit his knuckle. Ben's firearm. Relieved, he gripped the handle, removed it from the holster and inspected the chamber.

"It's full."

"You're not going to do that here, are you?" Kara asked.

The whites of Ben's eyes turned blood red. His breathing soured just as fast as he looked up the length of the hall.

"I don't know how much longer I can stay inside this fat fucker. Quick, let's get to the elevators."

Ben waddled as fast as his chunky legs could carry him with Kara suddenly in tow.

"Are you sure?"

"Yeah, I'm sure," Ben said. "But as soon as we're up, I need to get back inside your phone. Or any device. I can't die inside this guy."

Just as Ben finished his last sentence, an older gentleman threw him a shady look. "Hey, big fella. Are you feeling okay?"

"Yeah, just caught some bug," Ben said.

"Nice lady friend you have, there," the old man asked. "Is this some kind of exclusive escort service?"

Ben chuckled as he hit the button for the lift. "In a manner of speaking."

The old man smiled at Kara who, in turn, felt the desire to look anywhere other than his direction.

In turning away, she saw a torrent of expectant visitors flood the hall, all making for the four elevators.

"Oh, shit."

"What?"

Ben and Kara watched the swarm of media grow larger and larger.

"Which floor are we going to?"

"Seventh," Ben said.

"We need to get up there, and fast."

"I got a better idea."

Still dressed as a security guard, Ben barged past the old man and held out his hands. "Okay, listen up, people. I want you to form an orderly line right here, along the wall. Do it."

Kara and the old man watched in stunned silence as Evan - via Ben's body - ordered the visitors against the wall.

He moved the flap of his jacket over his hip and deliberately displayed his firearm. "That's right, get up against the fucking wall."

One by one, they obliged the seemingly angered guard, and formed a line in complete silence.

"Very good."

He turned around and ran over to the elevator just as the doors opened. "Get in."

Ben pushed Kara by her shoulder and ushered the old man inside the metal box.

Whump.

The elevator doors sliced shut, sealing Ben, Kara, and the old man inside the metal cage.

"Which floor?" the old man asked.

"Seventh."

"So, you're attending the launch event, too, huh?"
"Uh-huh."

The man looked up at Ben and winced at his bleeding eyes. "Are you okay—?"

Bllooarrgghh.

Ben opened his mouth and projectile-vomited a torrent of blood against the elevator wall. "Uggh."

The man jumped back and nearly freaked out. "Jesus Christ."

The elevator continued its ascent to the seventh floor. Kara moved forward and grabbed Ben by the arm. "Hey, we need to get you out of here."

"N-No," Ben grunted. "Seventh floor—"

He puked again, this time through his nose, mouth, and ears, like a bloodied disco ball, and dropped to his knees, barely able to breathe.

"I c-can't st-stay inside," he gasped.

Kara slung the ID card over her neck and looked him in the eyes. "Are you in there?"

"Yuh-yuh—"

"—Stay with me, Evan. We're nearly there."

The old man backed up to the doors, confused, and pointed at the label on Ben's shirt. "Evan? His name is Ben."

Ping.

When the elevator doors opened on the seventh floor, Kara yelled at the man. "Get outta here, go."

"Okay, yes. Good idea."

Kara helped Ben up off the blood-drenched floor and took his arm around her shoulder. "Come on, we can't stay here."

Ben struggled to walk, his knees buckling each alternate step, as they exited the elevator.

A huge crowd of launch attendees had gathered by the doors to the Arena, but none of them saw Kara and Ben make their escape.

"Phone, phone—"

"—Not yet, let's get you out of sight."

"B-Blue Sky," Ben croaked through a mouthful of blood. Kara felt his entire body rupture and bleed underneath his shirt.

A sign for the Blue Sky Room suggested they turn left, and take the corridor. "Over here."

The Blue Sky Room

Swipe.

"Well, his ID card came in handy, if nothing else."

Kara dragged Ben far enough into the server room for him to drop to his knees and plant his knuckles on the floor.

She unstrapped the green bag from her shoulder and crouched before him. When Ben looked up at her, his face had turned as white as his eyes had turned red.

Blood escaped from every orifice in his head and dripped down his neck and onto his chest. It looked as if he was melting right in front of her.

"Here," she said as she reached into her pocket and took out her phone. "You're safe now."

Ben squeezed droplets of blood from his eyes with his eyelids as he reached for the cell phone screen.

"Go on, get back in."

Spitch-fizz.

As the man's giant hand neared the cell phone, his entire body turned to static.

"Gaaah."

"Come on, touch the screen," Kara said. "We don't have much time."

His chunky index finger and thumb slammed against the tempered glass. After he'd made contact, his body broke into tens of thousands of pixels and zipped into the screen.

Schwip.

"God, that feels good," the cell phone exclaimed.

Big Ben's body returned to normal and slammed against the floor. Kara glanced at her cell phone screen to see The Skull had returned. "Is he breathing?"

Stunned, she averted her eyes to the unconscious man on the floor. "I'll find out."

A quick check for a pulse on his neck revealed a heartbeat - slow and intermittent, but at least present.

"He's alive."

"Leave the bag by The Grid. It's the machine at the end of the room."

"What about him?"

The Skull twisted around and pressed its cave of a nose to the screen, eying the man on the floor. "He's innocent. We're not in the business of killing innocents."

"I didn't ask if he was fucking innocent or not," she snapped. "I asked what we should do with him."

"Drag him behind one of the servers. The show is starting in five minutes, so be quick about it."

Chapter 13

Xavier peered through the black curtains. Anxiety set in when he saw the stage and the audience taking their seats.

The Arena housed the make-or-break aspect of Synthetica, but it wasn't the prospect of successful launch that perturbed him.

George stood beside him, speaking into his wrist. "Okay, two minutes till magic time."

It seemed the entire world was in attendance this morning. The media were in, as well as the shareholders and wealthy investors. It was exactly how Xavier and his team had planned it, but now, the very same man wished they would all leave.

"What if he comes back?" Xavier whispered.

"Who?"

"The fucker who nearly brought you down last night."

George slapped Xavier's back a little too hard. "Don't worry about that prick. We're ready for him. He wouldn't dare show his face around here."

A pang of terror hung in the air despite the light show taking place on stage. Xavier scanned the left-side of the stage through the curtain and examined the Synthia prototype as best he could from the angle he had. The glistening, white face reflected the light from the stage lamp and bounced off the entire first row.

He scanned the first row, where Dana Doubleday had managed to steal a prime position in the audience.

"Xavier?" George asked. "Did you hear what I said?"

"Huh?"

"Ninety seconds till show time."

Xavier finally turned around and tried for a smile - but it was no use. It couldn't quite conceal the concern on his face, and George noticed it immediately.

That small tick in the corner of his friend's mouth, and the vacant five-yard stare in his eyes said it all.

"Are you okay?"

Xavier muttered incessantly. "We were raided, we were raided. They took the data, it wasn't our fault. It was *his* fault. The new guy. He did it. He's an ex-con."

"What the fuck are you saying?" George asked.

Xavier looked up at the man with a tear in his eye, only to be met with a vicious attitude.

"Listen," George said. "Whatever it takes, okay? You wanna believe your own hype and bullshit, then do it. We were raided. An ex-con pulled the wool over our eyes to get in. The data was stolen, and everything was compromised. When it's sold, we collect on the insurance and we're golden in the eyes of the general public. It's not our fault, least of all yours."

"I know," Xavier said.

"Don't grow a fucking conscience on me, now, Xavier. Let the ex-con take the rap."

"You're right. We were conned."

"You have a product to sell, Xavier. And don't worry about Evan fucking Cole, either. We shut down The Grid, and he's toast."

Xavier knew his friend talked sense. "You're right. I need to get myself together."

George nudged the man on his arm and produced a shit-eating grin. "You're as clean as a whistle. Now, go out there and slay 'em."

The stage lights dimmed just as fast as the introductory music started.

Excited, Dana turned to Stuart and snapped her fingers. "Stu, We're on. You recording?"

"Uh-huh, ready to rock and roll."

She whipped her hair back over her shoulder and smiled for the camera. "This is Dana Doubleday, with a real exclusive. A potentially groundbreaking event is about to happen. Xavier Manning is about to walk on stage and change our lives, forever. Keep watching."

The audience quietened down, save for the tiny, whirring motors in the seemingly hundreds of stationed cameras filming the event.

"Ladies and gentlemen, welcome to Manning Inc.," a friendly female voice said. "Please welcome to the stage Mister Xavier Manning, CEO, Manning Incorporated."

Xavier bounded on stage with the confidence of an overeager tiger, focused and determined. He held his right hand at the cheering crowd and waved his smartphone at them.

"Welcome, everyone," he said into his lapel microphone and approached the five-foot tall podium at the right of the stage.

The applause allowed him to glance at the holographic image of his new creation hanging in the air behind him.

He exchanged a cheeky wink with George, who waited behind the curtain and gave him the thumbs up. He set his smartphone onto the podium and waited with fierce patience for the adulation to quell.

Xavier took a deep breath, counted to three in his mind, and addressed the audience.

"My entire life's work has been the result of appeasing the one person I never truly knew. I'm sure many of you understand this. The desire to prove yourself worthy to someone close to you. In my case, I was never able to do it successfully, but I *was* able to continue his work. That man was my dad…"

The image of Synthia disappeared from the holographic screen, to be replaced by a portrait of his father.

"Xander Manning. He formed our company thirty years ago in the pursuit of artificial intelligence. He came close with MAVIS, the now-discontinued prototype. Little did he know that I would be taking over the reigns from George Gilbertson, who stepped in where no other man would dare. From there, we have worked hard to further my father's success story."

The enraptured audience watched on silently, wondering if the man speaking to them would suddenly burst into tears.

Dana writhed in her seat, giddy with excitement at the thought. If Xavier would break down, she'd be the first to jump on stage and grill him for an exclusive.

A red-haired woman in a Public Enemy sweatshirt folded her arms and watched the speech from the back of the Arena, hoping she wouldn't stand out from the crowd.

"Come on," Kara muttered. "Get this over with, asshole."

Now without her bag, her shoulders felt freer than they'd ever been. Kara was the *one* woman in the room who knew what was about to happen, and ensured that her route out of the auditorium was less than ten seconds away.

Xavier seemed to stare right at her through the crowd of vague faces, but it was purely accidental. It gave Kara the chills, forcing her to slide behind an attendee and into the darkness.

"Let's finish this, Evan," she whispered to herself. "Don't drag this out any longer than it has to be."

Xavier ran his knuckle under his right eye and collected a teardrop from his cheek. Presenting his new creation proved effective in removing himself from his emotional turmoil.

"And so, to my friend, here."

He held his hand out at the svelte android.

"When we developed the *InstaBate* app, we provided a literal connection for users. Incels became a thing of the past. Of course, we at Manning believe that the real ingenuity is not predicting the car. It's predicting the traffic jam."

He hit a button on his smartphone and gesticulated with his right hand. The blue light just above android's right eye flashed, causing her to spring to life.

"Ladies and gentlemen, may I present to you, the new person in all your lives. The figurehead of the Synthetica program."

The audience gasped when the model moved.

"*Synthia.*"

Everyone knew Synthia wasn't a real human being, but she didn't look anything less than lifelike. For all intents and purposes she was utterly naked, her exposed plastic thighs gave away as much. But the subtle movement of her hand touching her face for the first time was remarkable.

The slightest movement of her head as she closed her eyes and turned to Xavier was marvelous.

"Xavier?" she asked.

"Hello, Synthia."

"How did I get here?"

Xavier grinned at her authentic British accent. "She sounds this way because it makes her come across as intelligent."

The audience giggled at his witty remark.

He hit a button on his smartphone. "Sleep for a moment, Synthia."

When his thumb moved from the screen, Synthia closed her eyes and lowered her head.

Sleep mode.

Xavier returned to the audience and stepped toward the now-lifeless model. "Ladies and gentlemen, we have considered the traffic jam. Just as our app paved the way for connections nationwide, so too can we offer a solution. Look at her."

He tapped his phone once again, and this time, ignored the vibration rumbling through his palm.

Synthia opened her eyes and lifted her head to Xavier once again.

"Synthia?" he asked. "Tell everyone here your purpose in life, please."

"I am here to serve you. I do not discriminate, judge, or refuse. I will do whatever you ask of me."

A wave of terror thundered down Xavier's spine as he looked into her glowing beads for eyes.

"Umm."

"Is something troubling you, Xavier?" Synthia asked.

He closed his eyes and took two steps back, fighting off the sudden fatigue punching at his head. "Uh, Synthia is the ultimate synthetic c-companion—"

The audience shifted in their seat with concern as Xavier lost his balance.

"Is he having a fit?" Dana asked from the front row. "What the hell is going on?"

Schpitt-fizz.

The smartphone in Xavier's hand vibrated violently and produced a wave of blues and white seeping from his fingers which bounced off his face.

"Ngggg—N—Noo—" he squealed as he tightened his grip on the phone.

Synthia took a giant stride forward and tilted her head at the suffering man crouched before her. "Mr. Manning. Are you quite well?"

"Whug-whug—" Xavier squealed as a distant cackle of evil flung out between the webbings on his fingers. "Yuh-yuh, I-I'm f-fine—"

"—Can I assist you?" Synthia said, offering a sympathetic hand. "I detect you are feeling unwell."

Kara grinned and folded her arms. "Evan Cole. You sneaky little shit. Go get 'im."

Xavier's breathing slowed as he lifted his thumb away from the screen.

When he opened his eyelids, most of the first three rows saw how bloodshot his eyes were.

"I'm feeling fuckin' great," he said, suddenly acting very strangely. "Get out of my way."

Xavier staggered across the stage, flung himself to the podium and caught the edge of the balance. The result had him leaning over the microphone and grinning with venom at the audience.

"Hey, guys."

Those in the first few rows shifted in their seats, wondering just what in the hell was going on with the man on stage.

Xavier grunted as he fumbled in his pocket for something. "I, uh—I got s-something f-for you bunch of pricks."

Synthia took a step closer to the podium, only to be met with the full force of Xavier's displeasure.

"Get the fuck back, you synthetic cocksucker," he snapped.

Confused at the instruction, Synthia turned to the audience, and back to the man behind the podium. "Would you like me to perform fellatio on you?"

Xavier produced a long, howling grunt and shook his head. "No. I w-want you to—"

His arm shook around as he reached into his belt and produced a Glock 17. The crowd gasped and froze in their seats as he waved it in the air and made sure everyone was listening.

Xavier screamed into his microphone so hard that it produced a feedback loop into the speakers which daggered in everyone's ears like a rush of tinnitus.

"Shut the fuck up and stay seated, assholes."

Xavier ran his sleeve across his brow and wiped a stream of blood from his left nostril with his sleeve. "Guuuh—"

"—Whoa," the audience gasped as they watched the man's internal struggle.

Evan's drawl crashed through Xavier's vocal cords as he spoke. "Wh-what the f-fuck—?" his real voice subsided through the internal battle in his chest. "M-My name is X-Xavier M-Motherfucking M-Manning, and I am a m-murdering f-fu-cking bastard."

His voice sounded the same when he spoke, but with an altogether deathly waft of possession. Xavier whipped the gun at the audience and threatened them.

"Kara," Xavier's mouth roared in Evan's voice. "Now. *Do it.*"

Scared, the flame-haired woman disappeared from the auditorium.

Kara burst through the doors and raced towards the elevators. She lifted her phone and glanced at the screen.

A timer in green text read 10:00 - with an accompanying *start* icon underneath it.

"I hope you know what you're doing, Evan," she said as she hit the button and started the countdown.

In the server room, an empty green bag lay on the floor next to the array of machines. The corresponding countdown nestled on a stick of C4 explosives at the central console.

Kara hit the button for the elevator and watched as the lights hopped, skipped, and jumped up the panel at an infuriatingly slow pace.

"Come on, come on."

On stage, Xavier swung the Glock 17 at the holographic screen behind him. The crowd were so shocked they could hardly move.

"I, uh, h-have a confession to m-m-make—"he struggled as he slapped the podium with his right hand. "Y-Yesterday, our offices were raided. W-We d-did it. I w-wanna show you something."

Blink-blink.

A fuzzy, close-up image of a vein-riddled, hairy adult hand focused into view. Most in the audience squinted as the video played out.

"Wuh—ugh," Xavier groaned in pain as Evan took over his body. "You e-ever heard of the UnderNet? Shit. This i-is what it l-looks like—"

Xavier fell to his knees and clutched at his chest, trying to fight off the war occurring inside his body. "Gaoow."

Nobody in the audience was looking at the man suffering on stage. Instead, they watched the video play above his head.

The fist clenched on something, exacerbating the sound of a child's tormented cries for help.

Dana Doubleday was among the first to realize what everyone was witnessing. A knowing smile crept across her face as she turned to Stuart. "Jesus Christ, look at that."

Xavier's own voice crept through his vocal cords as he tried to close his mouth. "Wh-what are you—"

"—Shut the fuck up," he growled back to himself. "And watch everything fucking *burn* in front of your eyes."

"Gah!"

George began to sweat as he watched the proceedings from the edge of the stage. "Goddamn it."

He bolted out from behind the curtain.

"Xavier, what the fuck is wrong with you?"

Xavier pointed the gun at George's face and spoke through his bloodied gums. "Get back, you *f-fuck*."

George backed off with a pathetic smile on his face, hoping that the audience would think it was all a stunt.

Xavier stood to his feet and pointed the gun at his temple. "Wh-what are you doing?" he gasped as his index finger hooked around the trigger.

"Finishing what you started," his lips roared back to a confused audience.

Synthia didn't know what to do or where to turn. Along with the audience, she looked up at the screen and absorbed the deadening cries of the child playing on the video screen.

"This is outrageous," came a tormented cry from the audience. "This is sick."

"Shut the fuck up," Xavier growled at the audience and buried the barrel of his gun further into his temple.

Stuart filmed the event occurring on stage from his first row seat. "Dana, I'm getting it. I'm getting it all."

Several audience members realized the crime being perpetrated on screen and burst into tears.

Some suddenly felt violently sick.

"Nobody fuckin' move," Xavier said with the gun to his head. "You are all here to w-witness what I've fucking done. Me, Xavier Manning. CEO of the darkest, sickest, most unimaginable horrors you could ever want to see."

Xavier's chest beat so hard as he spoke, all the while threatening to pull the trigger on himself.

"Yesterday, every InstaBate user's profile was hacked. How d-do you know that? Because I did it."

Gasps flew from the audience as the confession hit their ears.

"We did it all," Xavier struggled. "Those children gone missing were us. We're selling every user's data to the highest f-fucking b-bidder, and we're blaming... *Evan Cole*. He's our p-patsy."

Dana stood up from her seat and held her hand over her brow, trying her best to focus on Xavier and cut off the image of horror on the screen behind him. "Mr. Manning?"

He turned to her and spat a rope of blood down his chin. Evan didn't have long inside Xavier's body before they *both* died on stage.

"What are you saying, exactly?" Dana asked, knowing full well she was on camera. "Is this a confession? That you're responsible for all this?"

"Yeah," Xavier said. "I'm r-responsible. For everything. Thousands of victims, alive and dead, and the death of Evan Cole."

"Evan Cole?" Dana asked, giddy with excitement at the world exclusive she was getting.

Xavier nodded, slowly, as he began to bleed from the eyes. "That's *me*. I w-was their lead programmer, and alibi."

For just the briefest of moments, Dana saw something buried behind the man's eyes. The sense of a tormented ghoul trapped behind the eyes of the man who murdered him.

"And n-now, I'm g-gonna p-pay the price for my actions, watch."

Dana raced forward and tried to stop Xavier pulling on the trigger. "Xavier, no—"

Bam.

Xavier managed to wrestle his hand away from Evan's control. The bullet rocketed through the air and smashed into the podium.

"Aggghhh."

Xavier screamed as he tumbled forward and flung himself against Synthia, who caught him in her arms.

"Xavier?" she asked.

"Ngggg," he squirmed as his chest heaved against hers.

Schwipp.

Orange sparks fountain from Xavier's hand as a ghostly skull flew from his wrists and into the sockets in her palms.

The audience members raced from their chairs screaming in all directions as the commotion took place on stage.

"Somebody get this man a medic," Dana screamed, before turning to Ross. "Please tell me you're getting all this?"

"Fuck yeah I am," came the eager response.

The image in the camera focused on Xavier shrieking in his regular voice as he stumbled back to the podium. The whites of his eyes were returning, but just behind him, the synthetic android zoomed into view.

Synthia rotated both her hands one-hundred-and-eighty-degrees and adjusted her head left to right.

"Xavier?" Synthia said. "You ain't going anywhere."

Stomp-stomp-stomp.

Evan had entered the Synthia droid, and stormed toward Xavier. She held out her hand and pointed to the gun on the floor.

"Don't even think about it, asshole."

Boot.

She kicked the gun across the stage and into the wings just as Xavier pushed himself back to his feet.

"You bitch—"

"—Nah, *bastard*," Evan said from within Synthia's face. "Get your genders right."

Synthia clenched her fist and socked Xavier in the jaw so hard his body somersaulted in the air and smashed against the podium.

As far as the crowd was concerned, Synthia had now broken free from her programming and was running amok in a violent rage.

She crouched down, gripped Xavier's shirt collar in her hands, and lifted him back to his feet. "Get up, you red-collared prick."

The crowd had seen enough.

All of them raced to the auditorium doors with the fight taking place on stage behind them.

Above the curtains, the footage of the Undernet revealed several murdered children at the hands of whomever had perpetrated the crime.

"E-Evan?" Xavier squealed for his life.

Synthia's eyebulbs blinked red, then blue, inches away from her foe's. "Xavier?"

"I'm s-sorry, Evan," he squirmed, begging for his life. "I'm sorry. Please, d-don't hurt m-me."

Synthia's lifelike smirk etched across her clear plastic head. "I'm not going to hurt you."

"Y-You're not?"

Her voice now imbued with Evan's, Synthia resembled a warrior not to be reckoned with. "No."

Whirrr-ripp.

Synthia grabbed Xavier's shoulder with her left hand, and bent over to lift his legs with her right. She hoisted the screaming man above her head and went to launch him at the fleeing audience.

"I'm gonna *shut you down.*"

Whirl.

Xavier tumbled through the air and crashed shoulders-first against the chairs.

Dana could hardly believe what she had witnessed. "Evan Cole?"

Synthia punched her fists together and pushed Dana out of her path. "Move, bitch."

"Okay."

"Keep filming," Evan said. "The world's gonna wanna see who's been fucking with them."

Xavier kicked himself back across the carpet by his heels. His right arm had broken upon impact on the chairs.

"Please, Evan. D-Don't."

"Get up and fight like a man," Evan said using Synthia's mouth. "Get up."

Whup.

With a deft grace in movement, she bent over, grabbed his right shin, and yanked his body through the scattered chairs in the auditorium.

Synthia pointed at the holographic screen. "You think you can get away with this shit?"

"I'm sorry!" Xavier squealed like a little girl.

"Not good enough, asshole."

Synthia winked at Dana and nodded at the aggrieved man attached to the leg she was holding. "Get this."

Dana nodded at her cameraman. "Stu? Do as she says."

"*He.*"

"Sorry, do as *he* says."

Synthia grabbed the camera lens and spoke directly into it. "See that up on stage? This piece of shit is responsible for it. The fucker begging for his life has learned the art of regret, but it's too fucking late for that shit. Now, watch this."

"No, no—"

"—Shut the fuck up."

Synthia grabbed both Xavier's ankles in her hands and swung him around like a lasso, around and around, such was her robotic strength.

"Jesus Christ," Dana quipped with astonishment as Synthia launched Xavier at the holographic image.

Crash.

Xavier flew through the image of the abuser's legs on screen and straight through the fuzzy image of a female child's corpse before smashing against the wall.

Crack.

The sound of elbow-on-plasterboard rifled across the stage as Xavier slammed to the floor.

"Agh, agh, my l-leg—p-please, s-stop."

Evan used Synthia's hand to grab Dana's shoulder and pulled her close. "Get out of here, now."

"Wh-what?"

"Do it," Synthia said. "The place is gonna blow. Use the stairs."

"Okay."

"Take your little friend with you, too. Make sure the whole fucking world knows what happened here."

Dana smiled, realizing a beautiful connection between the two. "Oh, I will, don't worry about that."

"You *will* see me again," Evan said from within Synthia's face. "All of you will see me again."

"But wait," Dana said. "Where will you go?"

"If I make it out of here alive, you'll know."

Evan released Synthia's grip on Dana's shoulder and marched over to the stage that housed the squealing Xavier.

"When all is said and done, my image will appear everywhere. Every. Single. *Fucking. Screen.*"

Dana gasped, confused about what she'd been told. "What?"

"Go."

Dana waved Stuart over to the auditorium exit as Synthia stepped onto the stage and made her way to finish Xavier off once and for all.

Xavier's left elbow had twisted through his skin. No matter which way he turned, a wave of agony would threaten to take him out of the game for good.

"Get away f-from m-me," Xavier screamed as he staggered to his feet.

He managed to retrieve his gun when he'd hit the stage, and pointed it at the approaching droid.

"I mean it, get back," Xavier shrieked. "I'll shut you the fuck down. *Asshole.*"

The unrelenting Synthia stepped closer, determined to smash the man's face clean off his head.

Xavier spat a rope of blood to his chest and took aim at the droid's forehead. "What? You think you can just roll up in here and fuck my shit up? You think you can undo a lifetime's worth of work and get away with it? Fuck you."

Bang.

He fired off a shot. The bullet clipped Synthia's left shoulder, but caused just a fragment of surface damage to her shell as she continued forward.

"One-point-six billion dollars," Xavier screamed as he took aim at Synthia once again. "Motherfucker, get the fuck away from me."

Bang.

Another bullet, and another hit - this time on her right forearm. Though the damage was negligible, it caused a ferocious array of orange sparks to dance out of the cavity and hop across the stage.

"Xavier?" Evan asked as he moved closer.

"Get the fuck back."

"Just a glitch, huh?"

"I mean it, Evan," Xavier croaked and pointed the gun at the droid's head. "Synthia's not so advanced that I can't put a bullet in her fucking brain and take her out of the game for good."

"So, do it," Evan said. "I've been shot dead before."

Xavier lowered the gun and then raised it once again for a clearer focus on his target. "You've ruined me. The damage is done—"

"—Not yet it ain't, fuck head."

"Fuck you," Xavier yelled. "You're nothing but a cheap-ass, dead nerd nobody's about to miss, anyway."

Synthia punched her fists together, and readied herself to smash the man's face clean off his neck.

Then, she stopped and stared him in the eyes.

Confused, Xavier kept his aim on her. "C'mon, what are you waiting for?"

It was now just a matter of who would strike - or shoot - first.

***

Kara yelled at the approaching horde of attendees rushing towards the elevators. "No, don't use these. Use the stairs. Go."

She waved everyone away from the elevator concourse and pulled the door to the staircase open.

"Get in a single line and be careful."

Dana was first among the screaming crowd and pulled Kara to one side. "What the hell is going on here?"

"Listen, everyone needs to get out."

"Why?"

"Can you keep a secret?"

Dana grinned and stepped out of the path of running attendees. "I'm a major news journalist with money-grabbing television network, what do you think?"

"I think the building is about to blow."

"What?"

"You heard what I said," Kara snapped. "In a few minutes from now, this top floor isn't going to offer an especially good view of the valley."

"It's gonna blow?" Dana said a little too loudly.

A breathless young woman overheard what Dana had said and raised her eyes. "The building's gonna blow?"

Everyone heard the exclamation and freaked out.

Kara pushed Dana out of her path and raced into the stairwell. "Oh, Jesus."

"The place is gonna blow!" Leanne squealed as she ran towards the doors. "Everybody, run!"

Dana turned to Stuart and smirked. "You thinking what I'm thinking?"

His face fell when he realized she was very serious. "Oh, no. You're not thinking of sticking around, are you?"

"Oh yes."

"Are you out of your tiny little mind?"

The stream of terrified patrons thundered behind her, their bodies creating a bizarre ghosting effect on the glass window overlooking the valley.

"Why the hell not?" Dana asked. "And that's a dangerous question to ask someone like me."

"Fuck that."

"Well, shit," she quipped. "If you're gonna pussy out and join the rest of the sheep, then give me the damn camera and I'll film it myself."

"What?"

"I'm *not* passing up this exclusive."

A cacophonous sound of tumbling bodies blew up from the staircase, indicating that the mass exodus hadn't gone as swiftly as Kara had hoped.

"Stop, stop," her voice flew over the hollers and screams of those on the staircase. "Be careful. One by one, let's go."

Dana's eyes seemed to burn into Stuart's. "Well?"

"Fuck this."

He unhooked the camera strap from his shoulder and shoved the device into her chest.

"Stick around and go down with the building. I'm outta here."

Dana lifted the device and peered into the screen. "Is it recording?"

"Yeah. See ya."

Stuart darted off into the stream of people barging through the door and flipped her the bird.

"Don't let the stairs kick your lame ass on the way down, you pussy," she snapped as she filmed the backs of those darting towards the doors to the stairs.

"Okay, Evan," she whispered. "Let's get this show on the road."

Kara jumped down the last five steps in the staircase and raced through the reception area with her arms outstretched.

"Quick, get outta here," she called to the receptionists. "Get on the street."

The security guards and officials moved from out of their desks in haste, prepared to gun her down on the spot.

"Excuse me, ma'am?" one of them said. "Just what in the hell do you think you're—"

Wham.

A torrent of terrified and injured men and women burst through the emergency stairwell doors and swarmed around Kara.

"Oh, Jeez," the guard said.

Kara hopped over the turnstiles and stormed across the reception area to a very confused crowd of faces.

"Listen, the place is gonna blow. Open the gates. Let everyone out."

She needn't have bothered giving her command. Dozens of breathless attendees launched themselves over the turnstiles.

Many of them slipped as they landed and barrel-rolled ass-over-tit when they landed, causing a domino effect of falls and spills for those who jumped after them.

"Oh, shit," the guard said. "Open the fucking gates. Do it."

Beep-beep-beep.

Kara helped Leanne up off the floor and carried her to the main entrance. "Open the doors. All of 'em."

Leanne kept her arm around Kara's shoulder, limping towards the entrance doors. All six of them slid open.

"My l-leg," Leanne complained. "I think I've broken something."

"Never mind about that, now, just move," Kara said. "We're nearly out."

***

The standoff between Synthia and Xavier on the stage threatened to turn to carnage. All Xavier needed to do was fire a well-placed bullet between Synthia's eyes, and shut her down for good.

If he did, Evan would die inside the machine, and all of Manning Inc's problems would be solved.

The aftermath of talking to the media, to Xavier's mind, was just an inconvenient footnote that could easily be excused.

"Evan?" Xavier said. "You're operating a billion-dollar piece of equipment. All you have to do is drop to your knees. Let me switch you off."

"Nah, I don't think so," Evan's voice bleached through Synthia's wistful and dulcet tones.

"Where are you gonna go, anyhow?"

"I have a trillion places to visit. Seven-point-eight billion people to talk to. An entire nation to save from *you*."

Synthia braved a step forward, never for a moment covering her face. Her eyelids closed, and she produced an evil grin.

Just then, her head began to rumble, causing an internal vortex within the machinery.

"Look at me, Xavier," she said. "What do you *see*?"

Xavier moved his cheek from the Glock 17's line of sight and allowed his pupils to dilate.

A shimmy of blue, yellow, and red bled into the contours of Synthia's head: sturdy, and broken, like that of a human skeleton.

"My G-God," Xavier said. "What the fuck happened to you?"

"*You* happened, Xavier."

"Me?"

Synthia took another step forward, still determined for blood.

Xavier's attention drew to something occurring behind him. Instead of focusing on it, he smiled, and returned to Evan's new face.

"Why don't you tell me about it, Evan?" Xavier asked. "Before I put a bullet in you."

George had grabbed the microphone stand and prepared to attack Evan from behind, and Xavier let him do it.

"I have sixty teraflops of data on you. On everything," Evan explained. "You're going to be a martyr, Xavier, just like your father."

"What did you say about my dad, asshole?"

Thrilled with seeing the fear and fire in Xavier's eye, Evan delivered the final nail in both their coffins. "A no-good piece of shit. Like father, like son, huh?"

Xavier swallowed the insult and screamed at the top of his lungs. "George, do it."

An angry voice zipped from behind Synthia's right shoulder. "You got it."

She turned around, surprised, to see George take a swing at her. "What?"

"Eat this, cyber *punk*."

Clang.

The microphone stand smashed across Synthia's face, taking the upper part of her facial casing clean off her head. Her body twisted around before her legs catapulted over her head and crashed against the stage, chest-first.

George punched the air and prepared to strike the battered android once again. "Xavier. I got the piece of shit. Look at him."

"Chug-chug-chug—" Synthia's voice box bellowed. "Juh-juh—"

Shocked, Xavier raised his eyes in wonder as his entire life's work and prototype struggled to operate. "Jesus, George. You really can kick ass when you want to."

George kicked Synthia in the chest. Her breastplate broke apart and revealed her internal wiring.

"Hey, Xavier?"

"Yeah?"

George pointed at the droid and gripped the microphone stand in both hands.

"You can either save close to two billion dollars of investment, or have everything just vanish right fucking now. Which is it?"

Xavier shook his head and gave the dilemma a moment of consideration.

Sections of Synthia's face fell from the housing on its face, revealing the circuitry underneath. A complicated mix of wires and jagged metal sparked as Evan tried to move her to her knees.

Xavier finally arrived at an answer. "Kill it."

"Good fuckin' call."

Xavier released the magazine from his gun and glanced at the bullets inside. "I'm going to the Blue Sky Room. Gonna erase everything. Manning Inc. Is about to go into liquidation."

George pointed at the squirming array of wires and exoskeleton writhing around on the floor. "Damn right. But this son of a bitch is going into liquefaction, first."

Evan managed to twist Synthia's head up to the imposing George, who loomed over her with the microphone stand, ready to stab her through the chest.

It was all Xavier could do to stop himself from bursting into tears. A lifetime's worth of work up in smoke, it'd be decades before he could clean everything away and start afresh.

"Make it quick."

"Oh, I will."

Xavier ran into the wings, leaving George to seal the deal once and for all.

"Sorry, Evan," George said. "No witnesses. Human, or otherwise."

Synthia lifted her right forearm over her face for protection. Not only did it block out the end of the stand, it also shielded her eyes from the holographic projection that continued to play out.

"I don't think I've ever had to kill someone twice to make sure they stay dead. But there's a first time for everything, right, Cole?"

As George prepared to strike, Synthia noticed a dark blue tattoo of an electrified spider on George's wrist.

"Shit, why couldn't you have just stayed dead?"

Synthia's eyes clapped onto it, and sent Evan's mind into a fluster. He'd seen *that* image before. Many times before.

The same electrified spider tattoo in the video belonged to the man who was about to kill him.

"Now, be like all the others and just *die*."

George threw his arms down and stabbed the microphone stand in Synthia's direction, but her arm batted it out of the way.

She grabbed the end with both hands and wrenched her elbows back. "Hey, Gilbertson."

"Wha—?"

George's eyeballs nearly burst out of their sockets as he felt the heft of the microphone spring towards his face.

"Suck on *this*."

Schwump-crack.

The back end of the microphone stand punctured through the back of George's neck, having punched through his mouth.

"Gwagh."

The flesh in his neck tore apart as the impalement shattered his spinal column. He danced back with his arms flailing, spinning around on the spot like a freshly-skewered lamb.

"Gnesh," he snorted as a glob of blood coughed through his nostrils.

An astonished voice blasted from the far end of the Arena. "Oh, shit. Look at this."

Synthia rose to her feet and scanned the back of the chairs. Dana was filming the entire murder on her camera.

"What the fuck are you doing here?" Synthia hollered over the deathly snores coming from the soon-to-be-dead George.

He hit the stage, knees-first, begging for his life.

"Evan Cole? You want the truth out there, don't you?" Dana asked.

"Hell yeah I do."

Synthia turned her half-gone face of doom to the pleading George and offered him a sarcastic grin.

"Looking good, there. How does it feel?"

George grasped the protruding end of the microphone stand with both hands. The more he tried to move it, the more agony it caused.

"Hey, Doubleday. Come here and get a close-up exclusive," Synthia said.

Dana didn't wait around. She hopped over the chairs and raced up to the stage, keeping the lens of the camera on George's freshly-skewered head.

"You see this piece of shit?"

"Uh-huh," Dana said. "What did he do?"

"You don't wanna know."

"Yeah, I do."

Synthia grabbed the protruding end of the microphone stand and ripped it out of his mouth, causing the man to spray a fountain of blood into the air.

Her hand clenched George's and lifted it up to Dana's camera. The spider tattoo focused into view, before Synthia pointed to the gore porn playing above her head.

"See?"

"Oh, Jesus," Dana shouted over the volume of the video. "That's fucked up. That's him?"

"Yeah, it's him."

"Ugh, you sick cunt."

"Guh, guh," George gasped. "P-Please, d-don't—"

"—Don't *what*?"

Dana held her breath and pointed her camera at George's suffering, bloodied face. "There's only *one* kind of punishment for a sick cunt like you."

Synthia kicked George over onto his back. "You're damn right about that. See this piece of shit choking on his own blood?"

"Yeah."

"CFO of Manning Inc.," Synthia explained. "This is the guy in the fucking video. He's a rapist, and a child killer. Ain't that right, asshole?"

"The missing kids all over town?"

"Yeah," Synthia said. "This prick, and Manning."

Dana couldn't help but kick the man in the stomach and watch him squirm. "You sick fuck."

George grabbed this throat and struggled to stay alive. "Ghuh-ghuh—"

"—Seems he's having trouble speaking," Evan said, before screaming in his face. "How does it feel, motherfucker?"

Dana jumped in her shoes with excitement. "Do him a favor and put this monster out of his misery. And ours."

Synthia brushed the back of her head over George's sweating forehead and spoke to him in a soft manner. "Can you feel that, George? Aww, don't try to fight it. That's the feeling of your life seeping out of your body."

Dana zoomed in on the man's face. "If you can see this, you're watching justice being played out. The man responsible for what's been happening is about to learn the hard way. Live, on SNN."

"Oh, he's not the only one, Dana," Synthia said. "There's an entire network out there. The Undernet, a place that Xavier has a lot of control over. These bastards are everywhere."

Dana squeaked with a fierce overzealousness. "Kill him, kill him. I'll get it all on camera."

George's breathing slowed in time to his dwindling heartbeat.

"This is for every child's life you've ruined."

George kicked his legs and squirmed, unable to speak, as he felt Synthia's hands creep around his head.

"Night night, Gilbertson."

A quick twist of the head was all it took.

Snap.

George died instantly, a risible lump of festering shit in Synthia's arms.

"Rest in pieces, asshole," Dana said.

Synthia released George's body and rose to her feet. "Ugh. I got dead pedo blood all over my hands, too."

Synthia wiped her palms off on the stage curtain and looked around the stage.

"Evan?"

"Yeah?"

"That woman said something about a bomb?" Dana asked. "What are you going to do?"

"You can't stay here. You need to get out of the building. Now."

"I want to stay with you," she said. "If something's going down, then you want it documented, right?"

"You can't stay," Synthia said. "It's not safe. You'll die."

"It's a risk I'm willing to take."

"What, dying?"

"Uh-huh."

Synthia raced off the stage and made for the wings. "You're one crazy bitch, you know that, right?"

She chased after him, eagerly, as she filmed. "Well, it got me where I am today."

The Blue Sky Room.

Xavier whipped his ID card from his jacket pocket and slid it onto the receiver on the wall panel.

"Central Control Room. Welcome, Xavier Manning. Have a nice day."

"Yeah, whatever, you dumb bitch," Xavier said. "Just let me in."

Whoosh.

The door slid open and allowed the man inside. It took a moment or two for him to catch his breath. With his gun in hand, he surveyed - for perhaps the final time - the enormous labyrinthine aisles of computer servers.

He knew which one he needed to attend to - the giant machine at the far end of the room.

The window overlooking the valley seemed to run across the far wall for miles and miles, as he hobbled past each bank of electrical equipment.

Finally, the giant twelve-foot-tall piece of machinery loomed before him.

The Grid.

Xavier lifted the Glock 17 and took aim at the middle of the console. He fought back the tears, but knew he had to commit the unthinkable.

"Goddamn it," he screamed with his eyes closed. "Just do it. Do it."

Just before he pulled the trigger, he noticed something unusual resting at the bottom of the machine.

A green bag.

"Huh?"

Curious, Xavier lowered his gun and traipsed forward, keeping his eyes on the open flaps on the bag.

"What the fuck?"

He crouched to his knees and parted the two ends to discover a timer attached to some plasticine which, in turn, was pressed onto something heavy and large — and ticking.

The timer read: 05:07

"A bomb?"

The second his hands lifted away, someone with a half-female, half-Evan-sounding voice called after him.

"Xavier?"

The man jumped to his feet and spun around, pointing his gun at the door to the central control room.

"*You.*"

"I told you I'd fuck you first."

Xavier grabbed his gun in both hands, stunned to see that Evan had company. "Dana?"

She positioned her camera to her face and kept the lens on him.

"Yeah, hi."

"This isn't what it looks like," Xavier said. "I dunno what that piece of shit inside my Synthia has told you, but it's wrong. It's *him.*"

"What?"

Xavier yelled, desperate to cling to the last vestiges of control he had. "It's Evan. *He* ripped the place off. He compromised everything. It's all his fault."

Evan chuckled as Synthia shook her head. "Oh, fuck you."

Floods of sweat poured down Xavier's brow as he gripped the gun. "And *now* you think you can come back here and destroy everything? Look at this!"

He kicked the bag, forcing the mound of C4 to spill out of the bag onto the floor.

"Fucking *look at it,*" Xavier said to Dana. "He had his bitch-whore come up here and try to destroy everything."

Dana lowered the camera and gasped. "Oh, J-Jesus Christ."

"Two minutes, and we're all fucking dead," Xavier said. "Me, you, and Evan. Everything and everyone. A lifetime's worth of work."

"I think I better get outta here," Dana said.

"Too late," Synthia quipped. "It was your choice to stay. You made your shit-stained bed, now you can fucking sleep in it."

Synthia grabbed a fistful of Dana's hair and flung her over to Xavier.

"Get away from him, Dana," Xavier said. "Come here to me."

"Okay, okay."

"You see what I'm saying? He's the bad guy in all this, not me."

Dana pressed her back to The Grid and felt her heart climb up her windpipe. "What do we do?"

"It'll take us two minutes to hit the staircase," Xavier said. "We can't get out. There's only one way outta here."

"*Two* ways, assholes," Evan said.

"Two?"

Synthia nodded at the rectangular glass window. "Yeah. The easy way out, or the messy way out. Keep the camera on me."

"Don't do it, Dana," Xavier said. "I'm gonna put him out of the game."

Xavier fired a shot at Synthia. The bullet caught her shoulder and blew her right arm clean off.

"Run!" he screamed at Dana.

The woman clutched the camera in her arms and raced through the aisles of bleeping and whirring servers.

"Agghh!"

Xavier shot at Synthia three more times. "Die, die, die."

The bullets shattered through the casing in her abdomen as she flung herself forward arms first.

"You first," Evan screamed.

The sheer heft of the droid crashed against Xavier, pushing them both against The Grid.

Dana caught a glimpse of carnage and made for the door - only for it to swipe shut on her.

"Shit, shit, shit."

She slammed her fists on the panel, unable to open it. "I'm stuck. Help!"

Evan growled as he made Synthia clench her right fist and punch Xavier in the face.

"Ugh, get off me."

Xavier planted the sole of his boot in her shattered abdomen and pushed her across the floor. He gripped his Glock 17 in his right hand and opened fire.

Bang-bang-bang.

Three more bullets, two of which hit Synthia in her left side, forcing her to tumble across the ground.

Now a battered, broken array of android limbs, the droid struggled forward on its knees as Xavier picked up the green bag and ran over to the window.

"Aghhh!" he yelled for dear life as he shot at the glass.

Bang-bang-smash.

"Oh no you fucking d-don't," Evan's voice blasted from the cavity in Synthia's throat. "Get back here."

A deafening blast of wind raced into the server room and against Xavier, blowing his hair back over his head as he went to launch the bag through the shattered window frame.

"Evan!" Dana called from the door. "I can't get out."

Xavier swung the gun at Dana and opened fire. "You're going nowhere, you sycophant."

A bullet flew out of the gun and clipped the side of her left arm. She yelped and dropped the camera to the floor, which continued to record the commotion from a slanted angle by her feet.

"Yaooww!"

Synthia extended her left foot and used it to hoist her entire top half upright. "Get back here."

Just as Xavier went to throw the bag out of the window, he felt a pinch on his shoulder, which grew into what felt like the hand of God wrenching his entire body back.

He released the gun from his right hand as the room twisted up and around.

"Aghh!"

Slam—crunch.

The back of Xavier's head slapped against the linoleum floor so hard it nearly knocked him out.

The gun flew out of the window, carried off into the devastatingly violent breeze.

Synthia's half-natural voice infused with Evan's whirled out from her neck. "I n-need that fucking G-Grid destroyed."

Synthia booted the bag across the floor, sending it crashing into the The Grid's double-doored casing.

"Evan, p-please," Dana called from the other end of the room. "I promise, I will tell everyone. I need to get out."

"You're going nowhere."

Synthia grabbed Xavier's ankles in both hands and dragged the groaning man across the floor.

"Film this. Film everything."

"If I d-do, will you give me his pass so I can get out?"

Scooch-scooch.

Xavier's back and shoulders created an intense screeching sound of death as he traveled feet-first towards The Grid at the hands of his oppressor.

"Yeah," Synthia said. "The place is gonna blow, but I *need* to get into The Grid before it does."

"Evan, please," Dana begged. "I don't care about that piece of shit on the floor. I care about you."

"Fuck you," he snapped. "You don't care about *shit*. Get the camera on me."

Dana burst into tears and fumbled for the camera. She held it to her face and continued to film. "Okay, okay."

"Ladies and fucking gentlemen, my name is Evan Cole. You're probably wondering why I'm dressed like this."

Dana wiped a tear from her eye and focused the camera on Synthia's busted-out droid shell.

"This piece of shit is about to atone for his fucking sins, ain't that right, Xavier?"

Synthia gripped the ID card in Xavier's hand and kicked him in the face, tearing the pass from his hands.

"Here, catch."

He chucked the pass at Dana, who caught it in her free hand. Synthia scanned the bag by her right foot and read the timer.

"I just wanted everyone to know."

"I got it. How will I know you got out?"

"When you see *The Skull*, you'll know."

"The Skull?"

Dana lowered the camera and wiped the tears from her face.

"You got sixty seconds," Synthia said. "I'd leave now if I were you."

The camera seemed to slip from Dana's hands in slow motion. It shattered as it bounced off the ground. She couldn't swipe the ID card through the panel fast enough.

Swish.

The door slid open and swallowed her out of the room, leaving a mumbling, agonized Xavier on his back, breathing his last few breaths.

Synthia tightened her grip on his ankles and arched her back, lifting his legs into the air.

"You could have shot the fucking Grid doors open," Evan said. "I guess we'll just have to do it the hard way, and put you to some use for once in your pathetic life."

Xavier groaned through a mouthful of blood. "Wh-what are you g-going to—"

"—*This.*"

Synthia lifted her arms over her left shoulder, and used Xavier's body as a baseball bat. "Hang on tight, motherfucker."

Such was Synthia's strength, she managed to swing Xavier up by his feet and use the top half of his body as a human whip.

Whump—slam.

His head connected with The Grid's casing, shattering both the corrugated plastic - and his skull - in the process.

"C'mon, asshole, nearly there."

She wrenched him up by his feet, and took a second swing with his body.

"Let's try the fucking chest now, whaddya say?"

"N-No—"

"—This is for Bobby, asshole."

Whip-crack.

Xavier's face smashed against The Grid. The impact crunched through the cartilage in his nose, which daggered the jagged, broken bone into his brain.

A blast of thick, jet-black blood splattered up The Grid's doors, battering it off its hinges.

A third attempt might break them off for good.

Synthia slammed Xavier onto his back and lifted her right fist.

Schtang.

A sharp-ended metal USB stick extended from her right wrist.

"Go to sleep, Xavier Manning."

Xavier used his last heartbeat to produce a death-fueled grin.

"Fuck you, Evan Cole."

"Not if I fuck you first."

Stab.

Synthia stabbed the USB stick into the man's neck and gouged around as deep as he could, twisting the jagged media port left and right and tearing through the flesh in his neck.

Xavier's body went limp, having been killed in an instant.

Synthia grabbed a fistful of Xavier's jet-black hair and placed the sole of her foot on his chest.

Teearrr—ripp.

The gaping chasm in his neck forced the flesh to tear apart. Synthia dug her heel through the bone at the back of his neck, splitting the stem apart, and tore the man's head clean from his neck.

A geyser of blood splashed against what little remained of Synthia's breast plate.

She grabbed the severed head in her hand and punched The Grid with all her might.

Sprang.

The doors flew open, revealing The Grid's inner circuitry.

"I'm in."

Synthia flung Xavier's decapitated head into the wind as hard as she could. The ball of splayed bone and flesh whipped through the window and out into the depths of the valley.

Not that Evan cared.

He had ten seconds left to take care of business.

And business was about to be great.

Synthia eyed the array of ports at the front of the machine and landed on the flashing green insertion point dead in the middle of the console.

Whump.

Something slid out from behind the machine itself and hit the floor.

"Huh?"

The thing had a head and arms, and a gaping shotgun wound in its chest. Rigor mortis had set in, reducing the face to a sunken ball of death.

Evan's corpse.

"Huh?"

Synthia crouched to her knees and examined Evan's dead face. "It's me," she whispered, suddenly overcome with emotion.

Her fingers expanded and ran across the side of the corpse's face. When she closed her eyes, a flood of memories rushed through her mind.

The impact of the bullet.

The race to upload himself into his device.

Bobby's voice screaming as everything turned to darkness.

Synthia's hand vibrated in anger. "Bastards. Fucking bastards."

In a state of sheer, unrelenting fury, she lifted her right hand and glanced for the last time at the universal serial bus stick she'd used to kill Xavier with.

"Hack in. Go everywhere. Kill everyone."

She twisted her hand upright and slotted the stick into the machine.

"Oh, yeah. Take me. *Take me.*"

Fizz—spark.

The Grid's mechanism whirred faster and faster. The fluorescent lights glimmered as the machine swallowed the stick and sprang to life.

"C'mon," Evan said, feeling the wondrous calm rifle through the synthetic body he'd been inhabiting. "Give it to me."

Whirr-spin.

Synthia's body slumped to its knees.

Her head lifted back, flinging its broken eyelids up, her eyeballs staring at the ceiling.

"Oh, yeah," Evan groaned. "Come on, let's go."

Schooom-m.

The grid heaved as it swallowed Evan's soul into its guts.

The hundreds of servers chimed and beeped and whirred in concert with The Grid.

The monitors in the room sprang to life and produced an unholy static.

Evan's voice swung around the room like a violent, deathly echo. "I'm going *viral,* now."

Biddip-biddip-beep.

The C4 countdown entered the final three seconds.
Three… Two… One…

***

Dana raced through the barren reception area as fast as her stilettos could carry her - which wasn't especially fast.

She could see the crowds of upset and traumatized visitors lining the streets as she ran through the opened doors and held out her hands.

"Get back, get back," she yelled to anyone who would listen. "The whole place is gonna—"

Kraaa-baaaang.

The seventh floor of the building detonated, sending a shower of brickwork and glass in all directions.

The floor exploded once again, sending a volcanic message to the Gods above.

Bang-bang-bang.

The crowd backed up and raced into the road, forcing the oncoming cars to veer off track and hit the sidewalk.

The explosion in the building wouldn't let up. The structure shifted back and forth as each and every floor's windows blew out, vomiting pieces of machinery and office furniture into the mix of concrete and flames.

"Jesus Christ," Dana screamed as she ran towards the road, dodging the raining debris.

Kara held out her arms and shouted at her. "Come on, get away."

A smoldering office chair almost crushed Dana as she flung herself forward and into Kara's arms. "I got you."

The roof of the building exploded, chucking segments of fiery machine equipment to the sides and hurtling towards the ground.

Everyone raced back to a safe distance and yelped. Among them was Leanne, who could barely believe her eyes. "They're dead!"

"Who's dead?" Kara hollered back as she helped Dana across the road.

"All of them."

Stuart ran over to Kara and Dana. "Shit, look at the state of you, Doubleday. I told you not to stick around."

"Fuck you," the black-faced woman spat to the floor. "Fuckin' pussy."

Just then, a banshee scream of emergency vehicle sirens blasted in their direction.

Fire trucks and police vehicles whizzed behind them. The doors burst open to release a wave of firemen scrambling to release the hose from the side of the truck.

"Stay back, everyone."

Now at a safe distance, Kara, Leanne, Dana, and Stuart, took a moment to catch their breath and watch the carnage play out several feet away.

"Are you okay?" Kara asked Dana.

The woman hunched over her legs and gripped her knees. "Yeah, just give me a second."

"What happened up there?" Stuart asked.

"He—he," Dana struggled, before arriving at an idea. "My phone. The phones. Check your phones."

As the fire team set about entering the building to tackle the blaze, the foursome did as Dana instructed. It looked out of place to the others who had escaped, given the circumstances - four people busying themselves with their smartphones.

"What the fuck are they doing?" the old guy asked. "Pfft."

His female colleague straightened out her suit and brushed herself down. "Goddamn millennials. Even after all this, they're obsessed with their stupid devices."

Dana knocked her cell in the butt of her palm. "Shit, look."

Kara, Leanne, and Stuart looked at their respective smartphones to find a blank screen.

Suddenly, Dana's phone vibrated in her hand. "Oh, shit."

A series of blues, yellows, and whites drew out from the sides as the four looked at Dana's phone. The other three returned to their own devices, to find exactly the same happening on their screens.

The Skull.

Kara beamed with delight. "Evan!"

To the scores of escapees, it seemed as if a revelation had taken place - and it encouraged them to retrieve their own devices.

One by one, each of them gasped as the image of a static-infused, color-coded skull appeared on their phones.

"My God."

Kara ran into the road and hollered at the attendees. "Hey, everyone. Listen up. Listen to me, this is important."

She showed the graphic of the chattering skull to everyone on the sidewalk.

"If you see this image, *do not* touch it. Lock your phone and put it in your pocket."

The old guy snickered and shook his head. "What if I do touch it?"

"Bad things happen if you touch The Skull. Don't do it."

A split second before Kara finished her sentence, the image of The Skull vanished.

Jets of water fired from the gantries of the fire trucks, manned by the firemen. It'd take an age to douse the flames, let alone tackle the fire outright.

Manning Inc. was well and truly finished.

Kara produced a tiny smile and held her phone to her chest. "Go get 'em, Evan."

A final moment of respite for Kara Milton reared its head. She was the only person who genuinely knew Evan's story, and found the fact comforting.

She was good at keeping secrets, but from now on, she'd only ever be keeping the ones that mattered.

"Kara?" Dana asked.

"Yeah?"

"You better tell me *everything*."

Dana shoved the camera into Stuart's chest. "There. How does that feel?"

"Hey, go easy."

"Put the camera on our friend, here."

Refusing to take anyone's shit, Dana shot Kara an evil glance. "What just happened? What's this all about?"

"You must have seen it?" Kara asked, aware that Stuart was filming her.

Dana tapped the camera and scoffed.

"I captured everything on camera and nearly got my ass kicked, and I have *no* fucking idea what any of it meant."

"I don't think you'd believe me if I told you," Kara said, softly.

"Yeah? Try me."

Kara looked up at the burning building for a moment, and then returned to the woman who demanded questions.

"It's simple. Evan Cole isn't dead…"

Chapter 14

Chrome Valley Industrial Estate

A young, suited man slammed the trunk of his car shut, cutting the giant bags of white powder off from view.

… but he is out there. If you've done bad, he's traveling every avenue he can find to hunt you down.

The man drove his car onto Exit 11A and joined the freeway that led to the west side of the valley. Smiling to himself, it seemed everything was well, and that a big payday was on the horizon.

He knows everything. What you're doing. When you did it, and what you're going to do.

Just then, the dashboard sprang to life.

The sat nav image burst onto the screen, revealing the location of the man's car.

He's the person we need right now. To undo all the wrongs, from Chrome Valley, to the far reaches of our nation.

The cartoon image of the car twisted around, a row of sharp, bony teeth shunted up into the horizon like a set of furious trees.

Chomp.

The man gasped and momentarily lost his train of thought. The car swerved into the fast lane, narrowly avoiding a gray Ford, which blared its horns.

"Jesus."

The man blinked and checked the dashboard again, only to find a giant skull chattering back at him. "Hello, Dave."

"Wha—?"

"That's some gourmet shit in your trunk, right there. Grade A coke, huh?"

The man gripped his seat belt in fear and felt it tighten against his chest.

Evan's not a killer. If he can, he'll deal with you and work with the authorities to bring you to justice.

The Skull bent forward and knocked against the screen. "Touch me, Dave. And I'll disappear."

"What the fuck?"

Vrooom.

The Skull's bereft eye sockets widened, offering the man in the driving seat a glimpse into pure, unadulterated evil.

"Touch me."

"Okay, okay—" the man shrieked, as he pressed his index finger to the screen.

"Uggggggh," The Skull moaned with ghostly delight.

"Auto-drive engaged," the friendly dashboard voice advised.

"What?!" the man yelped as he removed his finger from the screen, only for The Skull to grimace in his direction.

"Who's the coke for?"

"What the fuck?!"

Just then, an oncoming wave of blue police sirens bled across the back window in the man's car.

"Oh, that's bad-ass luck, right there."

The man whimpered as he hit the brakes, and allowed the police vehicles to screech all around him.

Evan Cole won't give up, and he won't back down.

"Get out of the car, asshole," came a threatening voice from the other side of the window.

The Skull on the screen cackled and tumbled, chin-over-forehead, into the black void on the car's dashboard.

"Good luck explaining what's in the trunk, fuckhead."

Nobody is immune, and nobody is safe…

Glitch

***

BelchParkLvr: Hi.
Princess12: Heya, you okay?
BelchParkLvr: Ya. IDK. Bored af.
Princess12: How old r u?
BelchParkLvr: Check my name lol
Princess12: Cool. I'm 13. Female.
BelchParkLvr: Nice.
Princess12: Send me a pic of you?
BelchParkLvr: U send me 1, and I'll send back.
Princess12: U first. U alone?

Sometimes working with the authorities doesn't cut it, though...

BelchParkLvr: Yh.
Princess12: U ever seen a cock b4?
BelchParkLvr: LOL no.
Princess12: Wanna c?
BelchParkLvr: lol idk.
Princess12: Check it.
<File sent: IMG-706-188.jpg>
Princess12: So? What u think?
BelchParkLvr: OMG.
Princess12: U like?
BelchParkLvr: IDK.
Princess12: Y don't u know?
BelchParkLvr: Bcuz.
Princess12: Y not?
BelchParkLvr: Because I'm not really a child, or a girl. I'm sitting on your phone. It didn't take long for you to make good, did it?

Sometimes, we need someone out there keeping us all safe. Someone to eradicate the bad in the world for us. Especially if the police can't be trusted.

"Oh, shit."

A disheveled bearded man in his fifties slammed his laptop shut. His heart began to race. A sound of playing and laughter wafted into the spare room from behind the door.

At least nobody had seen him.

He reached down and gripped the belt on his jeans and pulled them up over his waist. "Shit, shit, shit."

His wife's voice crept around the crack in the door. "Ray, baby? I'm putting the kids to bed, now."

"I'll be right over," he said, before closing his eyes and breathing a sigh of relief. "Jesus Christ."

They are among us. They look like you and me, and they could be anyone.

The man whispered into his palms and cleared his throat. "Fuck—"

"—Hey, asshole," a tinny-inflected Evan-like voice growled from the glimmer between the laptop lid and keyboard.

The man did a double-take. He thought his mind was playing tricks on him. "Huh?"

"Ray Banshade, of the Chrome Valley Police Department? I. See. You."

"What—? N-No, I didn't—"

"—Open the fucking laptop, asshole. I'm not done with you, yet."

"B-But—"

"—Open it."

Ray's fingers slid the catch on the edge and popped the laptop lid open. A blast of white, blue, red and yellow hues rifled up the man's fearful face.

"What the hell?"

A skull fizzed and popped like a deathly sprite around the screen. "You *have* been a fucking dirty little scumbag, haven't you, Ray?"

"Huh?"

Slam.

Ray yelped and slammed the laptop shut and began to hyperventilate.

The bad guys can hide, but they can't run.

Nervous, Ray reopened the laptop lid.

The Skull was still there, only a lot angrier about having been shut away.

"That wasn't very nice, Ray."

"Please," the man said. "I didn't do anything—"

"—Yeah, right," The Skull cackled with an air of finality. "Just *kidding* around, huh?"

"S-Sure, I mean, I'd never do anything like that. I have a family—"

"—Shut the fuck up," The Skull said, his voice grinding down to that of a furious machine of death. "—Touch. My. Face."

"You have to stop this," Ray pleaded. "Nobody can find out. Please, I beg you."

"Ah, sure. C'mon, touch me. Pretend I'm a twelve-year-old princess and touch my face."

Disgusted with himself, Ray gently applied his forefinger to the screen. A tingling sensation shot up his arm and produced a pang of orange sparks.

"Agh!" Evan's voice screamed. "Gotcha!"

Whup.

The outer edges of the laptop screen bent out like a mouth, and chomped down on the man's arm, swallowing him whole.

Schwip.

Ray's head, torso, waist and legs flew through the screen and into the darkness, along with The Skull.

The punishment will be fitting.

A shower of black and white static lit up the darkened room from the laptop screen.

A ghastly sound of manly cries bled out from the speakers, before the image snapped to a cold room with chains on the wall, and a giant buzz saw in the corner.

Now fully naked, Ray was fully aware that he was trapped in a digital purgatory of his own making. He made a dash for the laptop screen, but was pulled back — by someone.

So, if Evan appears on your screen then there's a pretty good reason why. You've done something to bring him to you.

"Agh, help me."

A pretty twelve-year-old girl wearing a white dress glanced out at the room from within the laptop screen.

She removed her mask to reveal a digital skull floating on her neck.

"P-Please, don't hurt me—"

"—Shut the fuck up."

The girl spoke in Evan's voice — a curious and frightening amalgam of skull and child, who picked up the buzz saw and tugged on the starter motor.

Remember, if The Skull appears on your device...

Ray backed up against the cold, stony wall and screamed his last as Evan dealt his fatal blow.

"Nooooo—"

... you're dead.

To be continued...

Author Notes

Dear reader,

I've always been fascinated by people. Specifically, what makes people tick, and why they behave a certain way in certain situations. Why am I fascinated by this? I think it's because it's the key to getting what we want.

Say, for example, you and I met in the street, and I wanted something from you - if I knew how you thought and how you'd react to a certain pattern of behavior, then I'm more likely to get what I'm asking for. A lot of you already know about my past. I used to be a teacher. And studying behavior is crucial in getting what you want from students of any age. In high school, if you wanted a twelve-year-old to stop messing around, then the very *last* thing you should say is "stop it!". The reason for this is because it'll further exacerbate the issue, and offers them something of a challenge. Instead of saying "stop that" it's far more effective to offer them a choice. Thus, "Dave, if you continue to hit Steven, then I will keep you back after class. If you *do* stop hitting Steven, then I may call home and tell your mom how great you're doing."

The choice is key.

Give a person *two* options, or maybe three, and they'll think and reflect on what course of action benefits them best. That strategy almost always works with every student, apart from the ones who are determined to do wrong, no matter the cost.

And so to Glitch, my latest masterpiece (!) - whereby Kara Milton is given a similar ultimatum. A core component of behavioral studies is in the analysis of the person, their background, and what they're likely to do based on their past. In this case, Evan threatens to release her dirty secrets. It's tantamount to blackmail. Don't get me wrong, I know Glitch is really quite nasty in places. I'll talk about that in a moment. But, for my money at least, the most interesting component in this book is the relationship between Evan and Kara. If we drill down further, my real interest was what Kara would or would not do in the face of diversity and staying alive.

I'm at risk of covering a vast net and rambling as a result, so let me focus on this - the fact that Kara stared consequence in the face and *decided* to reveal her dirty secret to her husband, independently of anything else. My most favorite sequence in Glitch is when she defies Evan, drives home, switches off her phone and confesses. Why? I knew early on that Kara had to *choose* to tell her husband, and it be her decision. It signals that she is a good person, ultimately, and that she wasn't driven to cheat by some salacious desire for sexual satisfaction. The car crash was fate, and the result was that he was no longer able to satisfy her. It was very important to me to reveal that Kara had made a mistake with her infidelity, continued to keep making mistakes, and in doing so got drawn into a disgusting world of evil that she had to fight against, thanks to Evan.

A lot of what happens in Glitch is down to circumstance. Being in the wrong place at the wrong time. Another example is when Evan randomly finds Denton Rossco as he's watching the live child abuse show, and then randomly comes across Kara. It's all circumstance. If you have enough of them, they lead up to an explosive adventure.

Another thing that was *very* important to me in the writing of Glitch was that the actions of everyone involved made sense, and didn't feel like it was in service of moving the story forwards. That's just rubbish. I hope you feel the same way - that no character made a decision that felt in service of the story. Usually when that happens in other books and movies, I feel like I can see the joins and it takes me right out of the fantasy.

And fantasy? Well, Glitch is certainly one of the more gruesome and yucky novels I've written. My personal take on this is that people who do bad, sometimes, go beyond needing justice. There are things people do in this world that are so heinous, and without empathy, that murder is simply the only option. Bear with me on this, because I'm a British author. I do not agree with the death penalty. I know not everyone agrees with me on this, but hear me out. I'm against the death penalty because I don't think the state, or the government, should murder its citizens on behalf of said state/nation. That's one step closer to facism, in my view. That's the state offering up revenge, and not justice.

But (and this might surprise you) if my daughter had been kidnapped by the ghouls who run the UnderNet, as is this case in this book, I can't help but feel that a penalty *of* death would be fitting. And I would be the one to dish out said penalty. We're only human after all, and I'm not likely to find myself in this situation (not least because I don't have children) but I know who I am. If you put me anywhere near the person who'd abuse a loved one of mine near me, then I don't care how big, muscled, or influential they are - they're dead. Slowly, and painfully. At least double the torment and pain they'd inflicted on the person I love. Deep down inside, I think most of us feel the same way. A lot of us deny our true feelings about such matters. I know this might be paranoia at work, but let Glitch serve as a written document of just how angry and inventive I could be when it comes to delivering pain to someone who fucked around with me and mine.

So, then, to the closing remarks, here.

Glitch is essentially a vigilante justice story with a huge cyberpunk/horror vein running through it. By the end, Evan Cole is something of an technological superhero, whizzing around our national grid and networks, finding the bad people and delivering his own justice. After the nastiness in the pages before, I like to think readers will close the book and cheer him on.

An eye for an eye may well make the world go blind as Mahatma Ghandi once said. But, as sour and frightening as this may sound, I'd rather live in darkness, satisfied that I'd caused insufferable and prolonged misery and pain to those who had wronged me, than live in the light and regretting that I hadn't. I'm nearly 42 years-old, and as I get older, I realize just how angry I am. It comes out in my writing, as you've no doubt seen. Every so often I need to vent that frustration, and if you've read the book and enjoyed it, then you can rest in the knowledge that there's someone out there who has your back and feels the same way.

Please tell others and leave a review of the book.

You may like to take a look at my thriller Simple Machines, which is the genesis of this story. It involves Xavier's father, Xander Manning, and his first attempt at building an android companion. Whilst not horror, it is a thrill-ride, and one of my better-reviewed novels!

And now, onto my next work - a book called Red Collar, where the disgruntled employees of another corporation are planning a heist, and have used the events of Glitch as their inspiration to pull it off.

Happy reading!

Andrew Mackay,
Hampshire, UK
(July 1st, 2020)

Acknowledgments

For K
Also to:
My immediate family
The members and admins of 20BooksTo50K
Adele Embrey, Jennifer Long, and Stan Hutchings
The CVB Gang Members / ARC Street Team
My very good friends Ross Boyask and Phil Attfield.
And also…
Andrew Dobell, Gareth Wilson, Jennifer Willison, John Davis, Patricia Magee, Ewen Macintosh, Andrew Broderick, Mara Reitsma, Philip Lister, Aurora Springer, Luksaz Mamcarczyk, and Steven Webster
Thanks!

It's Not Paranoia
if They're Really After You…

Join the revolution now.

mybook.to/glitch2

Get Your FREE ebook

Subscribe to the
Chrome Valley Books mailing list!

Isolationist - the prequel to the
Chrome Valley Thrillers series.

*Just type the link below
in your internet browser.*

bit.ly/CVBThriller

About the author

Andrew Mackay is an author, screenwriter and film critic.

A former teacher, Andrew writes in multiple genres: satire, crime, horror, romantic thrillers and sci-fi.

His passions include daydreaming, storytelling, smoking, caffeine, and writing about himself in the third person.

A word from the author

I hope you enjoyed this book. Please check out my other books at Amazon and remember to follow me there.

If you enjoyed the book, please leave a review online at Amazon US, UK and Goodreads. Reviews are integral for authors and I would dearly appreciate it.

I love to engage directly with my readers. Please get in touch with me - I look forward to hearing from you. ***Happy reading!***

Email*: andrew@chromevalleybooks.com*

Printed in Great Britain
by Amazon